"It's terrific!"
> —Candace Bushnell, *New York Times* bestselling author of *Sex and the City* and *Is There Still Sex in the City?*

"The timing of Jacqueline J. Holness' story is perfect as the subject of 'black women finding a suitable partner' becomes the main topic of conversation when three or more of us gather. I discovered this to be true even among senior black women. I was a guest at a book club of professional women in New York recently where they went way off topic bemoaning the lack of mates for their daughters and nieces... Indeed, it is hard out there for a sister—which is why her book is important."
> —Brenda Wilkinson, Georgia Writers Hall of Fame nominee and author of *Ludell, Ludell and Willie* and *Ludell's New York Time*

"Jacqueline J. Holness has penned a delightful read that puts a new spin on the age-old dilemma of the beautiful, successful, single black woman finding a mate! Did I say beautiful and successful? Set in the Black Mecca—The ATL—*Destination Wedding* will have you asking, 'Why is this so hard?' I found myself in the moment, rooting for these women—and thoroughly enjoyed their journeys to happily-ever-after."
> —Monica Richardson, author of the Talbots of Harbour Island series

"In need of a getaway? *Destination Wedding* is the read you need. Filled with characters that will remind you of your girlfriends and unexpected adventures, it's the perfect vacation read."
> —Chandra Sparks Splond, author and blogger

"In *Destination Wedding*, Jacqueline J. Holness takes readers on page-turning twists and turns that hijack several friendships on the path to love. If you're eager for an entertaining read that will leave you rooting for the characters as if they're your friends, pick up your copy today."
> —Stacy Hawkins Adams, multi-published author of *Coming Home, Watercolored Pearls, The Someday List* and more

Destination Wedding

JACQUELINE J. HOLNESS

Soon Come Books

Fayetteville, Georgia

"Let us rejoice and be glad and give him glory, for the wedding of the Lamb has come, and his Bride has made herself ready. Fine linen, bright and clean, was given her to wear. (Fine linen stands for the righteous acts of the saints.) Then the angel said to me, 'Write: Blessed are those who are invited to the wedding supper of the Lamb!' And he added, 'These are the true words of God.'"

Revelation 19:7-9

Contents

Preface

. . . .

IN DECEMBER 2009, AFTER nearly seven years of preparing myself to meet THE ONE through prayer, self-help books, counseling, online dating, seminars, and on and on, I finally lost hope that he was even out there at all. I felt like Charlotte on my favorite single-girl television show of all time, *Sex and the City,* when she whined to her friends Carrie, Miranda, and Samantha, "I've been dating since I was fifteen. I'm exhausted. Where is he?" before dropping her head, face first, onto the table in front of her. A relationship that I had dreamed of having years earlier finally happened— only to dissolve like a dream too good to be true within a couple of months. I was devastated and despondent. After swearing off my small library of self-help books on relationships that I had lovingly acquired over that nearly seven-year period and declaring that not a single dollar would be spent on another one, I concluded that God's plan for my life did not include marriage and I would have to be okay with that.

It didn't help that I came to this conclusion during the Christmas season. Jesus is the reason for the season, but there is also another reason that Christmas romance books, movies, and music are popular year after year. Of all the Christmas gifts a single girl can get, an engagement ring tops the list for many, if not most! Something about the chill in the air creates the perfect setting for cozying up to someone new or old. And if you find yourself with no one to kiss under the mistletoe, there are a plethora of songs you can pull out from Christmas romance playlists to comfort yourself, from Wham!'s *Last Christmas* to Prince's *Another Lonely Christmas* to Luther Vandross's *Every Year, Every Christmas.*

But I was a single girl soldier at thirty-six years old. This wasn't the first time I was uncoupled at Christmas, and it likely wouldn't be the last—or so I thought (more on that later). I went on with celebrating the reason for the season, attending church, buying gifts for family and friends, decorating my home and more.

And then I saw an ABC News *Nightline* piece just before I nodded off for the night. It was December 22, just days before Christmas. I had nearly survived the season, although feelings of sadness and loss threatened to unravel my "Christmas cheer" that I put on like a coat when leaving my townhouse. But this piece—featured on one of the bedrock news organizations in the country, no less—packaged all of my fears and presented it to me like a gift that that I couldn't give back. "Single, Black, Female and—Plenty of Company" by reporter Linsey Davis was delivered through the television into my bedroom, the one place where I allowed my emotions to unfurl themselves without cover. Davis reported that 42 percent of black women have never been married, which amounted to double the amount of white women who found themselves in that dire predicament. And if that statistic by its lonesome wasn't startling enough, she pointed out that the number wasn't likely to improve, because of the overall black-male-to-black-female ratio at the outset. Additionally, many black men were unavailable or undesirable for marriage because they lacked a high school diploma or a job or were incarcerated, she said.

Then to illustrate all of this, Davis had to go and interview successful black women in Atlanta! Now, why did she have to do that? It was a death blow. My father never funded a dowry for me as far as I know, but I was just about ready to call him at nearly midnight (when the report aired) and tell him that any money that he had even thought about putting away for my wedding should be reallocated to his retirement, because he wasn't marrying me off anytime soon, if at all. ABC News had just reported that black women, specifically those in Atlanta, were on the fast track to spinsterhood.

But then, after the shock and sadness wore off, I was angry—angry that a reputable news organization saw fit to invade the lives of black women and lay bare our seemingly loveless existence. The notion of the "strong black woman" was always problematic, and now there was another misnomer that black women had to contend with: the "single black woman." One of my favorite novelists, Zora Neale Hurston, was onto something when she wrote that the black woman "is de mule uh de world so fur as Ah can see," in her 1937 masterpiece *Their Eyes Were Watching God.*

(And let me just insert this here in case some of you think I'm elevating being married above being single: There are worse things than being single. Being married to a creep is one of them. Also, being single does not equate to unhappiness. However, if you really want to be married, there is nothing wrong with that, either.)

Lest you think I'm being overly dramatic, there were many other think pieces, media conversations, books, and more about black women and our singleness that were publicized around the same time. In September 2009, NPR.org ran a story titled "Black Women: Successful and Still Unmarried." *The Washington Post* published a "Profile of Helena Andrews, Author of a Book About Successful but Lonely Young Black Women," in December 2009. "The Black Damsel in Dating Distress" was published in *The Atlantic* in March 2010. In June 2010, *Psychology Today* published "High-Achieving Black Women and Marriage: Not Choosing or Not Chosen?" And to follow up on the success of the ABC News *Nightline* piece in December, ABC News *Nightline* held a "Nightline Face-Off: Why Can't a Successful Black Woman Find a Man?" debate in Atlanta in April 2010. Critiquing the lives of single black women had become a commodity, babay!

I, as a single black woman at the time, felt bombarded, and I wanted to detonate some bombs in retaliation. As a writer, however, my words were and are my best line of defense. I wrote many blog posts about how all of this felt, and somewhere in the midst of all of that writing, God gave me the idea for a novel. Since I was primarily a nonfiction reader at the time, I just thought about these fictional single black women who decided to not let statistics define their worth as women or as marriage partners.

Even as the idea was slowly taking shape within my imagination, a real-life suitor showed up! We went on our first date on Valentine's Day weekend in 2010! Two years later, in December 2012, he proposed! I don't think it was a coincidence that this man (now my husband) proposed to me during the same month that I had declared myself destined for spinsterhood two years prior.

But even as I commenced with wedding planning in 2013, these fictional single black women stayed on my mind. After they kept pestering me, I finally decided to bring them to life while I was still single, so that all of the angst that I felt was still fresh in my heart and I could spill it onto paper. I planned my wedding and wrote the first draft of *Destination Wedding* simultaneously. Just as there were many twists and turns during my journey as a single black woman, there were many twists and turns in writing and now publishing my very first novel, *Destination Wedding!*

While it was ten years ago this very month that I saw that ABC News *Nightline* piece, I know that single black women who want to find love and get married still have it hard out here. In May 2017, just as I was finishing this manuscript, I read an article titled "Black, Single, and Waiting: For 15 years, *The Bachelor* Franchise Has Made a Caricature of Blackness. Could This Season Finally Be Different?" on Slate.com, in which the author referenced the ABC News *Nightline* piece from 2009. In the January 2018 People.com article "*To Rome for Love:* Host Diann Valentine on Why Black Women Are Going to Italy to Meet Eligible Men," Valentine referenced single black women outnumbering single black men as a reason for single black women to travel to another continent for love. And even as I write this, I read a funny yet heartbreaking piece, "Going on Dating Apps as a Black Woman Can Feel Like Searching for the Bare Minimum," which was published on Hellogiggles.com in February 2019. The author referenced dating app OkCupid's 2014 study in which it was reported that black women were at the bottom when it comes to non-black men's choices, and that black men had no racial preference at all when choosing women.

Despite all of this, I think finding love, no matter what race or gender, is undeniably tricky at best and downright hard at worst. But as a black woman, I wrote this book for black women generally and single black women specifically. One of my friends said this to me not long after she got married: "In my heart, I will always be a single woman." I didn't quite understand what she meant, as I was a single woman at the time. But now, as a married woman, I understand what she meant. I was single for quite a while, having gotten married at thirty-nine years old. The lessons of self-love, autonomy, and purposeful living are ones that I could not have acquired as a married woman. I came to my marriage as a whole person because of all of the time I spent as a single woman. I'm not saying that people who marry at younger ages aren't whole, prior to marrying. I'm simply saying that my singlehood, prolonged as it seemed and painful as it was at times, prepared me for marriage. And I don't regret one second of that preparation, because it led me to where I am today, happily (sometimes, at least ☺) married to THE ONE God had in mind for me all along.

So if anything from this long introduction appeals to you, read my love letter to single black women everywhere but especially to single black women in Atlanta. While this is a work of fiction, I'd be lying if I didn't tell you that many of the lessons I learned along the way aren't folded into the stories of Jarena, Mimi, Senalda, and Whitney. Hopefully, you won't have to learn them in real life like I did. But even if you have nothing to learn, *Destination Wedding* is a fun read, if I say so myself!

Prologue

ALL THEY COULD DO was stare. Although the restaurant was mostly illuminated by flickering lanterns, they could still decipher that Mimi was making out with one of Wendell's friends near the bathrooms, a dark and almost-secluded part of El Restaurante De La Playa. They groped each other as if they were lathering invisible soap on their bodies, which was apropos since it seemed only the shower of a fire hose could quench their heat. It didn't help that Mimi wore a tan sundress only a few shades darker than her skin tone or that Chauncy was nearly the same shade. They weren't naked yet, but the melding of their similar complexions suggested that was next. Their mouths smacked and limbs flailed so much that they fell against a cobblestone wall before disappearing into the men's bathroom.

Had this been a year ago, maybe they wouldn't have been so surprised. A year ago, Mimi wasn't married. And yet there she was—kissing a friend of the groom.

They were in Puerto Rico for Senalda and Wendell's wedding. About seventy-five people journeyed from throughout the U.S. and beyond to the tropical island where Senalda and her fiancé would say their vows on the beach at sunset just as she had always envisioned. Jarena and Whitney whispered to each other although loud salsa music probably drowned out what they were saying anyway.

"Should we tell Senalda that her matron of honor is locking lips and God knows what else one with one of Wendell's friends?" Jarena asked, trying her best not to make eye contact with anyone outside of the two of them who had witnessed Mimi's make-out session in the open-air beach restaurant. The palm-tree encircled restaurant was the site for the rehearsal dinner that just ended, as well as for the wedding reception the next day.

"I just hope that none of the parents or older people saw her," snarled Whitney. She picked up her glass from the table and sipped on sangria. "I mean, her behavior is beyond out of order. We may as well as be at a ghetto wedding, the way Mimi is acting."

Jarena lifted her glass of non-alcoholic sangria and shook it, causing the fruit at the bottom to rise before eventually descending again like flakes in a snow globe. *How are we going to tell Senalda that her recently married matron of honor is cheating on her husband during her rehearsal dinner without starting a fight?*

"One of us has to tell her," Whitney declared, jolting Jarena out of her contemplation. "I nominate you. Since you worked in public relations, you can come up with a PC way to tell Mimi she is making an ass of herself. I mean, I hate to be so crude, but there is no nicer way for me to say it."

"Can you believe I can't come up with anything?" Jarena said, shaking her head. "I'm just praying we see Senalda before Senalda sees Mimi."

"Why are you guys huddled up?" Senalda walked up to her friends at their table from behind, placing each arm around each of them. The plank wood floor hadn't warned them of her arrival.

"Nothing," Whitney said, maneuvering her neck upward and flashing a smile to her before sipping her drink. "Would you like a drink? I can get one for you."

"What are you talking about?" Jarena said, peering down at her arroz con pollo as she lifted her fork to eat.

"Senalda, I'm just going to be real with you," Whitney said as she moved Senalda's arm from her shoulder and rested her hand on the bride-to-be's hand. "Jarena and I saw Mimi kissing Chauncy a few minutes ago near the bathrooms. We hope none of the older people saw what happened."

"What?" Senalda screeched as her eyes grew large. In spite of her small frame, Senalda was not to be toyed with. Maybe it was the Bronx in her.

Maybe it was because she was in senior management at her company. Whatever it was, she did not hesitate to check anyone anywhere.

"I saw her flirting with Wendell's best man last night! This is going to stop right now," Senalda growled in the punchy edge of her Bronx accent that was pronounced when she was angry. She rushed toward the bathrooms.

Whitney and Jarena abandoned their table, running behind their friend. With her long legs, Jarena headed her off, putting her hands on Senalda's shoulders. "Wait," Jarena blurted, looking down at her before lowering her voice and slowing the pace of her words like she was talking to a cranky child who needed to be soothed. "You're about to get married tomorrow. Just think about it for a minute. This is not the time for confrontation. You need to be calm and serene tonight."

Jarena hoped she was saying the right things. Senalda looked at her for a moment before moving Jarena's hands from her shoulders. Thankfully, Mimi and Chauncy were not where they had been before. But they did find Mimi in the women's bathroom. While gazing in the mirror, she was reapplying her lipstick, her complexion nearly matching its red color.

"Just because you married someone you're not in love with doesn't mean that I'm going to let you make a mockery of my wedding." Senalda glared into Mimi's eyes in the mirror. "Last night you and Wendell's best man were flirting, and tonight you are kissing one of his friends. This is not a Tyler Perry movie. This is my wedding! And I didn't plan it this way. You are married, so act like it!"

Mimi rolled down her lipstick tube before turning around and responding to her diminutive accuser. "Why is da woman always seen as the home wrecker?" Mimi barked as she swiveled her neck, throwing her spindly dreadlocks which spread across her back like a shield. "Wendell's best man is married too. Did you ever think he was tryin' to get wit me? I don want dat man!"

"That's a first," Senalda snapped.

Jarena still didn't know what to say or do, which puzzled her because PR crisis management was one of her specialties. Senalda had a right to confront Mimi, but she wondered what the fallout of this clash would be.

"What you sayin'?" Mimi said, her arms folded and head cocked to the side.

"You've got a problem. I don't care if he did approach you first. It was obvious that you did not mind his attention. So how did you end up kissing another man tonight? Did he kiss you first, or did you just trip and fall on his lips? You're supposed to be my matron of honor and you're acting like a hoe!"

"Okay, okay," Jarena said, stepping between them. "Y'all, we cannot do this here. People can probably hear y'all outside. Maybe we should go back to the hotel and talk this through."

"Talk nothing," Senalda hissed. "I've said what I need to say except for one last thing."

She pushed past Jarena and marched up to Whitney, who was perched next to the portion of the bathroom countertop nearest the door. "Whitney, will you be my matron of honor? Clearly, Mimi doesn't respect the sanctity of marriage or give a damn about me or my wedding!"

Mimi opened her mouth like she was going to say something, but nothing came out. Instead, tears cascaded down her cheeks as she ran out of the bathroom. Jarena was about to run after her when the women heard rustling from the far end of the bathroom. A tiny, elderly white woman emerged from the last stall, made her way to the sink and plunged her hands under the faucet. As she washed her age-spotted, veiny hands, she looked up at the friends.

"I don't know which one of you is getting married, and pardon me for listening to your conversation, young ladies, but after fifty-four years of marriage, I believe I have some wisdom to impart." She dried her hands with paper towels and fluffed her silver curls before stepping to the center of the group of women like she was an impromptu keynote speaker. "It is true that weddings and marriages can change friendships, but sometimes it is our very own faults that push our friends away. And those same faults affect marriages."

As quickly as the woman began her speech, it was over when she parted the circle of women rendered catatonic.

"Thank you for the wisdom," Jarena finally managed to say with a smile. She held the door for the woman as she walked toward it.

"You're quite welcome," she said. She threw the paper towels in the trash bin and looked back. "I hope I helped. And congratulations to the beautiful bride in your group!"

Jarena thought about everything that had transpired. Over the course of their years-long friendship, the four women had obviously argued before. All of them had strong personalities so they were bound to rub each other the wrong way from time to time, but this felt different. Like they were at crossroads, and whatever happened at this wedding would determine their friendship going forward.

Having known Mimi since high school, Jarena knew that her boy craziness, now man craziness, clouded her judgment from time to time, but she had gone too far this time, even Jarena had to admit. And she also knew that Senalda, an unabashed control freak, had little tolerance for uncontrolled behavior. And while planning her wedding, her characteristic controlling and newfound-bridezilla ways were on display for everyone to see. Whitney was her girl, but she was not one to ponder the deeper questions of life nor come up with a way to fix this so that everyone would still be friends afterward. So it was up to Jarena, who prided herself on being the most balanced of their group, to fix this. And Jarena kept thinking, because she was convinced the answer would come to her. But she just didn't know how to fix it right then. All she could think of was the very moment that started them on their journey to this destination wedding.

CHAPTER 1

December

·····································

Jarena

OUR COLLECTIVE JOURNEY TO getting married started on December 22 at 11:30 p.m. Wearing my flannel PJs that had been softened into submission through several washings and a silk scarf wrapped around my plaits, I was nestled in bed, about to read a devotional book, when my phone rang.

"Girl, turn to ABC rat now!"

Although Mimi was screeching, I was determined not to buy into her frequent hysterics without a reasonable explanation.

"I'm about to go to sleep, Mimi," I whispered. I conjured up a yawn for effect. "Why?"

"There's gonna be a report on *Nightline* about why single black women aine gettin' married, and they interviewing women from Atlanta. You HAVE to watch."

"Okay, okay," I said, satisfied with her explanation as I rolled over and grabbed my remote from the other side of the bed.

"Alright, bye," she said.

One commercial later, I felt my eyes involuntarily shut, but ABC's Cynthia McFadden's words about successful black women not being able to have the proverbial "love, marriage and a baby carriage" opened them again. She asked if successful black women have too high standards, or if the small selection of black men was the problem. "Linsey Davis tried to answer that question."

I sat up, all of a sudden wide awake, so I pressed the volume button and leaned forward. The journalist, also a black woman, interviewed four women about being single in Atlanta. She started with a beautiful light-skinned black woman with shoulder-length hair, laughing with and toasting three girlfriends at a local restaurant. The journalist told us she was celebrating her thirty-first birthday. Next, she was working in a courtroom as a prosecuting attorney who was also running for state court judge. A clip from an Atlanta Falcons game in the Georgia Dome showed her on the sidelines shaking pom poms while wearing go-go boots. Beyoncé's hit song "Single Ladies (Put A Ring On It)" was the soundtrack connecting the scenes. *So this woman is an attorney running for state court judge AND an Atlanta Falcons cheerleader and she still doesn't have a man!* I groaned out loud.

At thirty-two years old, I was two years past when I thought I would be married, although the rest of my life seemed to be on track. In college, I decided that I wanted to be a publicist and made sure I was working at one of Atlanta's top public relations firms a month after graduation, and by the time I was in mid-twenties, I'd opened my own PR firm, 85 South Public Relations, representing up-and-coming hip hop artists in Atlanta. While I struggled to get a few major clients at first and constantly worked crazy hours, I had managed to carve out a nice career for myself. But here I was ten years after graduating, and I was as single now as I was the day I left school.

"Forty-two percent of black women have never been married," the journalist said, before explaining the statistic was *twice* the amount of white women in the same category. I jumped out of my bed like it was a trampoline and stood next to the television.

She broke it down even further. Of one hundred black men, subtracting men without a high school diploma, job, or who were in jail, only about fifty were even available for marriage, she said.

The rest of the women interviewed were just as beautiful and accomplished. One of them hadn't been in an exclusive relationship since college and she was almost thirty. *Shoot, that's my story too, except I'm two years older.*

I got back in bed and under the covers. *I don't need to see this before I go to bed. I'm probably going to have nightmares now.* I chuckled aloud.

"DEEP," I texted.

"Team Old Maid, beotch," Mimi responded. I laughed, despite being shaken up by the news report.

Steve Harvey appeared on the screen next. A picture of his book *Act Like a Lady, Think Like a Man* flashed across the screen as he spoke.

"How did Steve Harvey with his three-marriages self get to be a relationship guru?" I said. I had tried to avoid the book, but the buzz around it was strong.

Steve agreed that black women didn't have a lot to choose from, but he also said that some had unrealistic standards for black men. He pointed out that a black man doesn't have to be a C-level executive with the paycheck to match to be eligible for marriage. He surprised the four women, walking in on them during the group interview. He actually sang the chorus of "Single Ladies" before advising them to compromise instead of settle. He had a point: not everyone can marry a doctor or a lawyer. Somebody's got to marry the garbage man.

The journalist ended her story with the attorney's words. She said she wanted to get married, but she was not willing to settle to do it. And if that meant she would be single forever, so be it.

I rolled my eyes to heaven, picked up my remote, and hit the power button.

• • •

As I drove from my condo in Smyrna to my Midtown Atlanta suite near Georgia Tech the next morning, another cell-phone ring disturbed my thoughts.

"Good morning, Bossy," I proclaimed. My girls and I had christened Senalda with that name the moment we'd heard Kelis's song "Bossy." Senalda wanted to run everything.

"What's up, girlie?" Senalda replied. "Did you see *Nightline* last night?"

"Unfortunately," I said with a frown.

"Yeah, I know," Senalda said. "Pissed me off too. Especially that statistic that 42 percent of black women have never been married. And they interviewed black women from Atlanta, too. My question is, What about the black men in Atlanta? Why didn't they interview them? If you subtract the trifling men that don't want to settle down because there are too many women to choose, and the gay men—because you know this is the black gay man's capital—black women got it hard out here!"

"Preach!" I said while continuing to navigate rush-hour traffic.

"But you know what?" Senalda continued, "we can't go out like that. We can't be a part of that statistic."

"What do you mean?"

"Okay, I was thinking, me, you and Mimi got it going on, AND we can have men too. We've just got to focus on it. Remember when we first met? I thought I was the only one who mapped out a career in five-year intervals," Senalda said, recalling our first encounter as brand-new professionals in a Delta Sigma Theta Sorority alumnae chapter meeting almost a decade ago.

"Yeah," I said, scared about what was going to come out of Senalda's mouth next. She could make a project out of anything.

"Let's map out our love lives. Since it's December, it's the perfect time to plan for next year. I think we should commit to doing things differently and setting some achievable and measurable goals. And I think we should put our love lives first for once, or at least make them as important as our careers. If we do this thing right, I bet we can meet the men of our dreams AND get married by the end of the year."

"Are you crazy?" I piped. "You can't meet a guy and marry him in a year! Especially in Atlanta."

"Really? I thought you went to church every Sunday?" Senalda said. "What's that verse? All things are possible with God? I haven't been to church in forever, and I know that verse."

"Well, you got me there," I had to admit. "So what's the plan?"

"I was thinking we should meet every month and have monthly and yearly goals. And how about the name 'Destination Wedding' for our project?

That came to me last night. I've always wanted to have a destination wedding, and we are all on a journey to get married. Our first meeting should be a vision board meeting next month. We can have it my house."

"Leave it to you to have a plan," I said with a laugh.

"And Whitney can be our consultant since she's already married," Senalda said.

"Of course," I quickly replied, somewhat humoring her. When Senalda had her mind set on something, no matter how unrealistic, it was best to play along until *she* finally realized the futility of it all.

"Okay, I've got a meeting in a few so I gotta go."

"Holla at you later."

"I've been in the South for more than a decade, and I'm still not used to words like 'holla.' So country! Bye girl."

CHAPTER 2

January

Jarena

I EXAMINED HUNDREDS OF PEOPLE filing into Cascade Baptist Church's mammoth sanctuary in Southwest Atlanta, wondering what they hoped the New Year would bring. I had been in church all of my life, but I didn't let my faith dictate how I lived my life. Basically, I wasn't a holy roller.

I did want to meet someone special, but there was something else going on with me too. I loved my work and was making good money, but over the last few months, the music I was promoting was starting to feel unsavory or meaningless altogether. And all the schmoozing I had to do with the "sadity" and "bougie" folk in the A was getting on my nerves too. I found it hilarious that black people moved to Atlanta from all over since the 1996 Olympics and basically created new realities for themselves. Everybody was ballin' out of control on the weekends and working regular ole jobs on weekdays. None of that used to bother me before because it all seemed like a game that I knew how to play very well. But lately, I'd found myself wanting to stay at home rather than network at yet another party. As I sat in a pew, watching the megachurch fill up, I was hoping for some inspiration for the New Year.

And then I saw the devil out of the corner of my eye. I turned to the left and looked smack dab into the handsome chocolate-brown face of Percival Whitaker III. In the seconds it took for me to force myself to smile casually at him, his wife, and his two girls, the span of our "relationship" flooded my memory.

I met Percy, as he told me to call him, two years ago. After that year's Watch Night Service, I decided to join the church's homeless outreach ministry, and he was one of the ministry leaders. After we passed out blankets one Saturday morning in downtown Atlanta, everyone went for coffee at a nearby Starbucks. We were the last to leave. A natural-hair snob since I lovingly coaxed my once permed hair into a large, wavy Afro that framed my face years ago, I told him I loved his bushy, curly, black hair. He told me my face looked like it smelled like cinnamon. It was corny, but it made me giggle. Having coffee with him led to actual dates. He said he felt weird about dating me since he was a ministry leader and asked me to keep our budding relationship a secret. I was just happy to be dating a handsome Christian man who was at least five-foot nine like me, and I hoped for the best.

After one month of dating, I discovered the real reason why he didn't want anyone to know about us: he was married! But his wife and children were living out of town until she could get a job in Atlanta. I discovered this when they showed up in church with him one Sunday morning at the 8:30 service. I called him afterward, demanding to know what was going on. He explained and begged me to keep our secret. Since our "relationship" only consisted of a few dates without sex, I kept his secret and stopped seeing him immediately. I didn't need the drama. I dropped out of the ministry and began going to the 11 a.m. service instead. I hadn't seen him in over a year, until that moment.

Percy and his family sat in the pew one aisle over, but I willed myself to focus on the service. The four-member praise team began singing a few gospel songs. I was never the biggest gospel music fan, but the frenzied energy of the room convinced me to clap along with the congregation. I was surprised that I started to feel better almost instantaneously.

As they roared the last notes of their final song, the pastor strode up to his stand. "I don't know about y'all, but I don't need no club to get crunk on New Year's Eve," he shouted while moving his arms as if he were about to break out in a run. "I don't need no Dom Perignon to get my party on. This is my Happy Hour right now, and I'm so glad you saw fit to be with Cascade Baptist on tonight! Can I get an 'Amen,' church?"

A chorus of "Amens" rose like incense over the congregation.

"After that music, I know y'all expect me to deliver a powerful word," the pastor said. "The praise team really set it out, but I want to let you know hearing from God is not always about pomp and circumstance, although sometimes that may be the case. Sometimes God is in whisper church, and that is what I will be speaking on tonight. 'God Is in the Whisper.' Turn to 1 Kings 19."

I never took notes in church, but I felt compelled to write down the pastor's words.

"How many of you get tired from time to time? You feel like you have been doing all of the right things, but you're still being attacked. And now you're ready to give up. Well, that is what happened to the prophet Elijah. He was doing what the Lord wanted him to do, but all he was getting was opposition. How many of you know that when you are doing what God wants you to do, you will have opposition? Jesus will not bear the cross alone, but I digress."

My vibrating phone distracted me so I reached in my black Coach bag. "Hey, how are you? You look really nice tonight." I turned to look at Percy, but the devil was no longer sitting with his family. I scanned the rest of the sanctuary but didn't see him. Every now and then since we "broke up," Percy would text me. *I can't believe that devil is bold enough to text me from somewhere in this church with his wife and kids practically sitting next to me.* My phone buzzed again. "No need to respond. Was just saying 'hey.' I thought about you while I was in the bathroom." I cut my phone off, turning my attention back to the pastor.

"So read along with me, church. *Then a great and powerful wind tore the mountains apart and shattered the rocks before the Lord, but the Lord was not in the wind. After the wind there was an earthquake, but the Lord was not in the earthquake. After the earthquake came a fire, but the Lord was not in the fire. And after the fire came a gentle whisper.*

"Am I the only one who finds it fascinating that the Lord came in a whisper? The Lord is the creator of the universe, and He wasn't in the wind, He wasn't in the earthquake, He wasn't in the fire... And then came a 'gentle whisper.' And there He was! I've been meditating on this all week, and the Lord wants me to tell you, church, that some of you are looking for God to show up and smack you over the head. And He will do that sometimes, because some of you are so hardheaded! But sometimes you need to get real quiet so that you can hear God's whisper. And if some of you don't start spending time with the Lord outside of church, you will never hear from Him."

I couldn't believe it. The night that the *Nightline* episode aired, I had read in my devotional book that God's voice was sometimes as quiet as a whisper. I didn't know that passage was particularly special when I read it, but the pastor's words confirmed that it was just what I needed to get my New Year started on the right track.

I looked over at Percy, now back with his family, and beamed. *The devil thought he was going to take my word from me, but he didn't.* His wife smiled a nondescript smile that let me know that she didn't know me but wanted to be pleasant. Instead of looking away as I expected, Percy smiled broadly with his teeth showing and even winked as his wife leaned over to speak to their daughters. Something in my heart flickered, but I let my lips fall into a frown. I guess if the tempter could be in the Garden of Eden, he could be in Cascade Baptist Church. But right then, I claimed this year was going to be *the* year that married men or anything else that tempted me in the past wouldn't be blocking my blessings anymore.

Mimi

I'ma get dat bitch, I said to myself while smiling and holding a microphone in front of the stars of *As the Peach Drops*, the latest reality show filmed in Atlanta. I was one of two radio personalities from KISS 103 co-hosting the official viewing party at Opera Nightclub, and I had to interview the five-person cast. As each one of them chicks blabbered on and on 'bout fake conflicts on their stupid show, I asked questions because I was paid to. But when Jovan walked in the club, I had to stop myself from throwing down my mic, running up to him and kissing him in front of erebody. I loved how he wore his baseball cap to the side and how his sagging jeans hung from his slim frame. He was like a thirty-three-year-old vampire because he could pass for ten years younger or more. *Sexy ta def.*

Last night, erethang was perfect between us. I met him at his spot in Buckhead after he had a late-night session with one of his artists. We watched TV and killed our IHOP breakfast in his bed. As we chilled, eatin' pancakes, I realized I loved dis nigga. So I looked at him, with his curly black hair, copper-colored skin and slanted brown eyes, and said, "You know I love you, right?" I looked back at the television actin' like what I said didn't mean that much. He took a bite of his pancakes before replying. "I got love for you too."

He kept staring at the television, but my heart wanted to bust out of my chest! In the three years that we had been dating on and off, he had never mentioned the word "love" to me. I tried to be cool around him because he told me he didn't believe in monogamous relationships when we first met, but I could tell he was changing his mind FINALLY.

I couldn't help myself so I moved my long dreads from around my face and kissed him even though my mouth was sticky with syrup. I hoped my kiss said what I couldn't. He was the only man for me, and this was our year to make dis shit happen. He returned my kiss and much more. My body got warm all over again thinking 'bout it.

He came in the club tonight with Corazón "Chula" Ramirez, the artist he was with last night before we got together. Chula was the latest artist on his record label, A Shawty Records. He wanted her to be Atlanta's younger version of Mary J. Blige with a Puerto Rican twist, he told me. Since he was a record-label owner and music producer, I was used to seeing him around town with his artists, but as I checked them out while doing my interview, I got a crazy feeling. The way he was whispering in Chula's ear, I just knew he was sleeping with her. His lips touched her ear as he whispered, and she didn't even move away from him. She actually lifted her ear up like she wanted him to kiss it. Since me and Jovan were the same height—five-foot nine—she looked like an elf next to him. I guessed she was no taller than five feet. Her caramel-colored skin matched her hair, which she wore over one shoulder underneath an Atlanta Braves baseball cap she also wore on the side. *How cute. Their caps are both cocked to da side.*

As soon as my interviews were over, I left my bodyguard's side, walked up to Jovan and thumped him on his chest.

"Are you sleeping with dis chick?" I sputtered, knowing my face was probably all red but not caring.

"Mimi, calm down," Jovan said as his slanted eyes narrowed. "What are you talking about?"

"This is what I'm talkin' 'bout," I said, pointing to the two of them. "Y'all got your caps cocked to da side like y'all twins or something."

"I know you need to get yo hand out of my face," Chula said as she turned her cap backward.

"Heffa," I said, facing her and positioning myself between the two of them, "I wasn't talkin' to you, but now that I am, you betta learn how to keep your professional life separate from your personal life or you won't survive in this business."

I noticed then that the noise in the club had reduced by a few decibels as people started to crowd around and look at us like we were on stage. My program director, Angela Preston Locke, one of the few people in the club wearing a suit, walked over to the three of us.

"Mimi, may I speak with you for a moment?" she said with a strained smile. "Follow me over here."

I reluctantly followed her to the opposite end of the club. But I made sure I strutted, since I wanted to give erebody a show, especially since I had on my favorite ass-tight jeans.

"I don't know what that was about, but it needs to be squashed immediately," she said, her shoulder-length bob swinging from side to side. "I don't want the station to have to deal with another one of your fights."

"If you're talking about that last fight, I only told that woman that I would pull every strand of her hair out of her head because she backslapped me," I countered. "It wasn't my fault that woman's husband is one of my biggest fans."

"I didn't see the beginning of that fight, but I know that after your body-guard grabbed the woman, you still went after her."

"Because she was still hollering at me," I replied, but inside, just the word "bodyguard" was all Angela had to say to get me straight. When I worked at another radio station, my bodyguard was shot and killed by an irate listener who was aiming at another radio personality and hit him instead.

"I repeat: this needs to be squashed immediately."

"It is."

"Well, maybe it's time for you to go home since all of your interviews are done, right?"

"Yes, Angela, they are."

"I will see you in the morning, then." She motioned for my bodyguard to come over to us.

"Yes, you will," I said. "Goodnight."

As my bodyguard escorted me out of the club, Dee Daisy, an Atlanta gossip blogger, smiled at me. Only her evil smile didn't mean anythang good. I was sho she was going to blast what happened on her blog tonight.

Damn, I said to myself as I got to the door. It seems I wasn't the only one leaving the scene. Jovan and Chula had disappeared too. Why did Jovan make being with him so hard?

"Da fuck you staring at, Rambo?" My bodyguard stuffed a tissue in my hand and waited while I sopped up my hot tears.

Senalda

I had been reviewing my strategy for my appearance at the National Black MBA Association Atlanta Chapter's New Year's Mixer all day. I was the chapter vice president, but by year's end, I was going to be president. Next year, I planned to run for president of the National Black MBA Association, but I forced myself to focus on my immediate goal for the evening: greeting each and every person at the mixer with a firm handshake and a self-assured yet not stuck-up demeanor.

Just before I opened the doors to the hotel ballroom, I looked down at my navy pantsuit and ran my fingers through my short hair. I straightened my back to rise to my full height of five feet two inches and swung open the door. I scanned the room, estimating that at least one hundred fifty people were there. *It's going to be a late night,* I said to myself. All of the chattering and clinking of glasses would probably have intimidated some people, but I cut through the noise and power-walked toward the largest gathering in the room. About fifteen women had formed a circle around one tall, light-skinned, well-groomed man. I could smell the competition as each woman tried to talk over the woman next to her. *Atlanta men and Atlanta women.* I shook my head from side to side.

As I inched in the group, I looked up and locked eyes with the man the women had encircled.

"Dexter Bailey?" I said, my voice rising. His face looked the same as it did when were in college: model handsome.

"Senalda Warner," he replied with a smile.

I pushed past the woman who was standing directly in front of him and reached up to hug him. *I love a tall man, and he has to be at least six feet.* The woman scowled but moved to the side.

"What are you doing here?" I squealed. "Are you back in Atlanta?"

"Yes, I am." His doe eyes focused on me despite all of the other eyes on him. "Moved back from Miami in December."

"Wow, I haven't seen you since graduation," I said, putting my right hand on my hip.

I didn't wear a lot of makeup, but I hoped that my foundation still enhanced my chestnut-colored skin and that my chintz lipstick still looked fresh.

"I worked at Ryder for a few years in Miami, but now I'm a vice president at UPS. You know the headquarters is here, so I moved back. Plus I missed my family. And my hometown too."

While Dexter recapped the last ten years of his life, my mind wandered. I'd had a crush on Dexter when he was at Morehouse and I was at Spelman, but for whatever reason, we never got together. I tried to listen to what he was saying, but I was mostly examining him from head to toe. He really did look as good as he did then. Even better, actually. He was still slim, but now he had an extra layer of muscle, like a dancer. I suddenly realized that he had stopped talking.

"I'm sorry," I said, shifting my gaze. "What did you just say?"

He smiled.

"What's been up with you?"

"I'm a client manager at Wachovia," I said. "And I'm vice president of this chapter." I looked around the room like it was my domain.

"Impressed, but not surprised—so do you still keep in touch with the crew?"

"Here and there," I replied. "Whitney is still my girl. Did you know Richie Brannon? He was at Morehouse too."

"He was in one of my classes, but I really didn't know him that well. Why?"

"Whitney married Richie, and they have twins—a boy and a girl."

"That's nice," he said, nodding. "Whatever happened to Harley Whitaker? You know, the dude from Cali?"

"Well, I heard through the SpelHouse grapevine that he left his wife for a man!"

"What?!" Richie exclaimed. "I would have never thought he was gay."

"I guess his wife didn't either," I said with a laugh. "So speaking of marriage, what's your status?"

"Oh, me?"

"Really? Yes, you, Dexter," I said, while punching him in his chest. "Don't act!"

"I'm single, but I was engaged a couple of years ago. Obviously, things didn't work out."

His words were sad, but he didn't seem to be, so I forged ahead. "Awww, well, I won't get into all of your business tonight," I said, moving my hand from my hip and reaching into my purse. "We've got to catch up some other time. Here is my card."

I wrote my cell number on the back before pushing it into his hand. He slipped it in his pants pocket.

"Do you have your new business cards yet?"

"Yes, I do," he said while reaching inside of his jacket. "I just got them last week."

"I guess I should feel special since I'm one of the first to get one, huh?" I said with a grin while punching him in the chest again.

"I guess so," was all he said with a half-smile while moving back from my fist.

"Well, I hope to hear from you soon, but I've got to mingle and meet everyone tonight." I wondered if my prompt would elicit the response I wanted: he was going to call me and soon.

"I understand," he said. "It was nice to see you again after all this time."

"Yeah, it was," I said. "See you later."

Even after I moved on to another group and another, I was still thinking about Dexter. I sneaked a look at him to see if he was looking at me too. Another circle of women had gathered around him, and he was smiling over them like a celebrity. I decided then that Dexter was going to be mine. He was not going to be like other Atlanta men who couldn't decide on one woman because of all of the other women in Atlanta who wanted him. I made that decision for him.

Destination Wedding Meeting #1

The last Saturday of January, the single ladies gathered for their inaugural Destination Wedding meeting at Senalda's new home, in one of the new black upper-middle-class developments off of Camp Creek Parkway. Since she hadn't bought all of her furniture yet, they situated themselves on the living room floor.

"I love your home," Jarena cooed, surveying her surroundings. Senalda's dark-red-brick home was on a hill in a neighborhood oasis in the center of dense woods. The glistening crystal and gold chandelier in the foyer could be seen from down the street through a high bay window.

"It's a mansion, Bossy," Jarena noted.

"Really? This is so not a mansion," Senalda said. "It's—"

"Excuse me, you have five bedrooms and four and a half bathrooms for one person," Jarena interrupted her. "Ask someone in the Bluff if this is a mansion. I bet you they would agree with me. Shoot, ask someone who lives in Buckhead. This is a nice home, girl. If you didn't know, let me tell you. You have arrived."

"Okay, yes, I have arrived. But I want more," Senalda said with a laugh as she got up and sauntered to her kitchen. "I have red wine and white wine. Also, I have some brie, crackers and fruit if you guys want to nosh."

"Guurl, you shoulda tol me 'bout the wine when we first walked in," Mimi piped, loosening her multicolored wool scarf and matching knit cap and following Senalda to the kitchen. "What's up with that? I definitely need a drink or three."

"Something wrong?" Senalda turned and faced Mimi.

"Nothing she didn't cause herself," Jarena hollered from the floor.

"What did you do now?" Senalda said as she gestured for Mimi to pick red or white.

"Should I tell her or do you need to tell her?" Jarena said, meeting them in the kitchen.

"You know erethang as usual, so you tell her," Mimi spat back while pointing to the red wine.

"You need to be glad I'm even talkin' to you since you've got me doing work that was so unnecessary," Jarena said. She pulled her phone from her purse and clicked on the internet. "Here's what I was looking for. Right here on lowdownatl.com. 'KISS 103 Deejay Nearly Squares Off With Newcomer Chula Ramirez Over A Shawty Records' Jovan Parker.'"

Jovan Parker was one of Jarena's top clients. She didn't mean to introduce Mimi, Jarena's best friend since ninth grade, to Jovan, a known playa, a few years ago. But local media had been invited to a big dinner she'd hosted for Jovan and his artists at Shout in Midtown, and Mimi had been on the list. She had since told herself that they would have met anyway, since Atlanta was still a small town despite its big-city reputation.

Jarena read the story out loud.

"Really, Mimi?" Senalda said, eyeing Mimi as she handed her a glass of red. "You were about to start another fight while you were on your job? They must love you at KISS 103 if you haven't been fired by now."

Mimi chugged the liquid before responding.

"Dee Daisy is a crab," she stated, while staring at the wall ahead of her.

"Dee Daisy was just doing her job. Spreading gossip," Jarena said. "You created the news, and she had to report it. And then she had to call me to get a statement from Jovan. You could have at least warned me. It was almost midnight when she called."

"I really don need to be punished twice, Jarena," Mimi said. "My boss already wrote me up behind dat shit."

"Over a man that's not your man," Senalda said as she shook her head back and forth.

"Scuuuse me," Mimi said, "I don't see no man livin' with you in this big ole house. I was with Jovan last night. Who were you with?"

"Ladies, let's calm this down," Jarena said. "We came here to work on our man situation, not fight each other."

Senalda's scowl softened. "You're right. That is why we are meeting."

She momentarily disappeared into another room and then reappeared with three black binders, magazines, and poster boards. "Okay, ladies, let's get started. I made three binders; one for each of us. And we can make vision boards after we go through our binders."

"You are organized about everything, Bossy," Jarena said, taking the one with her name on it from her.

"Yes, I am," Senalda said, handing Mimi's binder to her. "I have decided to call our project 'Destination Wedding.'" Her friends nodded their approval as they perused the contents of their binders. On that first page was a sheet entitled "One-Year Plan." The page had several categories, including Immediate Steps to Reach My Goals, Personal Development Objectives to Meet My Goals, Personal Development Objectives That May Hinder My Goals, What Are My Current Skills, Abilities, and Training? What Are Some

Educational Activities That Will Help Me Reach My Goals? What Are My Development Areas and My Plan to Address These Areas?

"I've adapted this from my five-year plan sheet to meet my career objectives," Senalda explained. "What do you think, guys?"

"She's bossy," Jarena said.

Mimi laughed. "You aine neva lied. Seriously, dough, I like the sheet."

"Great," Senalda said. "Our immediate steps are our meetings each month, and I have some activities in mind for our future meetings, but it's all flexible. And I'm open to any ideas that you guys have."

"Because you're the project manager?" Jarena said with a laugh.

"You've got a problem with that?" Senalda retorted.

"I guess not," Jarena declared. Despite her overall dismal dating history, she felt strangely excited. "For better or worse, Destination Wedding, here we come."

She lifted her glass of water and touched the rim to the rims of the wine glasses of her friends.

"To Destination Wedding," the three women toasted.

CHAPTER 3

February

Whitney

ALTHOUGH BLANE AND BLYTHE were only barely five months old, I had a hard time imagining my life before my twin bundles of joy and poop arrived. Staring at them asleep in their cribs, I fought the urge to pick them up and bury my nose in the sandy curls they inherited from Richie. Their hair always smelled like pink baby lotion. But I couldn't wake my noisy cherubs up, as I had spent the better part of the previous hour trying to get them to sleep.

I had tried to rock them both at once, but I couldn't manage it because they kept squirming. So I put Blane in his bouncy seat on the floor and nudged it with my foot while I rocked Blythe over my shoulder in my wooden rocking chair. When Blythe fell asleep, I laid her down in her crib, but then Blane started whimpering. And then Blythe started whimpering after hearing her brother. So I had to start over. And then I realized that Blane pooped in his diaper. No, I couldn't risk them waking up again, so I inched out of their nursery and to my bedroom. Although my maternity leave had been over for a couple of months, I was able to spend time at home with them due to my law firm's flextime program.

As I sank into the pillows on our bed, luxuriating in my favorite gray cashmere robe from Nordstrom, I felt the weight that had accumulated around my midsection while I was pregnant. My twins were a double gift, but it was twice as hard to lose my baby weight. I had been back at the gym since December but my stomach was still paunchy. I thought about the letters Richie and I exchanged the night before our wedding six years ago. In my letter to him, I promised that I would always be his "girl" and "never ever look like a housewife." He promised that he would be my "knight in shining armor" and love me the way I "deserved to be loved."

We had kept our vows and our promises to one another. I kept my black hair long and straight like he liked. I tried not to wear scarves at night, opting to use silk pillowcases to keep my hair moisturized and manageable. I exfoliated my café-au-lait-with-crème-colored skin regularly, although my face still looked blotchy after I gave birth, and I used cocoa butter to soften my stretch marks. There was not an ounce of frump in my wardrobe—so much so that I was known as "Sexy Suit" at Brock & Johnson, where I worked as an employment and labor attorney. My firm was one of the most prestigious law firms in the city. Not that I was ever dressed inappropriately. But I did like to emphasize my femininity. Richie was an awesome provider, and we went on vacations, either domestic or international, every year. And he also made time to listen to me. My girls said we were the perfect couple.

But since the twins were born, I began to feel my husband slipping away. Not physically. He was there almost every day after work, helping me feed and bathe the babies alongside our au pair. We took turns on overnight diaper duty. He posted photos of us smiling with the twins on Facebook, bragging about his growing family. But he didn't initiate sex very much. I was thankful at first. But after I fully healed from my Cesarean, I was looking forward to making love to my husband again. We used to make love about three times a week until I was about eight months pregnant, but now we hadn't had in sex in two months or so and I had to work to get him in the mood the last time we did!

I thought about discussing what was going on with my girls, but my girls were still single. What did they know about marriage? Plus, I wasn't sure what was going on anyway. I noticed that he was leaving our bed almost every night and wouldn't come back for a while. I decided tonight I was going to get some answers.

I fell asleep around 9 p.m., but I looked at my phone when he came to bed. *11:12 p.m.* I closed my eyes, pretending to be asleep. I did nod off for a while but when I felt him rustling beside me, I awoke again but stayed still. I was able to see my phone. *3:47 a.m.* He padded to the bedroom door and was gone. Thankfully, the twins were sleeping for longer periods of time, so they wouldn't reveal nor interrupt my detective work.

About twenty minutes later, I rose from the bed and slipped down the hall. All seemed to be silent in our au pair Gwenaëlle's room, which wasn't too far from the twins' bedroom. I checked our two other bedrooms, but I didn't see anyone. With each empty room, I got more and more anxious.

Finally, I traveled down the stairs to the main level of our three-story home. I checked the living room, dining room, kitchen, den, my office and even the two main-level bathrooms. Richie had to be in the basement, where his office and darkroom were located.

Richie was an OB-GYN but also an amateur photographer. I thought it was a stupid hobby, but as long as he kept his priorities in order, I said nothing about it. I carefully stepped down the basement stairs. A sliver of light glowed from the half-opened door. I peered in.

There was Richie, hunched over his desk like a fiend, mesmerized by his computer screen. I turned my gaze to the screen and nearly gasped. There were two naked women having sex with a man. They were tangled, heaving like wild animals.

I followed him down to the basement for a few more nights. Every night, same spectacle.

On Saturday, I was supposed to be meeting my friends to be a marriage consultant on their Destination Wedding project. What was I going to tell them about marriage?

❦ *Destination Wedding Meeting #2*

Mimi, Senalda, and Jarena met at Jackson's for lunch for their second meeting, on Valentine's Day Eve. They each had reserved Valentine's Day in the last-minute hope that a real date would come through. None of them really believed that would happen this late in the game, but they wanted to give their new project the far-fetched optimism it deserved. Plus, Valentine's Day Eve was also convenient for their married-with-kids friend to meet them at the East Atlanta upscale soul food restaurant.

As Jarena entered the small restaurant, Senalda waved her hand, beckoning her toward their table.

"Hey, Bossy."

She spotted a bottle of champagne on the table next to a nearly full flute. Senalda's chintz lipstick was around the brim.

"Celebrating already, are we?" Jarena deduced.

"Yes dahling," Senalda confirmed with a laugh. "Just because we're 'manless' doesn't mean we have to be gloomy!"

"Is 'manless' even a word?" Jarena said, her Afro shaking as if to punctuate the incredulity.

Whitney, wearing oversized black shades with black leggings and a large, baggy pewter sweater exposing one shoulder, her hair twisted in a messy yet stylish chignon, approached, directed by the hostess.

"Hey, Whitney!" Jarena said. "Girl, how have you been? It's been so long since we've seen you."

"I know, I know," Whitney replied in a breath, carefully settling herself into a chair. "And I've missed y'all too. Alright, Senalda, pour a glass for me. I've got about two hours before I have to get back to the twins. Richie is alone with them, and I don't want him to drop them or anything. Gwenaëlle is off today."

"Drop them?" Senalda said, filling a flute.

"Yes, Bossy," Whitney said. "One baby is an adjustment but two, I mean, are a balancing act."

"Richie will be alright for two hours," Senalda stated, handing her the flute.

Whitney sipped for a minute, quietly.

"Dang lady, you alright?" Jarena said with a laugh. "You're guzzling over there. And can you even drink if you're breastfeeding?"

"I'm not," Whitney said in between sips. She drank again until the champagne was gone. "I tried, but they won't drink my milk. But enough about babies. Bring me back into the adult world. What's going on with y'all?

"Have you heard of La Leche?" Jarena offered. "One of my sorority sisters had the same issue, and she said the group helped her to find a solution."

Whitney took off her shades, laying them on the table before replying. "Is there nothing that you don't know something about?" Whitney asked. "Sweetie, I was trying to change the subject, but I guess that went over your sweet head. For your information, the time frame for breastfeeding has already lapsed. So let's try this again. What are y'all doing for Valentine's Day?"

Totally unfazed, Jarena quickly replied. "Absolutely nothing. This makes three years in a row that I haven't had a date for Valentine's Day."

"You work around all of those artists and you haven't met some hot and rich music executive yet? He doesn't even have to be hot if he's rich!" Whitney said, loose tendrils of hair moving about her face.

"I don't want to date anyone in the business."

"See, you need to get out of your own way!" Whitney said. "Lesson #1: If you meet a man who is rich and is hot, what else do you need? Why wouldn't you date the men that you work with? I mean, how are you going to meet men outside of the music business if you are always working anyway?"

"I tried dating a man in the business ten years ago, and as they say, you don't need to defecate where you eat," Jarena said.

"Really? I think the phrase is 'Don't shit where you eat,'" Senalda chimed in. "Damn, you were already a know-it-all. Don't tell me you're a no-drinking and no-cursing know-it-all now? If that's the case, you're in the wrong business."

"One man! Honey chile, please! You may think you want a man, but you're not acting like it. Senalda, what's going on with you, honey bun? Tell me more about this Destination Wedding project."

Before Senalda was able to respond, they spotted Mimi. Tall and slender with ebony locs nearly to her waist, Mimi was always noticed in any room. And today, she was wearing a black scarf that covered the roots of her locs, black leather pants, and a cutoff black turtleneck sweater that exposed the sliver of her white-chocolate skin between the top of her abdominal muscles and the start of her breasts.

"Have you committed a black-on-black crime?" Whitney quipped with a laugh. "Who are you hiding from?"

"Hey bitches to y'all too," Mimi said. She moved her locs to one shoulder and sat down.

They all cackled with the resplendent joy of being in the company of all of your best friends at once: a precious rarity as an adult. Mimi and Jarena were friends since their Banneker High School days, Senalda and Whitney since Spelman College, and the four since their early twenties. They'd clicked on their first meeting and hung together as a foursome ever since.

"Well, this is our second Destination Wedding meeting but the first with the old married lady here," Senalda said to Jarena and Mimi. "I'm just kidding. You know you can crash our meetings whenever you want to, Whitney."

"Old married lady?" Whitney repeated. "I'm a certified MILF. Y'all want to get where I am. Married with twins and sneaking out to drink with my girls! Seriously though, what's going on with you, Senalda?"

"Well, I did run into Dexter Bailey a couple of weeks ago," Senalda revealed.

"Dexter Bailey from Morehouse, the Alpha?" Whitney said. "What's going on with him? I haven't seen him since we graduated with his cute self."

"He was living in Miami, but his company transferred him to Atlanta last month. He's a VP with UPS."

"All of those initials I like! So is he married? Divorced? Does he have any kids?" Whitney said, in a flurry as she picked up a menu. "And let's order too."

"He almost got married a couple of years or so ago, but he's very single now with no kids as far as I know," Senalda said, "so we exchanged numbers. I called him, and he texted me the next day, but he hasn't called me back yet."

"And he probably won't call you back now until after Valentine's Day," Whitney concluded with a laugh. "You know how men are. Valentine's Day is too serious of a day for a first date. He will probably call you in a week or so."

"I hope so," Senalda said. "He looked good too. Just like I like a man. His suit was still crisp although it was after work. His hairline was still intact AND I noticed that he got into a BMW as everyone was leaving."

Senalda and Whitney clapped their hands together in a resolute high-five over the table.

"Y'all are too much," Jarena said with a laugh. "I'm not gon lie. I don't want a broke man, but he doesn't have to be rich to get my attention."

A pan crashed on the floor in the kitchen behind them and they all whipped around. The door was ajar, revealing two chefs bickering. Another chef jumped between them.

"What's going on there?" Jarena called to their waiter who rushed over to them.

"I apologize for the commotion," he said.

"Are those guys about to fight?" Senalda said.

"They argue all of the time," he said in sigh. "They're brothers and very temperamental. If you like, we can move you to another table so you won't be nearby the kitchen."

"No, that's okay," Senalda said to the waiter before turning back to her friends. "They must be good at what they do because their asses would have been fired a long time ago if they worked for me."

The waiter walked back toward the kitchen as the chef who had separated the feuding chefs came over to them.

"Scuse me ladies, my name is Chef Wendell Robinson," the rounded burly man said. "I want to apologize for what y'all just witnessed. I would be happy to provide free desserts for y'all to make up for interrupting you purrrty ladies. After y'all eat your meal, of course."

"Awww, that's so sweet," Whitney said with a smile. "Do y'all have bread pudding? That's my favorite dessert!"

"Unfortunately, we don't ma'am, but there are many other delicious desserts to choose from." He handed a dessert menu to each of them. "My favorite is our fried fruit pie. Just tell the waiter what you want when you're ready, and I will make sure he doesn't charge you. I wish you were on the menu, purrrty," he said, ogling Senalda without apology. "How can I get some of you?"

The three women raised their eyebrows and smiled at Senalda without uttering a word.

"Well, aren't you the aggressive one?" Senalda said with unflappable poise.

"I didn't mean to make you squirm," Wendell said.

"You didn't."

"I just wanted to tell you that you are the purrrtiest lady here, and I hope you have someone in your life that knows that."

"Thank you—Chef Wendell, isn't it?" Senalda said. "I appreciate the compliment, but I would like to get back to lunch with my friends."

"Got it purrrty," he said, with a smile and a salute. "Have a good lunch, ladies. My apologies again for the ruckus."

"I don even like big ole men, but dude got me squirming over here, gurl," Mimi said to Senalda. "Bossy, you betta get his number!"

"Hold up, Mimi," Jarena said, raising her hand in the hair. "He's a chef. He doesn't meet her criteria."

"No, he doesn't," Senalda said firmly, signaling that she was done discussing the flirtatious chef.

"Okay, there is something I've been wanting to tell y'all, but I wanted to wait until I had a good buzz going first," Whitney said, as she polished off her second flute.

"Are you pregnant again?" Senalda said. "Is that even possible so soon after giving birth?"

"Uh no," Whitney said. "I mean... we are done having children." She hesitated before continuing. "Well, there is no way to really say it without just saying it."

She filled in her girls on what she had observed in her basement. When she finished, the table was silent.

"Is that all?" Senalda finally said. "What man doesn't watch porn from time to time?"

"He has watched pornography every night this week. And we haven't made love in two months."

"I stand corrected," Senalda said. "I haven't had a steady man in years, but I have to admit this sounds like a problem. What are you going to do?"

"I don't know," Whitney said. "We've been married for six years, and I don't think he has ever cheated on me, but I wonder if that is next. Or what if he already has?"

Jarena opened her mouth to say something, anything that could reassure her friend, but Senalda quickly shook her head and mouthed, "No."

Although the restaurant din had disturbed the women just a few minutes earlier, they now were grateful for the noise. None of them knew what to say next.

Jarena

Although I was just at church two days earlier for Watch Night Service, I was still excited about returning for Sunday service. But as I swung my Acura into the parking lot and waited for directions from the parking attendants, I looked to the left and spotted Percy. Without thinking, I made a u-turn and left the parking lot. I had already switched services to avoid the man, and now it seemed he had followed me to the 11 a.m. service. Maybe he hadn't, but I didn't have the energy to fight the devil again while I was trying to be right with God.

So I headed down Cascade. I had no plan. I just drove. As I passed by the palatial homes that lined the street on either side, I could see why Southwest Atlanta, although weathered, was still a legendary hub for upwardly mobile black people in spite of new, affluent-but-not-storied neighborhoods like those in the Camp Creek area or Alpharetta. The homes on Cascade, though most were at least twenty years old, were well-preserved, and the area managed to maintain most of its hovering, lush greenery, unlike a lot of the newer neighborhoods that had huge homes but no trees for miles.

I passed by a few smaller churches but they didn't appeal to me. I was just about at the end of Cascade and about to get onto Fulton Industrial when I noticed a gravel road to my left. It reminded me of one of those pro-verbial deserted country roads on the outskirts of small towns like where I was born in South Georgia. I was intrigued.

I turned down the road and after about a half mile, I saw a small red-brick church with a white steeple. It sounded like the pastor was already speaking because I didn't hear any singing from outside. I contemplated whether to go in. I knew everyone would be looking at me as I entered. I decided to brave it anyway.

After straightening my skirt and fluffing my Afro, I walked in. It looked like the church was literally one room, and the room was packed. A tall, medium-brown-skinned man who I presumed to be the pastor, although he looked like he was around my age, was declaring, "God called me to be a minister when I was fifteen years old in Chicago where I grew up. I grew up in Cabrini Green, but my grandmother still took me to church every Sunday. And one Sunday, while the preacher was speaking in the pulpit, I literally heard God say to me, 'You will be speaking in a pulpit one day.'

"I tried to act like I didn't hear it for years, but I did. I even went to col-lege and graduate school before I finally acknowledged what God had said to me years before. On the day of my business-school graduation, I knew that I would never work in business. In fact, the next year I was in seminary. So why am I telling you this story? There is someone here today who needs to hear that God has a different plan for your life. You've been on the wrong path too long, and it's time to acknowledge that you have been called by God."

I sat on the last wooden pew near the aisle in case I wanted to sneak out. Although I was listening to and looking at the pastor, who I noticed had a nice set of teeth, I was filled with the memory of attending Redemption Baptist Church, another small red-brick church with a white steeple in my hometown of Vidalia, with my own grandmother. I'd had a special relation-ship with my grandmother, and from the time I was about six years old until she died when I was twelve, I would spend the whole summer with her.

Every Sunday morning, I would wake up to the smell of grits cooking and the sounds of gospel music, usually James Cleveland or the Clark Sisters, coming from her record player. My pastel Sunday dress would be hung up on the closet door and a matching hat and gloves would be on the dresser. I loved being with her every summer. Since I was living away from her ("up in the city" she would say), and I was her only grandchild, she spoiled me.

The sounds of hands clapping jolted me out of my reminiscing. I looked down and twisted the diamond and gold wedding ring that I inherited from G-ma. I wore it although there was a chunk missing from the ring since it had to be cut off of her hand after she died. *I need to get this ring fixed.* I quickly gathered my things and left. If this church was like Redemption Baptist, I would have to stand up and introduce myself before the service was over. I wasn't ready for that yet, but I would be coming back—if only to remember my grandmother.

And maybe see the pastor again too. He was cute.

• • •

Since I had ditched Cascade Baptist and stumbled onto Hidden United Methodist, I hadn't been back to either church. I didn't want to run into Percy at Cascade Baptist, but I didn't want to be the new person on display at Hidden United Methodist, either. So for about a month, I got my church on in front of the television, wearing my pajamas and a night scarf. But ever since I visited what seemed like a country church in the heart of metro Atlanta, I could not turn my grandmother's voice off in my head. Her voice was like a genie released from a bottle, emerging at the most inopportune times. When I didn't feel like going to church on Sunday mornings as little girl, she would say, "You did erethang you wanted to do six days of the week, the least you can do on the seventh day is give God thanks for six days to yourself!"

So on Valentine's Day morning, I decided I could still thank God for loving me. Plus, I had to stop that voice from scolding me as I stayed in my bed on Sunday mornings. So I ventured back to that small church at the end of Cascade. I chose to wear my red Kasper suit and oversized pearl jewelry set.

After drinking a smoothie, I hopped in my car, driving from Vinings down 285 to Cascade.

As I crunched through Hidden United Methodist Church's gravel driveway, I hoped I wasn't scuffing my Nine West heels. An usher gave me a welcome card and a program, and again, I chose to sit in the back.

I logged onto Facebook on my phone while waiting for the service to start. The cynical part of me smirked as I waded through mushy and gushy messages many of my married friends posted to one another. It seemed to me that if they were as in-love as they professed to be, they wouldn't feel the need to post a message for everyone to see, especially since they lived in the same household. *Why not just roll over in bed and tell him or her?* But then again, maybe I was being a hater because I was alone yet again on another Valentine's Day.

When Pastor Kirby Moore began to speak, I scanned his biography on the back of the program. He had four degrees! *I love an educated black man. I wonder if he is single.* But reading further, I saw that he was "married to the former Latrice Robinson, and they are the proud parents of a five-year-old daughter, Bailey." *Maybe all of the best ones are really taken*, I thought as I inwardly chuckled. I put down the program to focus on what the pastor was saying.

"As you know, today is Valentine's Day, the day that greeting card companies look forward to all year," Pastor Moore said with a laugh.

The congregation, particularly the men, nodded in agreement and laughed with him.

"On this day, every year, we focus on romantic love. We buy a card or a box of chocolates. We make reservations for the finest restaurants and spend money all over town to show our loved ones just how much they mean to us. And romantic love is a wonderful thing. Ain't that right, baby?" he said looking toward the church's front pew.

A petite, pretty, dark-skinned woman, adorned in a church hat, waved her hand in the air as if to testify to their love. *Wave it, girl!* I would be testifying too, as cute as he was. He was bald but his head was perfectly suited for it, as it was round with no indentations. His eyes were bright with intelligence, and he had the easy movement of a man who was physically fit.

"Believe it or not, there is a love far greater than romantic love. It's the love that we have from God. According to Revelation 21, we, the church, are actually the bride of God, and He wants to dwell among us, His people."

A phone beeped. I didn't realize it was mine until it beeped again. I scrambled to silence it while mouthing "Sorry" as people turned to look back at me. The pastor went on with his sermon. I tried not to look to see who was trying to get in touch with me, but I was too tempted to ignore it.

It was a Facebook friend request from Barry Simpson. I sucked in my breath. I hadn't spoken with Barry since he had called to tell me he was getting married, saying he wanted to tell me before I found out from someone in our network. We dated the last two years we were at the University of Alabama, and we'd broken up because he was ready to get married after college, and I wasn't ready to be someone's wife.

Since then I hadn't had a long-term relationship. Or a short-term relationship, to be honest.

I tried to focus on the rest of the service, but my mind kept drifting back to Barry. I lost my virginity to him. Although I felt kind of guilty because I had been taught to save myself for marriage, I always felt it was a good choice, even if we didn't end up marrying. And that wasn't his fault, anyway. It was mine.

I met him just after I pledged my sorority. I was at a campus fraternity party, and somebody started shooting. Everyone tumbled out of the student center into the parking lot, trying to dodge bullets. I literally ran right into him.

"Excuse me," I said as I backed away from a tall, light-skinned guy with curly blondish hair and blue eyes.

"Don't worry, I will protect you," he said as he held my arms.

I smiled while simultaneously trying to loosen myself from his grip. He was strong, in spite of his lanky frame.

"Just chill with me," he said, looking down at me. "I think the police are here now."

I looked around at all of the people who congregated in the student center parking lot after running out of the Alpha Phi Alpha Pajama Jam. It was strange to see everyone in their pajamas in the parking lot under the fluorescent lighting. I had on red satin pajama shorts and a matching chiffon and satin top. The shorts showed off my long legs, although I was nowhere near scandalous like some of the other girls who were dressed in negligees and garter belts of many colors. One crazy guy even on had a black fishnet type of thing with only bikini briefs underneath. I shook my head.

"You look beautiful tonight," the guy said, finally releasing me.

"Thank you." I continued to survey the parking lot. "I guess the party is over."

"Yeah," he said, still looking down at me. "But I can take you home."

"Wow," I said. "Usually guys don't come out with what they want. At least they try to act like they want something other than skins. I know it's some skeezers out here tonight, but I am not one of them."

I started to walk away. The guy pulled my arm, and I turned to look at him, before snatching my arm back.

"I'm sorry," he said. "I didn't mean to come off like that. Let's start over. My name is Barry Simpson. I'm an Alpha, but I just transferred in from a community college in Huntsville."

He extended his hand toward me to shake it. I looked at him for a moment before speaking.

"My name is Jarena Johnson. I just pledged Delta Sigma Theta, actually. The fact that you're a transfer student explains why I haven't met you yet. I pretty much know all of the Alphas since I was an Alpha sweetheart freshman year."

"Well, I want to know you better," Barry said with a smile. "Can I get your number so I can call you later?"

I studied his face before writing down my number on his hand. When I got back to my dorm room, Barry had already left a message on my answering machine, asking me to call him so that he would know if I got home safely. For a second, I wondered if this dude was going to be a stalker and if I should call him back. But I took a chance and dialed his number. He answered after the first ring.

"Hi, is this Barry?"

"Jarena. So you made it in okay," he said.

Just then some music started blaring, and I heard some voices in the background.

"What's going on there?" I said.

"Can y'all hold it down?" Barry said. "My lady is on the phone... Sorry about that. It looks like my roommates want to continue the party over here."

"Your lady?" I said, smiling into the phone.

"Yeah, one day." I could hear him smiling too.

"Wow, you must think you're all that!"

"Naw, I just recognize when a good thing bumps into me," he said with a laugh. "You want to go to the movies tomorrow night?"

"Okaayyy," I said. "What time?"

"I'll pick you up at 6:30. Alright, sweetheart. I will let you get your beauty sleep, even though you don't need it."

At the time I thought he was laying it on thick to get in my drawers, so I was on guard for the first month or so, but over time I realized what my mother said was true: When a man really wants a woman in the best way, he shows it from the very beginning.

It had taken a few years to get over the end of the relationship. I was the one who didn't want to get married; I loved him, but I wasn't sure what was waiting for me after college. I wanted to be free enough to do whatever I wanted when I wanted. I wanted to meet more men. Maybe even better men. But now it felt like I had scored the jackpot in college, but I was too young and dumb to know it at the time.

A heavyset woman in the pew in front of me shouted, "Hallelujah," the rhythmic, hypnotic jiggle of her flesh transporting me back to the present. I had seen Barry's Facebook profile in the past but had never requested his friendship out of respect for his marriage. But since he had reached to me,

I accepted. He had always respected my boundaries, and I reasoned that nothing would be different now.

Senalda

I forced myself away from my laptop, closing it before sitting down to eat dinner at my brand-new mahogany dining room table. I usually stayed at work until 7, but I had made a New Year's resolution to try to leave by 6. I had also resolved that I wouldn't try to work every spare moment and that I would take better care of myself.

My dinner, baked chicken and sautéed green beans, wasn't a home-cooked meal, but at some point, I reasoned, I would build more time into my schedule to make my meals instead of always getting takeout.

"Baby steps," I said out loud. And then my BlackBerry buzzed.

"Senalda Warner."

"Hey there," a breathy male voice uttered.

"Who is this?" I shot back.

"Am I that forgettable? This is Dexter. From Morehouse."

"Oh, Dexter. Why didn't you identify yourself in the beginning? I thought somebody was playing on the phone for a minute."

I examined myself in the mirror on the wall across the room as I spoke. I couldn't wait for my weekly hair appointment on Saturday morning. My naturally curly hair was starting to curl again, although I preferred a bone-straight look for my pixie cut. As if Dexter could see me, I ran my free hand across my hair.

"How are you, lady?" Dexter said. "I'm leaving work to go home and do more work, but I thought I would call and say hello."

"I know how that is," I replied. "I'm trying to be better about that in the New Year. I want to cook more too, because I get tired of eating restaurant food all of the time."

"You, cook?" Dexter said with a laugh. "You don't look like the type."

"Really?" I retorted. "I can cook. I just don't very often."

"Well, don't get upset with me, lady," he said, still laughing. "Besides, I wanted to take you out to eat anyway. This weekend, actually."

"Oh really?" I said. "That would be nice. Eating out on the weekends is allowed." I laughed.

"Alright. How about 6 on Saturday? Text me your address, and I can pick you up."

"Okay," I said. "See you Saturday. And since you probably don't know the best restaurants in Atlanta, why don't we go Sambuca in Buckhead?"

"Sounds like a plan," he said.

Right after we finished our conversation, I called Whitney to debrief. "You were right, girl," I said, my hand still playing with my hair.

"Right about what, Bossy?"

"Dexter called me a few minutes ago. We're going out on Saturday," I said. "So what does it mean?"

"What does what mean?"

"I'm just wondering what you think about Dexter calling me today instead of a full week after Valentine's Day as you predicted. O married one, please tell me your thoughts."

"Hmmm," she pondered aloud. "I would say that he is definitely interested, since he called only three days after Valentine's Day. But on the other hand, don't call the wedding planner yet, since he could have called and asked you out for Valentine's Day. This is one of those wait-and-see situations. So what are you going to wear? You need to wear something girly. Bright colors. And no pants!"

"Really? What are you saying, Whitney?" I said. "No sugar-coating, either."

"I'm just saying that your wardrobe tends to be... How do I say this? If you're serious about marrying a man this decade, you have to take it up a notch. Isn't your mother Puerto Rican? Add some caliente to your wardrobe!"

"Okay, Mami, you're crazy," I said as she snickered.

I surveyed my closet. After going through my clothes, which were grouped by colors and style, I conceded that Whitney was right. About 90 percent of my wardrobe was from Ann Taylor. If I was serious about Destination Wedding, I would have to add some caliente to my wardrobe.

I had hired a business-image consultant a few years before, when I was positioning myself for a promotion and wanted to make sure that my credentials and appearance were beyond reproach. I wondered if there was an image consultant for sexiness. Maybe this image consultant could come to my house and teach a master class on dressing sexy to me, Jarena, and Mimi. It wasn't that my friends' clothing was drab, at least to me. I've just always believed that if you wanted to get something you've never had, you've got to do something you've never done.

"If we knew how to attract the right guy, we would have been married by now," I said, taking a final look at my closet. But until I could find an image consultant, what was I going to do about Saturday night?

• • •

I picked up Starbucks coffee for my staff at the bank. I loved getting to work early, sometimes by 6, to get started on my daily to-do list before being distracted by everyone else in the colossal building.

I caught my reflection in one of the mirrored panels of the building, digging out my security badge from my purse. My brown pantsuit with a cream silk shirt and leather ankle boots was one of my favorite outfits. As a teenager in New York City, I admired the men in business suits on Wall Street that I saw when my girlfriends and I went shopping downtown. While they dreamed about pretty dresses and marrying the cutest boys in our neighborhood, I dreamed about wearing business suits and having the kind of jobs the men had. That vision stayed with me as I completed high school, graduated from Spelman College, and earned an MBA from Emory University. What I was wearing was proof that there was more than one way to be a woman in this world. I smiled and then I sighed. *What am I going to wear on Saturday?*

"Good mernin, Mizz Warner," a syrupy, high-pitched Southern voice said, interrupting me as I worked on a client's report at my desk.

"Huh?" I answered, temporarily confused. "Oh, good morning, Nashaun. I'm sorry. Is it already 8?"

As I waited for her answer, I realized a solution, albeit temporary, to my dilemma was in front of me. My assistant Nashaun Nance was ghetto gone good. Although her "outside" voice—which she used everywhere—and country twang sometimes irritated me, she was the best assistant I had ever had.

"Izz something wrong?" Nashaun said. Her carefully sculpted, painted-on eyebrows wrinkled while she swung her long wavy weave from her shoulders to her back. *When did weaves become everyday wear?* When I was at Spelman, a few girls had weaves, but most of them only wore them for special occasions. Now, it seemed that Atlanta women were divided into two groups: those who were going natural and those who wore extra-long weaves. Short, permed hairstyles like mine weren't as popular as they were in the '90s when everyone wanted to look like Halle Berry and Toni Braxton. Jarena was always telling me that my natural curls needed to be released instead of relaxed, but I had a corporate image to maintain.

"Nashaun, I'm going to a restaurant on Saturday night," I said, eyeing her blue dress, which was lace at the top and solid at the bottom. *I'm so glad her blazer covers her big, round behind.* She was overweight, but she didn't carry herself like an insecure big girl. "I want to look hot but not easy. You always look so nice at work, so I thought you could help me out."

"Thaaank you, Mizz Warner," Nashaun sang as she twisted all of the way into my office. "I don't want to get all in your bizness, but are you going on a date? I hope you don't mind me asking." She put her hands on her hips and scrutinized me right back.

"Yes," I said, wondering if I was going to regret the conversation.

"A new guy?" Nashaun asked.

"Yes," I replied.

"Well, you know I like to be jazzy, but I know you're on the conservative side," she said as she walked around me. "How about a wrap dress? Wendy Williams wears them all the time on her talk show, and she always looks guud in them. I bet you would too, even if you're not working with all she has."

I rolled my eyes. I remembered Wendy Williams when she was just a big-boobs-with-a-mouth-to-match radio deejay in New York. She was not known for being a fashionista.

"What is a wrap dress?" I said, trying my best to keep my voice neutral.

"Guuurl, I mean Mizz Warner," she squawked, "can I use your computer?"

"Can you?" I said. "You mean, 'May I.'" I waited for her to catch on.

"Oh yes. May I use your computer, Mizz Warner?"

"Yes, you may," I replied.

She sat down in my chair while I stood and looked over her shoulder.

"Ooh, this chair feels soo guud, Mizz Warner!" Nashaun said with a smile as her hips spread in my leather chair as if she had already had a long day. I always had to fight the urge to stare at one of her side teeth, which was framed in gold. *What makes her think that is cute?* "Don't worry. I won't get too comfortable."

I nodded as I saw wrap dress examples pop up on my computer screen. Nashaun was right. Wrap dresses were conservative and sexy at the same time, and they looked good on every body type I saw.

"You should get sum nude platform heels to go with a red wrap dress," she said, swiveling my chair to look at me.

"I don't know about platform heels, but I think I will look for a wrap dress later today, probably after work," I said. "Thank you, Nashaun."

"Anytime, Mizz Warner," she said as she got up and walked toward my door. "I hope you have a good time on your date."

"Me too," I said as I sat down.

I would buy a sexy wrap dress after work, but I had no idea how to actually be sexy.

• • •

An hour before Dexter was scheduled to arrive, I called Mimi for a few tips on being sexy.

"Bossy," Mimi stated after the first ring. "What's good?"

"I'm fine," I said, sliding my left hand through my hair before snatching my hand away, remembering my manicure an hour before. I walked into my closet and pulled out my red wrap dress.

"So what you call me for, den?"

"Must you always be ghetto when I know you know how to speak?"

"Heffa, you called me!"

"Yeah, yeah, you're right," I said. "I need your help. I have a date tonight with a guy that I ran into at a networking event. Remember, I told you guys about him. He went to Morehouse, so I met him in college."

"Oh, are you recycling him?" Mimi hollered. "You gotta be careful when you do that."

"No, I didn't date him in college. We were strictly friends."

"Oh okay, so what's up?"

"Well, you are my sexiest friend," I admitted to her. "So give me some tips about being sexy tonight. But tastefully sexy, Mimi."

"You know you crazy, right?" Mimi said as she laughed. "Off da top of my head, make sure you smell like sumthin other than soap. Look into his eyes like erethang he says is interesting, and laugh A LOT. Be bubbly. Also, you want to be confident and vulnerable at the same damn time. It's tricky, but you can do it if you think about it."

Half an hour later, after realizing that I didn't have any perfume, I opted to wear some Frederick's of Hollywood lotion that Nashaun got me for Christmas. I hoped my scent was "sexy, not stank," as Mimi would say.

A stickler for punctuality, I tried not to be annoyed when I realized Dexter was fifteen minutes late. When the doorbell rang, I thought about effervescence, confidence, and vulnerability.

"Hey, lady," Dexter said with a confident smile as he wrapped his muscular arms around me. "You smell good."

I returned his hug and smile. Between my all-red ensemble and his black sweater and slacks, we could be Falcons fans. I loved football.

"We look like we're going to a Falcons game," I said.

"I may have to take you to a game next season," he said while walking with me to his car. "I love football."

He's already thinking about next year!

"I have concluded we are twins," I said while sinking into the plush black leather passenger seat of his BMW. "We have the exact same car, except I have tan interior."

"Hopefully we will discover we have even more in common tonight," he said, looking at me.

I was glad my skin was dark brown, so he couldn't tell I was blushing.

Despite Atlanta's always-heavy traffic, we made it to Buckhead in forty-five minutes. I couldn't resist checking myself out in the mirrored wall outside the jazz club and restaurant. Although I had a naturally small frame, I wasn't as petite as I was in college. I hadn't gained weight, but 118 pounds at twenty-one years old looks different than it does at thirty-two. I wondered if Dexter noticed. I hated going to the gym, but maybe hiring a trainer would help me to get into a regular workout routine. I sucked in my stomach as we were shown to our booth. I tried to judge how far to sit away from him and decided to leave enough space that another person could sit between us. First date etiquette was so tricky.

"So update me on the last ten years," Dexter said as he laid his BlackBerry next to a menu. "You look the same as you did back then, except when we first met you had glasses. Whatever happened to your glasses, by the way? They were gone by junior year."

I slowly exhaled before responding.

"I got rid of them after I pledged Delta—or rather, my Delta big sisters got rid of them. They had an image to maintain at Spelman," I said as I chuckled.

"So, back to the present," Dexter said, looking directly into my eyes. "I'm sure you have conquered the world by now. I heard from my contacts that you are on the short list for president of the National Black MBA Association."

"Who told you that?" I said, wondering about his contacts. "I just want to run for president of the Atlanta chapter. Maybe I will run nationally one day, but first things first."

Dexter's BlackBerry buzzed on the table, and he looked down to check it.

"I'm sorry. What were you saying?"

"I was saying that working at the national level of the association feels like a natural progression for me, although I'm not sure how I would make time for my responsibilities with the association and my work."

"Lady, I'm sure that you can handle it like you handle everything else," Dexter said. "So are you ready to order? I hope they have a good steak. I heard this place was a nice jazz spot, but I hope they have good food too."

"I've been craving steak all week myself," I said, marveling at how much we were alike. "I'm trying to eat less red meat, but one night won't hurt. I think I'm going to order the rib eye."

Had I been alone, I would have eaten my entire meal, but I decided to leave a few bites on my plate. Dexter, on the other hand, ate his whole meal. He asked me to dance after we both declined dessert. Mimi told me that you can tell how a guy is going to be in bed based on how he dances, and I was eager to hit the dance floor.

The restaurant's house band sang a variety of songs, from modified hip hop to bona fide slow jams. Dexter pulled me to him and swayed as the band performed a competent rendition of D'Angelo's "Lady." He sang the lyrics as we danced. I almost gasped when I felt his pants vibrate before realizing it was his BlackBerry again. I liked his rhythm.

We sat back down at our table to rest for a second. When the bill arrived, I reached for it while simultaneously reaching in my purse for my credit card.

"I got it," Dexter said, putting his hand on mine and shaking his head. "Is that how Atlanta women roll nowadays? I know I haven't lived here since college, but have things changed that much?"

"I can't speak for all Atlanta women, but I can afford to pay my own way when needed," I declared. "I make six figures. Do you?"

He almost frowned but then smiled instead. "You don't need to tonight," he said. "If you let me be the man, you can be the woman. And yes, I am working with six figures too."

Later that night, as I tied my hair down in my scarf, I smiled, remembering feeling Dexter's breath in my ear when we were dancing. I studied his LinkedIn page before going to sleep. Based on his profile, he had made all the right moves since college. And now he was employed by one of the country's top Fortune 500 companies. Plus, he had a powerful network. *He was vice president of the Miami chapter of the Black MBA Association! I wonder why he didn't tell me. Wow, we really are alike.* I made a mental note to ask him about that the next time we talked.

So far, Destination Wedding was on track. Tonight a first date. Six months from now an engagement. And Puerto Rico in December would be perfect for a wedding.

CHAPTER 4

March

···

🦋 *Destination Wedding Meeting #3*
_____

SENALDA CORRALLED THE WOMEN for their third Destination Wedding meeting at The Veronique Experience, where the owner, Veronique Carter, would help them select sexy but age-appropriate clothing. Senalda's former business-image consultant highly recommended her. Her clothing boutique was located in East Atlanta Village, a quaint assembling of refurbished brick buildings, busy eateries, and brightly painted wooden shotgun homes, with major retailers sprinkled in.

Spring was still days away, but Atlanta weather changed without warning. Mimi wore cutoff jean shorts, a baby-doll T-shirt, and thong sandals, while her friends were still covered up. The women chatted as they bustled through the door.

"Hi ladies, come on in," called out a tall, elegantly thin, light-skinned black woman with silky, very long black hair draped over one shoulder. It seemed the only makeup she had on was bright red lipstick, which wasn't even necessary to enhance her refined beauty. She wore a baggy green print dress that flared at the sides and sparkly gold flats, an understated yet stylish ensemble.

"I'm Veronique Carter. You must be Senalda Warner," she said, walking up to Senalda and extending her hand toward her.

"You are correct," Senalda confirmed, removing her sunglasses with one hand and shaking Veronique's hand with the other. "And this is Jarena and Mimi."

"Good," she said. "Let's get started. Judging by what you're wearing, I've already got a good idea about your personal styles. My specialty is helping women define and enhance their personal style. I don't want to change what you wear. I simply aim to enhance it."

"Perfect," Senalda chimed in. "I'm more of a conservative dresser, so I'm usually in black, brown, or navy pantsuits for work, but I have been experimenting lately with other colors."

"Jarena, I can tell your style is conservative too, but with a twist," Veronique said, gesturing toward her. "Your clothing is pretty conservative, but your hairstyle shows me that you have some alternative thoughts or ideas."

"I cannot believe you just described me!" Jarena said, stealing a look at her fluffy, defined Afro in one of the mirrors. Some days her curls refused to separate, and her hair looked like clustered black cotton balls affixed to her scalp, but today they stretched themselves into shiny ringlets. "I don't know if anyone has been able to do that so quickly. So what do you have in mind for me? I think—"

"Well, you probably wear a lot of solid clothing in primary colors," Veronique said, interrupting Jarena. "But I think you should explore wearing prints."

She walked over to some silk blouses hung on a nearby rack. "You could pair this black-and-white leopard-print blouse with this red pencil skirt," she said, picking up the skirt and placing it next to the blouse. "The solid bottom is conservative, and the black-and-white colors are conservative, but the leopard print shows that you have a wild side. Do you want to try these on?"

"Okay, but I was thinking—" Jarena replied.

"Where is your dressing room?" Senalda said as she stepped to Veronique, took the clothes from her, and handed them to Jarena while rolling her eyes.

Veronique smiled while pointing toward the back of the store.

"I got next," Mimi piped. "Lemme save you some time by telling you that my style is tomboy chic/ATL playa. So whaddaya think?" Senalda and Jarena nodded while chuckling.

"Exactly," Veronique confirmed. "But I know you're a radio personality for KISS 103, which mostly plays 'urban' music. Your style is fine for a rock 'n' roll radio station, but I would imagine that you probably stand out at work or industry parties."

"I wanna stand out," Mimi blurted.

"Yes, you should, but in a good way," Veronique continued. "No disrespect, but I think we are all in our thirties. You also have to allow room for getting older or more mature in your clothing choices. Your coloring and body frame are very similar to my coloring and body frame, although our personal style is different. I think you should wear more form-fitting but conservative clothing in pastel colors. What about this baby-blue dress? It would accentuate your curves so that you would stand out, but the style of this dress is more R&B and mature."

"Miss Thang Mimi already gets men in baggy or ripped clothing, so I don't know what will happen if she wears that dress," Senalda nearly shouted.

"I can tell she is flirty, but this style would attract a different kind of man," she said, handing the dress to Mimi.

"Wow, are you a life coach or a clothing stylist?" Senalda said. "You know what you're talking about! Girl, get back there and try on that dress!"

"Okay, okay," Mimi said, "but I already got da man I want. And I do wear tight stuff to radio events sometimes, but not in dis color."

Senalda rolled her eyes before looking at Veronique. "So what about me?" She spun around, perusing the store. "I've been wearing red lately since I started dating a new guy, so I think I may have a head start in changing my wardrobe. Of course, I am open to a more informed opinion."

"I've been envisioning your style since we spoke on the phone," Veronique said. "Obviously, you are a very polished and professional woman. You are strictly business. Wearing red goes with your skin tone, but have you ever thought about adding some other jewel tones? Like fuchsia, blue, or green? Colors that pop!"

"Me in all of those colors?" Senalda exclaimed, pointing to herself. "I don't want to look like a rainbow!"

"I think they would soften you a bit. You mentioned that you're looking for love this year in our initial conversation, and I think these colors are very feminine but strong."

Senalda's inner feminist wanted to shut down the stylist, but she had been sneaking peeks at Veronique's colossal diamond on her slender wedding finger. She was apparently engaged to someone wealthy enough to buy her a beautiful solitaire that could be the down payment for a home. Her personal style was flawless. And her store was beautiful.

"How about this fuchsia chiffon dress?" Veronique walked to a black wardrobe bag hanging on a stand behind the cash register and unzipped it. Senalda took the dress from her and held it in front of her body as she looked in a full-length mirror. It was the type of dress that you wore to party with a man, as it was short enough to be flirty but with enough material to be respectable.

"I would have never picked this for myself, but I will give it go, I guess," Senalda murmured.

Mimi burst into the main room as Senalda headed to the back of the store.

"You in hot pink?" Mimi shouted.

"You in one color?" Senalda retorted. "But you look good, I must say."

Senalda and Veronique evaluated how Mimi looked in the dress. The fit gave her a more finished look while still framing her body. The door of the store opened then, and a tall man, who was the color of white-bread crust, came inside. Although it was Saturday, the man wore a crisply ironed beige dress shirt over creased blue jeans. He was handsome in a buttoned-up kind of way.

"Hello," Veronique said, marching up to the man. "Actually, my store is closed until noon. I forgot to lock my door, so I apologize for the mistake. Would you mind coming back in thirty minutes?"

"Sure, no problem. I'm trying to find a gift for my mother. I saw all of these beautiful women in here, and I figured I could find the right gift for her here. I'll be back."

Pushing his rectangular wire-rimmed glasses up on his nose, he stepped to Mimi and said, "I usually don't do things like this, and I hope you don't think I'm being a jerk, but if you're wondering if you should buy the dress, the answer is yes. And if you like, I can take you to dinner tonight so that you can have somewhere to wear it."

He paused, noticing the other's women's eyes were fixated on him. "Okay, ladies, I will let you get back to your shopping." He made a half turn to leave before turning back. "I have a business card if you want to call me later." He smiled, put his card in Mimi's hand, and walked out the door without Mimi saying a word.

"Whoa," Senalda said. "Let me hurry and try on this dress. Maybe if I do, another cutie will step up in here unannounced and ask me out in front of everyone. Let me see his card."

She snatched it out of Mimi's limp hand.

"His name is *Dr.* Ian Goodman. Jackpot! Now you can dump that zero you been booed up with for way too long and get with this hero. You better call him today or I will be mad. Veronique, you have proven you have skills."

"Shut up, Senalda," Mimi said, scrunching up her face like she smelled spoiled milk. "Dat man was corny. And I don know 'bout this dress, either. You see my whole ass. What lil bit I have, anyway."

"I know you just didn't say that. You always find a way to show your ass. Need I remind of the fight you started over Jovan? You didn't mind showing your ass then, did you? At least this time you will have a man at the end of the day!"

"Jarena, you betta come get yo girl," Mimi said raising her hand in the air, "cuz she's fun to get cussed out."

"Senalda, you are in rare form, even for you," Jarena said, emerging from the dressing room. "And on the other hand, Mimi, I didn't hear you say anything to that man. I've never seen Jovan show that much emotion for you in the whole time y'all have been 'kickin' it.'"

"See, that's what's I'm talking about," Senalda said, interrupting Jarena. "Nobody should be 'kickin' it' if they are not in college. We are too old to be 'kickin' it.' If you don't call that man, I will."

"Ladies, y'all are hilarious!" Veronique declared, giggling, relaxing her carefully cultivated professional veneer.

"I'm sorry," Senalda said, pivoting toward the counter where the stylist had positioned herself. "We've been best friends for years, and we can get out of hand sometimes. I hope we haven't embarrassed you. You've been so gracious to meet with us and shut down your store for us. Let me go try on this dress— and there better be a man waiting for me when I come back!"

Whitney

It had been a month since I discovered Richie's secret, and I had been debating when to confront my pornography-addict husband ever since. Maybe addict was too strong of a word. You can only be addicted to drugs. And everyone knows that only people who do not have enough willpower or class are addicted to drugs. My Richie was nothing like that, but something was going on, and I couldn't ignore it anymore.

Years ago I had found a recipe for "engagement chicken" in a magazine. The author of the article promised that men who ate this chicken would ask their girlfriends to marry them within months. So one day I decided to make the engagement chicken. Just a few weeks later Richie proposed to me, on Christmas Eve.

I found a chicken and the rest of the ingredients in the refrigerator. There were some russet potatoes in the pantry and some asparagus in the freezer. Two-and-a-half hours later, the meal was simmering on the stove. I changed the twins' diapers and set them in front of the den television set while I searched for the right flouncy dress and heels, since I was pathetically short at five feet, two inches.

I heard the garage door opening. Richie was home. I felt a warm sensation inside of my chest. Even after six years of marriage, I still thought he was one of the most scrumptious guys I had ever seen. He was almost six feet tall with solid muscles, although he hadn't played baseball like he did in college for more than a decade. We both had the same complexion. Some of our friends even thought we looked like we were brother and sister, though our hair color was different. Richie's hair was brown with sandy highlights. He had a perfect smile made possible by years of braces while he was in prep school. He practically looked the same as he did when we met as seniors at Spelman and Morehouse.

"Whit," he called, louder than he needed to since I was also in the kitchen. At times, the bass in his voice made it seem like he was angry even when he wasn't.

"Hey, sweetiekins," I said, walking up to him and planting my lips on his. I felt my hair whip across my back which made me shiver a little. "How was your day?"

"I'm just glad it's over." His chest deflated as he dropped a folder on a table. "I may have to go back at 7 again tomorrow morning, but it's over for tonight. At least I think it is."

Although I was disappointed that he would probably have to work on the weekend, we always tried to be understanding with each other about our demanding careers. And an OB-GYN's schedule was especially unpredictable, but I never complained. No one gets to the top working regular hours.

"How are the twins?" he said, walking into the den. "Awww, look at my big man and my little lady!"

The babies started squealing as he picked them up. I smiled at my family from the doorway. He placed Blythe on his right arm while balancing Blane on his left.

"Is that my favorite dinner cooking?" he said, settling onto one of our den couches.

"Yes." I smiled and sashayed past him.

"I know this isn't our anniversary." He looked at me over the babies' heads while nuzzling their faces. "Did you go out and buy a car or something? What's up?"

"It's been a long time since I made your favorite dinner, and I just wanted to surprise you," I sang as I sat down on the couch, snuggling up to him and the twins.

He shifted, moving away from me. "Okay, take the twins while I get a shower, and I'll be back in fifteen."

"Okay, sweetiekins," I said, positioning the twins in my arms after he thrust them toward me.

As promised, fifteen minutes later, Richie appeared in the formal dining room where I had set the table. The twins were in their high chairs opposite where I positioned our place settings. Richie moved their chairs so that they were between us.

"I don't want the twins to think we're ignoring them." He straightened their chairs before sitting down while I stood, looking at him. "Have they eaten? Where is their food? Do you want me to get some baby food from the kitchen?"

He didn't wait for me to answer. Instead, he got up and breezed by me, ignoring the fact that I was still standing with my hands on my hips. He ambled back into the dining room with their peas and green apples and set their food down on the table as he asked, "Do you have my favorite beer? I need one tonight." He started to go back to the kitchen, but my words stopped him.

"Richie, why are you watching pornography in the basement every night? Are you a pornography addict now?" I was tired of buttering him up. I just wanted the truth at this point. The words flew from my mouth as if I had involuntarily thrown them up. I tightened my grip on my hips, waiting for him to respond.

"Whaaat?" Richie barked. "Porn? Me? What are you talking about?"

"Yes, you and pornography every night! That's what I'm talking about!" The twins began to whimper, but I charged on. "Don't try and deny it. I had been wondering where you were going nearly every night now for months. At first I thought you were changing the twins' diapers or rocking them to sleep or working or something. Anything that would make sense. But you are gone for hours so I started to worry. So I've been letting you get up and leave our bed, and then a little while later I follow you."

Richie didn't say anything for a moment. "A lot of men watch porn every now and then," he finally muttered.

"Do a lot of men watch pornography INSTEAD of making love to their wives?"

He said nothing.

"What's wrong?" I said, hearing my voice go soft. "Are you not attracted to me anymore? I guess I'm not your hot chick or your girl anymore, since I gained weight." I pinched the extra skin around my waist.

"It's not that," he said, looking at me briefly. "You're beautiful."

"In a mother kind of way, right? You don't even want to make love to me anymore unless I initiate it. So you would rather get all hot from naked pictures online rather than be with your wife?"

"Whitney, I've been so stressed out. Sometimes a man just needs..." He shook his head. "I just need to—"

"Oh, oh, so giving birth to TWO babies at the same time and being a lawyer at one of the top firms in the city is not stressful? I mean, that's all you've got?" The venom in my voice even surprised me. The twins' whimpering turned into crying. I was glad Gwenaëlle had the night off.

"Would you calm down? All of this took me by surprise, Whit," Richie offered in a more conciliatory yet still defensive tone. "Can you understand that?

"What took you by surprise?" I screeched, knowing that my tone would make my reserved husband shut down any second.

"Being a father," Richie admitted. "We've been by ourselves for years, and now we have two other people to take care of."

The twins wailed beyond the point of return. "What are you saying? We waited six years to have children. Grow up. I'm going upstairs."

I picked up our babies and stomped up the stairs to their nursery. I plopped down in the rocking chair with a twin on either shoulder. As we rocked, their wails reverted back to crying and then to whimpers and then they were asleep. I was calm again too, at least on the outside, but I was more confused than ever.

Mimi

A whole week had passed since Jovan and I had seen each other, and now I had to see him with dat trick Chula. I don't know what it was 'bout her that made me so crazy! Jovan had worked with other young female artists before, but I just couldn't shake that feeling that something was different this time. But I tried to roll wid it because I know in my bones that what we have together when we are together, he couldn't have with any other female. Three years had to mean something, especially since he could pull any chick he wanted. And whatever chick he found himself with from time to time didn't even matter because he always came checkin' for me in the end.

So I sat in the studio trying to psych myself up to be nice, since I had to interview her in about ten minutes. Jarena, Jovan, and Chula were coming up to KISS 103 to be on my show "Mid-Day Motivation with Mimi." Her album *Wassup Señorita?* was dropping today, and my station was one of their stops for media coverage throughout the day. Jarena had called me early in the morning with a special request.

"I know you don't like Chula, but please, for the sake of my business, please promise me that you will be professional with her, at least on the air. Please."

I mumbled, "Okay," after laughing about how many times Jarena said "please." But now that they were on the way up, I wasn't sho if I could keep my promise. Luckily, I saw Jarena first. Her eyes locked with mine as if to remind me. But she only smiled and said, "Mimi, so nice to see you again."

"Hey gurl," I said, hugging her while looking over her shoulder at Jovan and Chula. They stood side by side looking like a modern-day Aaliyah and R. Kelly. If Aaliyah was short and stubby, with about twenty more pounds on her. I noticed that Chula's thighs looked chunkier than they did on the album cover. Like sausages stuffed into jeans. Jovan told me that she had to lose twenty pounds before they could take promotional photos, but it looked like she had eaten at least ten of them back on.

"Ms. Mimi Gayle," Jovan said, reaching his hand to me to shake mine. Jarena had trained Jovan to be professional when it came to the PR business, regardless of how well we knew each other outside of the station. I shook his hand and gave it a little extra squeeze. His lips loosened into a tight smile, but I could tell he wanted to return my cheesy grin.

I said nothing directly to Chula, but I asked the three of them to sit down opposite of me. After they sat down, I noticed Chula's thigh was touching Jovan's, and she did nothing to stop it. I picked up the album cover, examining it again.

"Chula, those papas fritas, frijoles and all that Puerto Rican food must be real good."

Jarena must have trained Chula well too because she didn't say anything for a second, but then when I puffed out my cheeks, she had words for me too.

"You know, you're a real bitch," Chula hollered. "I didn't even want to come to this lame-ass station anyway. You mad because I'm 'bout to blow up and you stuck here talking to stars instead of a being a star like me."

Jarena opened her mouth, but before she could say anything, I launched the interview. "This is Mimi, your mid-day motivator, reminding y'all to Elevate, Celebrate, Not Playa Hate. Guess who we got in the studio today? Corazón, better known as 'Chula,' Ramirez, the latest artist from A Shawty Records."

I asked all of the right questions and gave Chula the chance to recite her rehearsed answers. But a second after the interview was over and her first single, "I♥U," was playing, I braced for the fallout. The station's phone lines were slammed with people calling about Chula's going off on me before the interview. As Jarena, Jovan, and Chula were getting their stuff together to leave, Angela rushed in.

"Hi Jarena, would you mind waiting here for a few minutes?" Angela said. "I want to speak with Mimi in my office for a few minutes, and then I will be back to speak with you."

Since Angela had exactly six commercials to speak with me, she made it quick.

"What the hell was that?" She crossed her arms and waited for my answer.

"What, Angela?"

"We don't have time to play games. Why was the mic open before you interviewed Chula? The whole city heard her call you a bitch. But the funny thing is, no one heard you say anything to her first."

"She did call me a bitch," I said. "And she called KISS lame. I don't think we should promote her album, since she obviously thinks we're beneath her anyway."

"So you said nothing to provoke her?" Angela probed. "And you happened to turn on the mic seconds before you started interviewing her?" She shook her head in disbelief before continuing. "Your spontaneity and sassiness are two of the reasons why you're one of the best personalities I've ever had. But lying won't be tolerated."

I sighed. Angela was the coolest boss I've ever had. I had to be straight with her.

After filling her in, it was Angela's turn to sigh.

"So what are we going to do about this, Mimi?"

I didn't say a word. I wasn't giving her the gun to shoot me.

"Finish your show and come back to my office when it's over. We'll talk about it then."

I went back to the studio, bracing myself for Jarena's reaction next.

"Have you lost your mind?" she started. "I asked you to be professional with Chula this very morning and you do the exact opposite. I would go off on you, but I'm guessing getting fired is punishment enough."

"I didn't get fired."

"Hmmpph," she said. "Well, it's coming if you don't figure out a way to be professional with Chula, because she is Jovan's top artist right now. And she's not going anywhere, either. And I didn't want to say this before, but obviously I need to get through to you now. Jovan is not your man. He has never been. And the sooner you can accept that, the better off you will be."

I felt my face getting red, but I didn't allow myself to cry. My producer signaled that it was time for me to get back on the air then, so I didn't have time to think about what Angela or Jarena said until the next commercial break.

My boss was mad at me. My gurl was mad at me. My man was mad at me. I kept waiting for a call or text from Jovan, but after a while, I figured that Jarena smoothed over everything with him. I knew I could count on my best friend.

At ten till 2, I closed out my show. "This is Mimi, your mid-day motivator reminding y'all to Elevate, Celebrate, Not Playa Hate. And I'm out."

I got my satchel and walked to Angela's office.

"Come on in, Mimi," she said without up looking up from her desk. "And close the door."

I did as she asked.

"Have a seat." She eyeballed me then while motioning to the chairs in front of her desk. "In spite of everything, you had a good show today, and after that drama you created, we probably got good ratings, but that is beside the point. This is the second time you've had an issue with this artist. I'm not going to get into your personal life, but I suspect this has something to do with your little crush on that producer Jovan Parker. But that's your business. My business is this radio station. After thinking about what happened, I've decided I won't fire you THIS time, but I do have to suspend you. For three days. Effective immediately. I've already scheduled a fill-in jock for the next three days. So, do you have anything to say?"

I moved my head from side to side.

"Okay, well I do," she said. "If I were you, I would not see these three days as a vacation; I would see it as an opportunity to get my priorities in order. Do you want your career or do you want this man? From where I'm sitting, it looks like you could lose both."

CHAPTER 5

April

·············(·················

🎀 Destination Wedding Meeting #4

ON A WHIM, SENALDA swung her BMW into the Barnes & Noble parking lot on Camp Creek Parkway on her way home from work. Since she was always reading books on how to effectively manage her team, generate new clientele, and advance in her career in general, she thought she could browse the bookstore's self-help department for books on relationships and how to meet and catch a mate. The rows and rows of relationship books were overwhelming, but she was undeterred, scanning until one title, *How to Get a Date Worth Keeping*, seemed to separate itself from the others. The author, psychologist Dr. Henry Cloud, became a dating coach for a woman who hadn't been on date in two years. He bet her that with his help, she would be dating in six months. Only five months later, she was in a "significant dating relationship!" He also ended up officiating her wedding!

She hadn't ever considered that a psychologist could also be a dating coach. So she mined her network until a woman recommended Dr. Catherine Cleghorne, a psychologist who also specialized in dating and/or romantic relationships. The woman said the psychologist's counseling helped her to meet her husband. After perusing Dr. Cleghorne's website and a quick telephone interview, Senalda set up a conference call for the psychologist to explain her services to the Destination Wedding group. The conference call would be their fourth Destination Wedding Meeting. Whitney decided to be on the call too. Now that she had confronted Richie about his pornography, she wasn't sure what to do next and hoped the psychologist would have some ideas.

"Hello ladies, we are in our fourth month of our Destination Wedding project!" Senalda began the call with enough enthusiasm to spare. "Can you guys believe it? Last month, we worked on the outside, and I hope all of us incorporated what we learned at The Veronique Experience. But now I think it's time to work on the inside. Dr. Cleghorne, would you mind telling my friends more about you and what you have to offer?"

"Not at all." She cleared her throat and took a noisy, prolonged sip of some liquid. "I apologize. This Atlanta pollen kills me every year! What was I saying? Oh yes, where do I start? I guess my name is a good place to start. My name is Dr. Catherine Cleghorne, but everyone, including my clients, calls me CC. I am a licensed psychologist. I opened up my own practice, Cleghorn Counseling, in 2008—or was that 2007? Menopause makes you lose your mind! I specialize in romantic relationship counseling, but I'm also passionate about career counseling, so that is one of my other specialties. That's the abridged version of my bio. Do you have any questions for me? I'm better at answering questions than reciting information these days." She cackled and then was quiet.

"Yes," Whitney chimed in. "Do you counsel married couples or just single ladies?"

"With the divorce rate like it is, most of my business is married couples," CC said with a laugh that ended in a snort. "How can I help you, dear? Are you married?"

Whitney paused for a beat before she replied. "Yes, I am. Seven years in August." The tone of her voice was suddenly artificially high-pitched, as if she had inhaled helium from a balloon.

"Oh, coming up on the seven-year itch, are we?" CC chortled. "Who's cheating? You or him? Don't answer that! In all seriousness, the seven-year itch phenomenon is very real. Many couples divorce after being married for that amount of time, so if you and your hubby have anything going on, I highly recommend that the two of you get counseling, even if it is not with me."

"Nobody's cheating," Whitney declared. "My husband has just been watching naked women online and—"

"Don't kid yourself, dear," CC interrupted. "Call it what it is. Is he watching pornography? That can be very destructive to a marriage, but it doesn't have to be a death knell unless it is ignored. So is that what your husband is doing, dear?"

"I guess so, but I only think it's only been going on for a few months."

"That you know of. Have you spoken to him about it?"

"Yes." The tone of Whitney's voice now seemed as deflated as a popped balloon.

"Again, no need to despair. If you husband is open to counseling, I would like have the two of you come into my office and flesh everything out. Let me get my appointment book. Hold on, dear."

The women heard rustling papers, what sounded like a belch followed by deliberate footsteps, but there was radio silence on their end.

"Awww, let's see. Luckily for you I had a cancelation for a 5 p.m. Monday appointment. Otherwise, it will have to be on April 15 at 6. Which would you like dear?"

"Dr. Cleghorne—" Whitney started.

"Please call me CC," she interrupted.

"CC, let me speak with my husband about his schedule. He's an OB-GYN, so his schedule changes frequently."

"Fine, dear, but don't delay too long. These types of issues only get worse, never better, if they are untreated. Senalda dear, I have another appointment that I need to get ready for, but I hope your group has a good idea about my services."

"Yes, thank you very much." Senalda said a little too loudly as if she had been awakened from a trance.

"Thank you again, dear, for inviting me. Goodbye to all of you. Whitney, dear, a time bomb is ticking in your marriage. Don't let it explode. I'll be expecting your call. And one more thing for the rest of you: So many modern women plan their professional lives but don't plan their personal lives. And then they wonder why, when they are finally ready to marry, there is no one left to marry, or they are too old to have a baby. Alright dears, I really must go."

CC hung up then.

"Dayum." Mimi expressed the collective reaction of the group as the rest were silent.

"I really thought that CC was too kooky to take seriously until her last words about modern women," Whitney finally said. "But she is right. I knew that I wouldn't graduate from college without having met my husband. If y'all had planned to meet your husbands back then, there would be no need for this project now. You will never have as many good men to choose from as you did in college."

"You may have had a plan to get yo man, but what's yo plan to keep him?" Mimi retaliated with a snicker.

Mimi

I scrolled through emailed invites on my phone. As a radio personality, I received hundreds of them to events all around the A, from block parties in the hood to upscale parties with celebrities from Atlanta to Hollywood.

Today, I deleted one invite after the next. None caught my attention until I got to the very last one. ABC News was coming to town to host a "Nightline: Face-Off" to debate "Why Can't a Successful Black Woman Find a Man?" on Friday in Decatur. After its interview of the four single black women in Atlanta went viral, they thought it would be educational and entertaining to have a live debate. Steve Harvey, Sherri Shepherd from *The View*, actor Hill Harper, journalist Jacque Reed and author Jimi Izrael would be on the panel.

"Now, I gotta go to this," I said out loud. After confirming with Angela that I was going to do a live broadcast from the debate and setting it up with ABC reps, I forwarded the press release to my girls.

Senalda responded first: "Definitely coming! Sounds like a perfect outing for our Destination Wedding group! I still can't believe that single black women in Atlanta were singled out on *Nightline* in the first place!"

Jarena's text arrived next: "Count me in. I don't know if there is anything new to debate, though."

. . .

After my show was over, I drove from the station to my condo near Piedmont Park. Every few days I changed my route because fans can be crazy sometimes. A few times some even followed me home. While I was driving, I wondered what Jovan was doing that very second. He told me that he and his son were in Florida this week for spring break, and the following week he was flying out to L.A. for business meetings.

I had met his son once, when his baby mama dropped him off at Jovan's Fayetteville house, but I had never spent any time with Jovan Jr. For the first year of our relationship I didn't mind, since we only saw each other every now and then anyway. But two years later, I thought he would have officially introduced to me to Junior by now. But then again, maybe Jovan thought at ten years old, Junior was too young to be introduced to a woman who was not his mother. Who could blame him fa dat?

Just then, my phone rang. For a second, I thought I conjured up my man.

"What's up?" I said softly, disappointed when I didn't recognize the number.

"Hi, may I speak with Mimi? This is Ian."

"This is me," I said, regretting that I answered the call.

"Oh, I could barely hear you," Ian said, "so I didn't know that was you."

"Yeah," I said. "I wasn't sho who was on the other end myself."

"I'll try not to be offended that you don't recognize my number yet," Ian said with a laugh that I didn't return. He didn't even take the hint and kept right on talking.

"So I can take you to dinner sometime this week?"

Since my girls told me I should call Ian after he pretty much hunted me down in Veronique's store, I followed through because I didn't have anything else to do that night anyway. Dude took out me to dinner. I cannot even really remember where. When I'm bored, I forget details. I even fell asleep for a hot second when he went to the bathroom, but I played it off. When he walked back to the table, I told him I had to rub my eyes because somethin' got in em. If a nigga didn't make me feel like I was bungee jumping or riding my Harley or anything that pumped up my adrenaline, it wasn't even worth getting to know him. So I didn't call him again and avoided his calls the couple of times he called me. But this time, he caught me off guard.

"Oh, I'm booked at events all week long so I won't be able to have dinner with you."

"Sorry to hear that, but I understand," Ian said. "Maybe we can meet sometime next week then."

"Okay, I will give you call next week," I lied. "Talk to you soon. Bye."

"I'm looking forward to it. Goodbye."

Although I was known for being off da chain and not afraid to look crazy if the situation called for it, ereone thought I would say anything, anywhere, to anybody. The truth was that I had a hard time being mean to nice people. That was my weakness. I was just sensitive like that. So sometimes I lied just to be nice. I just hoped that when I didn't call Ian next week to meet him for dinner or anything else, he would finally get the message and leave me alone.

• • •

On Friday morning, I texted my girls: "Bitches, if y'all plan on coming w/ me, y'all need to be there at 4:30 because the radio station will be setting up then."

The day couldn't go by fast enough. All week I had been thinking 'bout how my dating life got to be where it was. I was gonna be thirty-two years old this year, and I didn't want to celebrate my birthday with work friends, my girls, or alone, especially since I had a man. Except in the three years I had been dating Jovan, he always found a way to not see me on my birthday. The first year he told me that he wasn't serious and just wanted to kick it. The second year he was on vacation with his mama and son. The third year he texted me "Happy Birthday," but he was in New York working. I wondered what was up for this year. I decided if he dodged me on this birthday, I would finally admit to myself that he was not my man.

As my booth was set up for the live broadcast, I saw women were already in line to get inside of the Porter Sanford III Performing Arts and Community Center auditorium. The line was damn near around the whole building, and the debate wasn't going to start for two more hours. And I bet all of them, including me, couldn't figure out this man thang. Jarena, who rode with me to the auditorium, went outside to look for Senalda.

This is gonna be da shit!

I spoke into my mic. "Heeey laaadies, we gonna get right tonight!" I waved my arms from side to side like I was performing at an old-school rap concert. "Holla if ya hear me! I need a good man to stick by me. Aine that right, ladies? And we gon work that situation out tonight!"

The women cheered like they were at a football game.

I waved toward Senalda and Jarena as they walked into the center, directing them to the area of the auditorium that was sectioned off for the media.

"Y'all, I just noticed that we all have on our outfits from Veronique's store," I said, checking out my girls' clothing as I adjusted my baby-blue booty dress. Every now and then I had to make sure it wasn't ridin' up too high on my ass.

"You're right," Senalda said. "I'm usually talking about your outfit by now in my mind, but I hadn't noticed that I wasn't doing that."

Senalda put her hand on Jarena's arm, and they laughed together.

"You know what, heffas? If I didn't love y'all like sisters, y'all would be good and cussed out."

"Seriously, though, you look really nice tonight," Senalda said. "We all do. Since there are so many women out here tonight, I'm hoping some men will show up too."

"I thought you were trying to get at Dexter, Bossy," I said.

"Nothing wrong with a few backups in case your first choice doesn't work out. You should think about that too."

"Senalda, that wasn't nice," Jarena said.

"I aine even worried about her," I said. I laughed to show Senalda hadn't fazed me, but maybe she was right.

An hour later, the auditorium was so packed that people were being turned away. The energy in the room was off da chain. Finally, the debate host, ABC's Vicki Mabrey, announced she was ready to start. She began by asking how many single black women were in the audience. Over half of the room raised their hands as they laughed. She explained that ABC was hosting the debate in Atlanta after the Linsey Davis report went viral. The crowd applauded as Linsey Davis stood up. She said Linsey Davis was looking for a man too which is how she came up with the idea for the report.

A few minutes later, Vicki Mabrey hit the panelists with questions. As she listed all of the negative statistics, the same kind of negative statistics from the December interview, I felt lucky to have a relationship with Jovan at all.

She said that by the time they were thirty years old, only 50 percent of black women will get married, black women outnumber black men in higher education by two to one, and that there are almost two million more black women than black men. She asked if black women were too picky or were black men the ones with issues.

Jacque Reid's answers hit me hard. She said that some men think they shouldn't be even expected to have one woman because it was in their nature as men and that some women let their men cheat because of that.

"Ummm hmmm," some of the ladies said to each other as they hi-fived and nodded.

I'm a real fool for Jovan. For all I know he's probably with some other woman right now. He aine never gonna feel 'bout me the way that I feel 'bout him.

But then I remembered all the late-night conversations me and Jovan had. Ereone was always telling me he wasn't my man because of how he acted in public, but in private he acted completely different. It was like we had a spiritual connection. One Father's Day, he was at my place and we talked about our fathers. He told me that his first priority was being a good father to Junior because his father, who had several women around town including Jovan's mother, was never there for him. I told him my father was there for my family physically, but I could tell he didn't want to be there. In my mind, I knew he loved me, but I just couldn't feel his love. He never said it, and when I tried to hug him, he always got all stiff like I like made him uncomfortable, so I stopped trying. My parents divorced months after I graduated from high school, so that told me I was right. He was never happy with us—my mom, my older brother, and me. Jovan held me as I cried and I even noticed a tear or two on his face. Those were the moments that nobody saw, and I knew they meant something. They had to.

I interviewed women in the audience for the station too. Some thought that the women were the problem.

"Sometimes we are our own worst enemies when it comes to criteria. If a woman has an MBA, she has to marry a man with an MBA. Or a man has to be appealing to my girls," said a woman who called herself Donette the Dating Diva. Donette told me that she met and married her former husband when she was a Coca-Cola executive and he was just a meter reader. "I looked for someone with character. Formal education is not equivalent to intellect. I know a lot of educated fools." But they did get divorced after seventeen years. She said it wasn't cuz of the different status levels though. "I'm better because of the marriage."

Nadia Night, a flight attendant, told me that she started checking for white men because some black men did her wrong. She met her husband, a white man, at Johnny's Hideaway, a club in the A, and they have been together ever since.

Senalda and Jarena talked about my interviews.

"I can't see myself supporting a man. That's why I want a man to make what I make or more," Senalda said.

"And even though I haven't had one in years, black men got so much swagger," Jarena said. "I can't see myself living without that. And I don't want to explain why I tie my hair up every night or don't wash my hair every day."

I was halfway listening to them because the Jovan I knew in public and the Jovan I knew in private were battling each other in my head. In that moment, surrounded by hundreds of women who wanted what I wanted, real love, I realized I wanted—correction—I needed a man who wanted to be with me everywhere in public and in private. Shit, I deserved it. I interrupted my friends. "Y'all I think I'm gonna finally do it," I said. "I think I'm gonna stop seeing Jovan."

My girls smiled at me but didn't say anything.

• • •

As I was driving home on I-20 in my Jeep Wrangler with Jarena, we kept talking about the debate. Jarena admitted she learned something, and just as I was about to respond, I spotted a White Expedition that looked like Jovan's. "It figures that I would see a car that looks like Jovan's when I'm trying to forget about him."

When I got closer, I saw the license plate was MUZAC1.

He told me he was in LA. I sped up to see who was driving just to be sure. I crossed a lane in front of a car to get beside the SUV. *It's him.*

"What are you doing?" Jarena squealed, her body swaying as I shifted gears.

I turned down her passenger side window and leaned as far as I could. I screamed at him although his window was still up.

"What are you doing here?"

Then I saw Chula lying on his shoulder asleep. Her body was curled into his, and his head was lying on top of hers like he wanted to touch her in every way that was possible as he drove. I finally realized what had been pissing me off for the last few months when I saw them together. Jovan never even touched me in public because he didn't want to give anyone the wrong idea, he told me. Obviously, that rule didn't apply to Chula. And if he allowed that in public, there was no telling what was going on when no one else was around.

I felt like I had been struck by lightning. Jovan looked, but I could tell he didn't recognize me at first. I drove my Jeep into his lane so that he could see me clearly.

"Mimi, what's going on?" Jarena shrieked, but I ignored her. I was on autopilot, no longer responsible for what was going to happen next.

Jovan pounded on his horn while turning down his window.

"Hey, what the hell?" he shouted just before he recognized me.

His face changed. First, I saw shock in his eyes and then fear. I felt more powerful than I had in the whole three years we had been together. He sped up, jerking his vehicle into another lane. I slammed my foot into the accelerator, going 100 miles an hour to catch up to that nigga and his trick.

"If this is your suicide mission, I choose not to accept it," Jarena yelled while holding the edges of her seat and moving with the zigzagging of my Jeep. "Let me out of here."

I didn't realize I was crying until my whole face was wet.

"I'm so tired of his lies, but he gon learn tonight!" I shouted.

It was the ultimate adrenaline rush! After driving on his bumper for a few miles, I took it one step further. The front of my Jeep smacked his SUV with a BOOM. The car screeched as he sped up again. I sped up too and hit his car a second time.

"You and that bitch gon die tonight!!! You HEAR me Jovan?" I yelled as loud I could. "DIE bitches!!!"

After hitting him for the third time, Jovan flew across five lanes to escape and got off at the next exit. I thought about chasing after them again, but each time I'd hit his car, I'd felt a little better.

I was ready to go home. I hoped the front end of my Jeep wasn't too damaged, but it would be worth it if I could finally prove to Jovan that you couldn't play with my feelings and get away with it.

"You better be glad I'm a praying woman, because God was the only one who saved us," Jarena screamed in my face. "And you better pray that Jovan and Chula aren't hurt! I can't believe this! Are you trying to get arrested?"

"I told y'all I would be done with Jovan after tonight, and I am," I said calmly, turning down my window and letting the cool night air that flooded in dry my tears.

CHAPTER 6

May

Jarena

AFTER THREE MONTHS OF being a visitor at Hidden United Methodist Church, I placed my membership at the country church hidden in the middle of the city. My decision came in stages. The first part happened when I decided to stop being a visitor at the back of the church the Sunday after Valentine's Day. Instead of sitting in the back as I had for the two Sundays I had visited before, this Sunday I sat in the middle. I just felt the Lord had a word for me, as my grandmother would say.

When the devotion was over, a deacon ambled over to me. His dark skin was slack and folded with age, but his curly Afro, although all white, was as full as the head of hair of a man decades younger. His best feature was his watery but smiling eyes.

"Ma'am, before you run out of this church for the third time, I thought I would introduce myself," he said, reaching out his hand toward me.

"I didn't know that anyone other than maybe the ushers had noticed me," I said, as I shook his hand.

"Young lady, you may be able to get away with not being noticed in those megachurches we have all over the city, but here we see everybody, whether they want to be noticed or not," the man said as he chuckled. "My name is Deacon Stanley."

"Jarena Johnson."

"Ms. Johnson, I don't know if you plan on staying for the whole service, but we're having a visitors' luncheon after church," he said. "We do this periodically, so you came on the right Sunday. I hope you join us."

"I think I will," I said in spite of myself. I guess there was no turning back now. I was going to get to know these people whether I wanted to or not. I kept listening for the word the Lord had for me during the service, but I didn't hear anything.

The church was so small, I wondered where it could possibly have enough space for a luncheon. But I was led down a rickety spiraling stairway at the back of the church to a very clean but still musty-smelling basement. It was like Thanksgiving—fried chicken, macaroni and cheese, collards, sweet potatoes, apparently all for one visitor—me. The smells of my favorite food spread out on a long table, unruly kids tagging each other from one side of the basement to the next, and everyone smiling and chatting made me feel like I was being hugged.

As I sat on a folding chair, eating from a paper plate on my lap, the deacon came up to me again.

"I want to invite you to our Bible Study" he said. "We're getting ready to start studying the book of Acts this Wednesday, so you haven't missed anything. It starts at 7 p.m., and it only lasts an hour."

I smiled. "I just may come. I'm pretty busy during the week, and unfortunately I have pretty long hours, so we will see."

After getting home and shedding my suit, I decided to check out Barry's Facebook profile on my laptop. I had been lurking on his page every day since I accepted his friendship request a week earlier. I purposely only posted a few pictures on my page because I didn't want everyone knowing my business, but that didn't stop me from scouring my friends' pages to piece together their lives through what they shared online.

According to Barry's profile, he lived in Charlotte, North Carolina, and was a Coca-Cola Bottling Consolidated senior brand manager. As I scrolled through his pictures, I saw that the woman who appeared in at least half of them was his wife, Naomi (Sweet) Simpson. And she looked sweet too. She had the perfect toffee-brown skin with the perfect congenial smile and long, thick hair that she wore feathered. She looked perfectly coiffed, the opposite of me with my long limbs and massive curly Afro. I clicked on the link to take me to her profile page, glad to discover that she hadn't made it private. Even her career was sweet. She was a fourth-grade teacher. And they had two adorable kids—a boy, Bartholomew IV, and a girl, Amber.

A sound on my computer interrupted my investigation. Barry was trying to chat with me. I almost got up and ran away from the computer to look in the mirror first, before remembering he couldn't see me. I debated for a second about responding, and then I decided to take a chance.

What's the worst thing that can happen on a computer?

"Thanks for accepting my friend request, Jarena," Barry typed.

"Of course man, how are you?" I typed.

"I can't complain," he wrote. "So are you running the world yet?"

"LOL," I typed. "Hardly. I do have my own company though."

"I know. 85 South Public Relations, right?"

"Oh, so you been checking up on me, huh?"

"Every now and then I Google you," he typed.

A tingle started in my chest and went to my fingertips. I typed a response but deleted the words, wondering how to be casual with a guy that I used to love.

"You there?" he typed.

"Yes," I typed. "I'm sorry. Got distracted for a second."

"Oh I'm sorry. Are you busy? I just wanted to say hello. If you need to go, I understand."

"Naw, I'm fine. So what's up?"

"Just wasting time on Facebook!"

"I know, right!"

"So why are you wasting time on Facebook? Shouldn't you be hanging out with your wife and family? I guess you have a family by now."

"I do. A boy and a girl. I'm supposed to be working! LOL. Got caught up on FB for a sec. So do you have a husband and family? I couldn't tell from your profile."

"Nope, not married, no kids. Working on it though. Just fabulous friends and a career for now. :)"

"If you're like you were in college, when you're ready to get all of that, you will."

"Well, I don't want to keep you from your work, plus I'm sleepy."

"Yeah, I need to get back to work. Nice catching up with you. Bye."

I wasn't sleepy. I figured that if we kept communicating, I would inevitably unload about my relationship issues. And then he would probably think about how he proposed to me and I turned him down and never looked back.

And then I started thinking about Hidden United Methodist Church. The elderly deacon looked like an older version of the pastor of Redemption Baptist Church, the church I went to with my grandmother in Vidalia. I remember the pastor, Dr. Baker, always made time to ask me about my schoolwork or living in the "big city of Atlanta." He would bend down to my level, looking me in the eyes as he spoke to me. Reminiscing, I realized how special it was for a pastor to pay attention to even the youngest of members that way. And I wanted to feel special again. Like I belonged somewhere. Had a family that missed me when I wasn't there. Hidden United Methodist didn't have all of the people and programs that Cascade Baptist offered, but that wasn't what I needed then.

• • •

A meeting with Jovan in my office in March also propelled me to join Hidden United Methodist. Although music producers were notorious for being night owls and not showing up anywhere before noon, Jovan was on his grind any time of the day. That singular quality was my top reason for taking him on as a client. His hustle made it impossible for him to not earn money, and that would earn money for me. Our meeting was scheduled for 10 a.m., but he sauntered into my office twenty minutes early.

I studied him as he walked. It always made me smile that he dipped from side to side as he moved, almost as if music played in his head at all times.

His gold-and-diamond studs in each ear seemed to glint on beat with his rhythm.

"J.J., I hope I'm not too early," he said.

"Naw, you're alright." I turned my swiveling desk chair and stood up to greet him. "How are you?" I gave him a side hug and sat back down.

"Chillin'. What you know good?"

"Working, that's all. Have a seat."

He sat down in one of my chocolate leather couches.

"So I just want to make sure everything's tight for Chula's album release."

"So far I have ten press events scheduled, and Mimi has agreed to interview Chula on her show."

"Good. Do you think Chula's accent is too strong? She grew up in Southwest Atlanta, but her parents are straight Puerto Rican. Like they just off the boat. They don't even speak that much English. Her English sounds like Spanish sometimes."

"You've met her parents?" I said, moving my chair closer to my desk.

"Yeah, my son and I kicked it with her folks a few times. Good people, too."

"What? Hold up," I said as I went over to the couch where Jovan was sprawled and sat down.

"In the five years or so that I have known you, I have never heard of you hanging out with any woman's parents, and you definitely don't take your son around any woman. So that's why Mimi is freaking out. You really like this girl."

I tried to focus on his eyes through his dark shades, but I couldn't see them clearly, even up close.

"She's a nice lady."

"Naw, it's more than that," I said, my voice rising higher. "If y'all are dating, I need to know so that if anyone asks, I know what to say."

"J.J., I meet beautiful women all of the time. You know that," he said slowly, as if he was carefully considering what words he used. "But Chula is a different kind of chick, I gotta say. She's just really sweet, even though she really wants to be a star more than anything. She's ten years younger than me, though."

"I thought you were one of those bachelors for life. You know, the type of man who is married to his career but sees women on the side. But if you are considering marrying Chula, she is grown."

"I aine say nothin' 'bout marriage," he said as he laughed. "I just like being around her."

As I looked at him, I knew he was downplaying his emotions. I had been telling Mimi for years that Jovan was not the settling-down type. But the way he looked when he was talking about Chula was the way Barry used to look at me just before he asked to marry me.

"Are you still seeing Mimi?" I said, forgetting that this was supposed to be a business instead of a personal conversation.

"Ere now and then," he said as he looked down.

"Anyone else you're seeing?"

"Damn, you worse than my mother," he said as he pulled down his shades a bit. "I got a few in rotation. Chula's stock is rising, but I'm not trying to get married. All of this is between us, right? Attorney-client privilege?"

"Well, I'm not your attorney," I said with a laugh. "But yes, this is between us. And I'm not trying to advise you on your personal life since I'm just your publicist, but since you are 'seeing' one of my friends and your brand-new artist at the same time, I'm telling you that you need to be careful. I don't want to see Mimi hurt, and you know she would be."

"I'm not lying to anybody, and I never have." He took off his shades completely. "I like variety, and I've always told every chick I see that monogamy is not my thing. What else can I do?"

"Nothing, I guess." I shrugged my shoulders and returned to my desk. I guided our conversation back to the promotion campaign for Chula's debut album, but inwardly I reflected on our conversation and my career in general. I sensed this love triangle between my friend, my client, and his protégé was going to get messy before it got better, and I wanted no part of it. But that wasn't the only thing that was irritating me. It was becoming clear that I wanted no part of the whole PR industry anymore. That thought had been on the periphery of my mind for a while, but it crystallized and came to the center during my conversation with Jovan.

When I was in college, I wanted to be in public relations because I loved communications, writing, and being persuasive. And I wanted to get paid well. And when I watched Atlanta hip hop blow up all over the world, I knew that PR in Atlanta hip hop was where I needed to be. But in retrospect, all of my hard work was feeling meaningless. A lot of the lyrics in the songs I promoted now were explicit without reason or just foolishness. If my mother and grandmother were still alive, they would be shocked that I was affiliated with that kind of music. Not to mention that very few of the men that I met in the industry over the years were worth anything.

The first sermon I heard from Pastor Moore came back to me. He preached about how he was called into the ministry. God had told him, "You will be speaking in a pulpit one day."' He wasn't the only one that heard those words. I felt like God told me that when I was six years old. One Sunday, I told the pastor at Redemption Baptist that I wanted to speak, like him, to lots of people about God. I remember him and the rest of the church laughing because they probably thought that I was a precocious but misguided kid. And on top of that, I never saw any women speaking like he did, so in my child's mind, I figured women couldn't do that. Whatever my calling was, whether I was called to be a speaker of some sort or not, I knew I wouldn't find it promoting *Wassup 'Señorita* or any other hip hop album.

• • •

"Aine no such thang as a Lone Ranger Christian. The devil gets you when you by yourself," was another one of my grandmother's homespun proverbs. After the last Friday in April, I knew I couldn't be a Lone Ranger Christian anymore. I was finishing up a press release just before lunch, but I was also logged into Facebook, and Mimi's show was playing on the radio too.

And then I heard a sound from Facebook. It was Barry messaging me. Since February, we had been messaging each other a few times a week. Not conversations: a "Have a great day" or "Happy Friday" or "What are you doing?" here and there. Nothing deep. Over time, my boundaries loosened like the elastic in my old sweatpants I used to wear when we studied together in his apartment. One day, I posted a rant about being stuck in traffic and he sent me a direct message that made me laugh out loud. "Better to be stuck in traffic than in traffic court." I got so many speeding tickets in college, some of the courthouse personnel knew me by name. After that, it was clear we were just old friends catching up online, and I no longer flinched when he messaged me. It was like being surprised with a piece of candy every once in a while. His messages sweetened my day and made me smile.

"Happy Friday, Jay! What do you have going on this weekend?"

"Nothin' much, hopefully nothing, Bama," I replied.

"Jay" was his college nickname for me, and "Bama" was my college nickname for him, since I thought he was country and the fact that he was born and raised in Birmingham, Alabama.

"Do you have Skype?"

"Why?" I raised my eyebrows and frowned.

"I want to see you. Let's Skype. I'm at my home office today so I've got some time."

I paused and then decided, *Why not? It's Friday.* Within minutes I was face to face with the love of my life, who I hadn't seen since I was twenty-one.

"You look good," he said. "I love your hair."

I reached up to touch my Afro and smiled. "Thanks. I've come a long way since my permed hair in college."

"You would look good in any hairstyle."

"Still Barry, I see."

"Is that booty shake in the background? At work? Oh, I forgot you're the boss! I haven't heard booty shake in a minute. What station is that?"

"KISS 103. They have a special deejay on Fridays who plays straight booty shake for an hour. You can listen online on their website if you want to."

Barry started dancing in front of his webcam, wopping and other dances from the '90s. "Dance with me!"

I sat in my seat, just looking at him until I heard these words. "It's time to ride out. Ride out. Party! Party! Shake it! Shake it! That booty! That booty," blared from my system. The bass boomed behind the lyrics.

"Awww junk!" I pushed my chair away from my computer and dropped my behind low in front of my desk like it was a man. I laughed out loud at myself. For the next ten minutes, I was transported back to my college days when booty shake music dominated the Southern rap music scene. Although the music could be degrading to women, the beats forced you to move. It was one of the reasons I named my company 85 South Public Relations. I was a big fan of 95 South, a Miami bass group, in high school and thought I should honor Atlanta-bred rap music by naming my firm after a main thoroughfare in Atlanta like the group 95 South did. For ten minutes, I forgot that promoting Atlanta-bred music wasn't as fulfilling as it once was.

"That was good," Barry said, as he laughed. "We haven't danced like that in a long time."

"No, we haven't," I said. "I have to go now, Barry. See you on Facebook."

I closed my laptop and sat back down in my chair. Sweat trailed down my stomach as if I had been to a party. *What just happened? Was that wrong? What does this mean?* Questions permeated my thoughts the rest of the weekend until I got to church on Sunday, the first Sunday in May. Pastor Kirby got in front of the altar after finishing his sermon, raised his arms and said, "Don't let this opportunity to trust God as your personal Lord and Savior pass you by. I know we got a bunch of hypocrites in the church, but we got room for one more. You won't be perfect this side of heaven but at least you can be saved and let God help you. If you need God's help or even if you want to join Hidden United Methodist, we've got room for you."

I don't even remember getting up and walking down the aisle. I had the thought I should get up and then I was in front of Pastor Kirby. He reached out his arms to hug me while the church clapped behind us. When he asked me what I had come up for, instead of saying, "I need help," like I wanted to, I said, "I'm ready to join Hidden United Methodist Church." But when I thought about it, they were one and the same anyway.

"Praise God," Pastor Kirby shouted. "We're happy to have you."

He embraced me, and I felt more optimistic than I had all weekend. It was obvious that Barry and I still had a connection, but I hoped that God and becoming a member of this church would help me leave our relationship where it ended—in the past.

Senalda

If Dexter thinks I'm going to throw the election just because we're dating, then he doesn't know me at all. Although I was making progress on my to-do list for the day, I felt more and more anxious every hour that went by. For the first two months Dexter and I dated, I really had nothing to complain about. Sometimes, he was a few minutes late for a date or didn't call me back as quickly as he told me he would, but it was nothing a straight-up conversation about my expectations couldn't fix.

And then in April, he blindsided me and told me he was running for president of our local Black MBA Association. I was furious at first and asked him why he didn't tell me sooner. He told me that since he had just moved back to Atlanta, he wasn't sure that with his new job he was going to have time to be president.

That calmed me down for a while, but now that it was election day, I was upset again. But not because he hadn't told me sooner. I didn't know what the election was going to mean for our relationship. As I was promoted from one title to another at my company, I noticed that men treated me differently. They either treated me as a colleague and not as a woman, which wasn't entirely a bad thing most of the time, or they took the male chauvinism route: ignoring me or grumbling when I spoke in meetings.

So far, Dexter didn't seem intimidated by me, but we had yet to compete with each other. And I intended to win the election.

I guess I will have to wait and see what happens. Since consulting with Veronique, I bought more clothes in jewel tones for my wardrobe, but tonight I reverted to one of my trusty power suits: a black pantsuit with a crisp white shirt underneath to show that I meant business. When I arrived in the SunTrust Plaza lobby, I saw association members congregating in groups. I spotted Dexter and was about to go to him when a guy I had lusted over last year got to me first. He was so fine with his bald head and dark black skin.

"Leonard! Heyyy," I said as I hugged him. His suit stretched over his swollen muscles. In addition to being an IT professional, Leonard was a body builder in his spare time. I flirted with Leonard all last year and even asked him out, but nothing happened. Just then Dexter walked up. I turned to speak to him, but he was facing Leonard as if he was waiting to be introduced.

"Dexter, this is Leonard. Leonard, Dexter." I looked at both of them.

"What's up, man?" Dexter said.

I noticed Dexter's voice was deeper than it was when we were alone. *Was this some of kind of male territory thing?*

"I see you are running for president too," Leonard said.

"I am," Dexter said with a smile. "I don't know if I have what it takes to beat this little lady, but that's not going to stop me from trying."

"May the best candidate win," I said. I laughed although there was nothing to laugh about. They kept talking as the election chair came up to me and explained how the meeting would proceed. After introducing each of the candidates, members would be instructed to go the MBA website and cast their vote.

"Did you already know Leonard or something?" I said as Leonard walked away.

"No," Dexter said, looking down at me. "What made you ask me that?"

"The two of you were talking like you were old friends," I said, moving closer to him.

"Oh no, but he is frat so I invited him to my weekly Men's Night Out at J.R. Crickets."

For the entire three months that Dexter and I had been dating, he always met up with a few of his boys on Friday nights and hung out at the Crickets on Camp Creek Parkway. One time, I even asked to join him and his friends just to see what was going on, but he said they called it "Men's Night Out" for a reason. With my anxiety about the election specifically and being annoyed about "Men's Night Out" in general, I was about to be pissed off. But then Dexter kissed me on the cheek and whispered into my ear.

"Hey sexy, maybe you can wear that suit when we go out this weekend. I love a woman in a power suit."

I smiled although I tried to frown.

"Don't tempt me," I said with a laugh. "I love my power suits too. So how would you feel if I won and had power over you?"

"I just told you I love a woman in a power suit," he continued to whisper in my ear, his breath tickling my ear. "If you beat me, I will surrender."

An hour later, after the election results were calculated, Dexter wasn't whispering in my ear or even speaking to me. When I was declared the winner, he stuck his hand toward me stiffly like we were just colleagues, shook my hand, and barely mumbled "Congratulations."

I said, "Thank you." I attempted to hug him, but his arms stayed at his side.

Since it was Thursday night, I knew I wouldn't see him the next day, and now I wondered if we were still on for the weekend. *If he didn't know before, now he knows just who I am.*

Destination Wedding Meeting #5

Something was up with Jarena and Mimi, but Senalda didn't know what. The ladies were supposed to run and walk the Active Oval at Piedmont Park for their fifth meeting. In April, Dexter convinced Senalda to start training with him for the July 4th Peachtree Road Race, the world's largest 10K race and an Atlanta tradition, and a month later, she noticed that her stomach was starting to look as flat as it did when she was in college.

Jarena agreed to the workout because she said she had been eating too much soul food lately and not getting to the gym as often as she should. And Mimi, who sometimes went hiking with her "granola buddies" in the North Georgia mountains and didn't like "organized exercise," agreed to meet at Piedmont Park only since she lived practically across the street. Dexter and

Senalda had been meeting on Saturday mornings for their runs, so when he told her that he was going to Miami the second weekend in May, she figured that would be the perfect day to meet her girls instead.

But by the time she parked her car at Piedmont Park, Jarena had called to tell her she couldn't make it, and Mimi had texted her saying, "shit came up." Senalda debated heading back to Camp Creek, but since she was already there anyway, she decided to take on the Active Oval by herself.

Since the six-month mark of the Destination Wedding project was coming, it was a good time to take inventory of their progress. She was having a good time with Dexter, but he had never said anything about where they were going. Although he had apologized for his attitude about the election, she didn't have a clear direction for their relationship. If Senalda was going to meet her goal of being a wife by the end of the year, she needed some answers.

She wanted to stop running but forced her limbs to keep moving forward. She was ahead of the other women: Mimi still seemed like she was into Jovan even if she was never going to be his wife. And Jarena hadn't mentioned a single man at all. If Senalda had to grade them on their progress for their project, she would have to give them a "C," and there was nothing average about any project that Senalda had ever led.

She realized then that she was awash in sweat, even if she had only been running in circles.

CHAPTER 7

June

· ·

Whitney

AFTER TWO MORE MONTHS of trying to solve our intimacy issues on our own, Richie let me make an appointment for us with CC. Neither of us wanted to go, but it was either counseling or forego having normal intimacy altogether. We tried a few times, but he seemed like he was forcing himself to be interested. And the indignity of it all was as insulting as the rejection.

Our counseling session was scheduled for a Saturday morning. That morning, I attempted to make everything as pleasant as possible. Since we had to drive to the Perimeter Mall area from Henry County, I woke up extra early and made breakfast: scrambled eggs, crispy bacon, creamy grits, and juiced oranges. I hoped the aroma would bring Richie downstairs, but after sitting at the table by myself for twenty minutes, I went upstairs to see what was going on. He was still asleep with a blanket in between his legs. I smiled. I stood there looking at him for a few seconds, still not believing that we, the perfect couple, were going to counseling. I finally sat down on the bed next to him and caressed his shoulder.

"Good morning Richie, time to get ready." I spoke in his ear as gently as I could. "I've got breakfast downstairs."

He rolled over, rubbing his eyes before opening them. "I'm not hungry." He rolled back over.

All the warmth I felt evaporated immediately, and something in me snapped. "You know what? I'm glad we are going to counseling today because you are getting on my nerves. I don't know what's going on with you, but you need to tell it all today because I don't know how much more of this I can take."

He rolled over again and looked at me. "Are you really getting mad at me because I want to get a few more minutes of sleep after I worked a twelve-hour shift yesterday?" He walked to his bathroom and slammed the door behind him.

• • •

According to my Cartier Tank diamond-and-white-gold watch, it took us forty-five minutes of uncomfortable silence in his silver Range Rover to get to CC's office. I used the time to obsess about what we were wearing. I had selected a Tory Burch floral-print shift dress while Richie was wearing his signature weekend attire: chino pants and a Polo shirt. The psychologist had to have a good first impression of us because I couldn't predict what she would find out.

When we arrived, I jumped out of the Jeep ahead of him and walked into the office building. I didn't wait for Richie to catch up with me as I got on the elevator to go to the seventh floor of the twenty-story building. I wandered down a long, ominously bland hallway, searching for CC's office. I heard the elevator doors open behind me and waited for Richie to catch up to me.

"Found the office yet?" He frowned while removing his shades.

"I think this is it." I pointed toward the door in front of me. "Are you ready?"

CC looked just like she sounded on the phone. Like a disheveled librarian with her wispy, shoulder-length gray hair that had been dyed brown and her matching tortoiseshell glasses. I felt myself exhaling after scanning the numerous degrees on her office walls. She directed us to a large couch while she sat down in a reclining chair.

"How are the two of you this morning?" She flipped through papers stacked on her legs. "Would you like some water or tea? This English breakfast is delicious." She gestured toward a teacup on a table next to her.

We shook our heads from side to side in unison.

"Let's get started then, shall we?" She looked down. "Richie, you are addicted to watching pornography, and you are no longer interested in having sex with your wife. Is that a fair assessment?"

Richie shook his head. "I don't know if that is a fair assessment, but I have been watching porn for a few months now. Don't most men watch porn?"

"And when was the last time you made love to Whitney?"

Neither of us answered.

"Sounds like a pretty long time ago," she concluded, scribbling in a notebook. She put the notebook down and took off her glasses. "Well, Whitney dear, why don't you tell me about how the two of you met and got married. I like for my couples to remember the happier times before we get into the nitty gritty." She threw her head back and laughed.

I described how we met at a party his fraternity, Kappa Alpha Psi, had at the beginning of our senior year in college and how we became a couple almost immediately. But we had a long-distance relationship while he was away at Harvard Medical School and I was still in Atlanta at Emory Law School.

"But the distance that we had to contend with during our five-year courtship melted away like hot candle wax once we lived in the same city again. Isn't that right, honey?" I turned to Richie and attempted to hold his hand, but he wouldn't allow his fingers to interlock with mine. So I faced CC, put on a smile and continued.

"We got married before his first year of residency at Morehouse School of Medicine. The theme of our wedding was 'A Royal Wedding.' We said our vows at the St. Louis Cathedral in the French Quarter in New Orleans, where I'm from. It's one of the oldest Roman Catholic cathedrals in the nation! I was a princess. I had sequins imported from Paris for my wedding dress. Richie was my prince in his black tailored tux! Ambassador Andrew

Young, who used to be an Atlanta mayor, was one of the officiants! Everyone was there. Actor Samuel Jackson. Congressman John Lewis."

"So you were together for five years before you got married but lived apart for years?" CC said, interrupting me.

"Yes," I said, carefully, wondering what she was thinking.

"Before the last few months, Richie dear, did you ever dabble in pornography?"

He was quiet for a moment before replying.

"I watched some flicks with my boys in college but nothing serious."

"Well, how do you think this all got started? You watching pornography, that is."

He sighed and shook his head. "I had gotten off of work pretty late one night, but I wasn't ready to go to bed yet," Richie started. "I checked on our twins first and then I decided to go to my office in the basement. I got on my computer to just kill some time until I felt sleepy enough to go back upstairs, and then a screen popped up with a naked woman. I clicked on the site and then it went from there."

"So in the beginning, Richie dear, did you watch pornography on your computer every night after coming home from work?"

"I'm an obstetrician so my schedule changes sometimes," he explained, "but I usually only did it when I came home from work late at night."

"So now you watch pornography during the day too?"

"Yes."

"Every day?"

He sighed again. "Yes."

"So your pornography watching has been progressive," CC said while looking down and scribbling faster than before. "Do you only watch pornography at home?"

During CC's line of questioning, I tried to be as quiet as possible so that Richie would feel like I wasn't even there. I wanted him to reveal everything he refused to tell me. I almost stopped breathing. But then I leaned forward on the couch, accidently bumping into his knees.

"I'm sorry," I said. *Oh no, he's going to stop talking now for sure.*

He looked at me, inhaled and turned back toward CC.

"I've started watching some porn at work too when I have a little down time between patients," he confessed.

"You do what? Have you lost your mind?" I spat, unable to contain myself any longer. "What if you get caught? You could lose your job!"

"You don't think I know that, Whit?" Again, he turned to me briefly, like I was a fly that needed to be swatted away, before turning back toward CC. "I've been trying to stop ever since you asked me about it!"

"That's because it's an addiction, dear," CC said calmly, unfazed by the outburst. "I want to continue to see the both of you, but in order for my services to be effective, we're going to have to address your pornography addiction too, Richie dear."

After placing her notes on the table next to her, she got up and walked over to a large file credenza. She pulled out some multicolored pamphlets and handed them to Richie before she sat down.

"That is information about Sex and Love Addicts Anonymous," she said. "It's a twelve-step program to help people recover from those addictions. You must commit to going to these meetings."

"Twelve-step meetings?" I exclaimed. "I thought only crazy people went to meetings. Why can't you address this issue in counseling?"

"I can address some of the root causes in counseling, but he is going to need support from other addicts to help him get well, because he is sick."

"My husband is not an addict, he's not some dope fiend, and he is definitely not sick," I said, trying to summon all of the persuasive authority I used in a courtroom. "Look at him. He's a doctor at Grady Hospital. He helps sick people get well. He is not sick."

"Dear, just because you cannot see his injuries doesn't mean he is any less sick than one of his patients at a hospital. And all addicts are sick. His drug of choice just happens to be pornography."

I wanted to continue to argue my case, but I noticed Richie hadn't said a word in his own defense. I looked over at him, and he was actually engrossed in reading the pamphlets CC had given him.

"If everyone is talking about sex, how bad it can be?" he said with an annoying grin. "I could at least try one meeting, right Whit?"

"Well, dear, you're in luck," she said, clapping her hands together. "There's a Sex and Love Addicts Anonymous group that meets just down the hallway from me. I gave you a schedule so you can go to their next meeting if you like."

"Thanks," Richie said.

• • •

When I woke up the next morning, I felt groggy with oversleep, but I jumped out of bed, realizing that I was late to make breakfast. But then I smelled food and heard laughing. I plodded downstairs and into the kitchen where I saw Richie with the twins and Gwenaëlle. The babies were babbling, moving their chubby arms up and down while Gwenaëlle fed them in their high chairs. Richie's back was turned to me, but he must have heard me because he spun around.

"Whit, I didn't want to wake you up because you looked like you were getting some good sleep," he said as kissed me on the cheek. "I've saved some bacon and eggs on the stove for you. I wish I could eat with you, but I'm heading out in a minute."

"What?" I rubbed my eyes. "I thought you only golfed on Saturday mornings."

"I'm going to one of those meetings," he whispered in my ear before pinching my derrière.

I wanted to be happy because of his change of attitude, but I was more annoyed than ever.

Mimi

Erebody had been calling me crazy for the longest, but no one called me a felon until April. An hour and a half after I got home from the *"Nightline:*

Face-Off" debate, while Jarena was in the bathroom getting ready to crash at my place since she said she was too nervous to drive home, a police officer showed up at my door. I thought about ignoring his knock, but I figured he knew I was there because the front-desk security officers of my condominium building probably told him so.

"Hello Mr. Officer," I said, slinging my locs and putting my hand on my hip. "Can I help you with something, sir?"

"Are you Mimi Gayle?" the thick white officer said, without changing his expression.

I nodded.

"You are under arrest for aggravated assault and terroristic threats."

I kept nodding like a bobblehead as he read me my rights and brought out handcuffs. I tried to think of somethin' I could say to make him smile, especially since I knew he didn't know Mimi the Mid-Day Motivator. But all I could think of to say was, "At least I have on clean drawls." I saw somethin' change in his eyes, but no smile.

Damn.

"Mimi, this is not the time for jokes, and please don't say anything else PLEASE," Jarena said she walked up to us and looked at his badge. "Hello, Officer Lucas, I'm Mimi's friend Jarena Johnson. If you don't mind, I will follow the two of you to the police station. On second thought, would you mind giving me a second to call her attorney?"

• • •

In a heartbeat, I was booked into jail. When it was time to take my mug shot, I smized when the camera flashed so my mug shot would at least be sexy. The worst part was the full-body search. But my attorney worked it out so that I could get out in a few hours because I posted a property bond with the special condition that I not have any more "violent contact" with Jovan and his hoe. So after all dat bullshit, I was allowed to go home. My attorney also worked it so that I didn't even have to go trial. I paid a fine and had to do some community service. I was surprised that I didn't regret anything I did, but maybe I was numb, because it was like watching a story from someone else's life.

And that wasn't the end of the story. Being that I am kinda a celebrity in town, my mug was all up in *The Atlanta Journal-Constitution*, splashed on the local television news, and talked about by all of the jocks at the other urban radio stations the next day. But the blogs really did me in, specially Dee Daisy, that trick...

> ### "Mimi Gayle Wears Butt Pads to Jail"
>
> KISS 103 Jock Miriam "Mimi" Gayle was arrested last night for aggravated assault and terroristic threats after she allegedly rammed her Jeep Wrangler into A Shawty Records owner Jovan Parker's Expedition. Mimi, in a jealous rage, hit Jovan's car several times as he was allegedly in the vehicle with his recording artist and girlfriend Chula Ramirez... One of my sources at the police station told me that a full-body search revealed that Mimi was wearing butt pads, and she begged officers not to reveal her secret.

I didn't wear butt pads all of the time, but I wore them sometimes to events so my booty would be on point. It's hella hard being a black girl with a flat booty.

But that wasn't the end of the story. Before I saw Angela, I already knew it was the end of my career at KISS 103, but I showed up at the station two days after I was arrested anyway.

"Well, Mimi, you've had a quite weekend."

"I guess you could say that." I tried to crack a smile, but the look on her face stopped me.

"Mimi, I hired you because of your talent, even though I heard how you crazy you were at V-104. And I have tried to harness that talent since we've been working together. I don't know if you see me as a mentor, but I have seen you as a protégé."

"Angela, I'm so sorry. I didn't mean to disappoint you." I didn't even try to stop my tears. It was the first time I felt anything since that night.

"I know you're sorry, Mimi, and I hate to do this, but I'm going to have to let you go. You're a dynamic radio personality. One of the best. But this isn't what you need to be doing with your life. You need to straighten out your personal life, and once you do that, I know that a career will be waiting for you."

She handed me some tissues and a business card. I blew my nose and tried to look at the card.

"That is a card for a career counselor and psychologist I know. Her name is Dr. Catherine Cleghorne. Please make an appointment with her. She can help get to the bottom of what's going on with you, Mimi."

I hadn't thought about calling CC when Senalda introduced us to her on a phone call at the beginning of April. But now that her card was handed to me while I was getting the boot from my gig, maybe God was tryin' to tell me something, as Jarena would say.

• • •

During my first career counseling session with CC weeks later, she recommended that I start going to Sex and Love Addicts Anonymous meetings.

"Anyone who continually pursues a romantic relationship that puts their safety and security in jeopardy is not in love. That person is in addiction, dear," she said.

At first, I was like, *Bullshit*. But then I read the pamphlet with questions for self-diagnosis. Some of those questions described me for real.

"Have you ever threatened your financial stability or standing in the community by pursuing a sexual partner?"

"Does your sexual and/or romantic behavior affect your reputation?"

"Do you find yourself unable to stop seeing a specific person even though you know that seeing this person is destructive to you?"

Shit, that's me.

• • •

I was scared as hell to go to my first meeting, so I didn't go until June. But I got a sponsor, Victor, my first day. The first thing that Victor recommended was that I attend ninety meetings in ninety days. So almost two months had passed since shit hit the fan, and I felt better. But like they say in the rooms, *"While I'm in a meeting, my disease is out in the parking lot doing push-ups."*

Destination Wedding Meeting #6

Luckie Lounge was the spot for their sixth meeting. Whitney convinced Senalda that a club outing would allow her to observe her single friends in action with men and give them some feedback about how to successfully interact with them. Senalda wasn't convinced that was Whitney's real reason for wanting to hang at the club, but Jarena and Mimi agreed to meet there, so it was go. Plus, it was Friday and Dexter was with his boys at J.R. Crickets as usual.

Seated in a plush black-vinyl booth, Senalda, Jarena, and Mimi attempted to catch up over the club's booming music until Whitney rushed toward them.

"Do my ladies run this mutha?" she said rolling her neck and yelling loud enough for other people to turn and stare at her. "Hell yeah!"

The three women looked at each other with their eyebrows collectively raised. Not only was Whitney's language out of the norm for the self-professed Southern belle, she was wearing a strapless black leather dress with her breasts nearly spilling out, and spiked heels.

"Have you been drinking?" Jarena asked.

"Really? All you need is a whip, Whitney the Dominatrix!" Senalda said. "I know you like to be sexy, but you look sexy scary! What's going on with you tonight?"

"And you have nothing to say?" Whitney said to Mimi as she reached the table.

"Sho don't," Mimi said after she sipped water.

The three of them turned to Mimi and stared for a moment before Senalda and Jarena refocused on Whitney again.

"What's up with your new look?" Senalda asked.

"I mean if Richie can look at pornography anywhere or anytime he wants to, then I can wear a black leather dress and spiked heels. And I might just to have to buy a whip too! Maybe that's the type of woman he wants anyway." She sat down with a thud in the booth. "So what is everybody drinking?"

She motioned for a waitress to come over. "Please refresh all of my friends' drinks, and I want a vodka martini."

The waitress nodded and left the table.

"Drinks on me for the rest of the night, ladies," she said. "It's been so long since I've been to a club. Where are the cute boys? I'm going to dance with somebody tonight."

"You never answered my question," Jarena said. "Have you already been drinking!? Because you are off the chain tonight!"

"Married ladies know how to have fun too," she said. "I see a cute boy over there. Watch me in action, ladies. You may need to take notes. I'll be back. Or maybe I won't!"

In silence, they watched Whitney slither out of their booth and over to group of men who looked young enough to be in college. She stood directly in front of the light-skinned, curly-haired one who looked like he could pass for a younger version of Richie.

• • •

"You are so cute," Whitney said to the young man in front of her. "Do you want to dance with me?"

"Are you talking to me, ma'am?" the young man said, pointing to himself before looking at his friends on either side. He was still young enough to have that skittish colt look that young men who haven't had a lot of experience with women have.

Whitney nodded. "Yes, you," she said with an overexaggerated smile.

His friends chuckled and hit him in the chest, egging him on.

"Okay," he said, returning her smile with a demure one.

She gyrated in front of him, maneuvering her hips from side to side while the young man stood a few inches away. He danced too, but his motions were measured, obviously practiced before the club outing with his boys.

"What's wrong?" Whitney asked. "Never danced with a grown woman before? Let me show you what to do."

She reached out her arms, placing her hands on his shoulders. "Move your hips with my hips." He attempted to follow her lead, but his slim hips never caught up to her fuller ones. Suddenly, he stepped away from her, stopped dancing and shook his head.

"I knew you looked familiar!"

"What are you talking about?"

"You're Mrs. Duvernay-Brannon, aren't you?"

Whitney stopped dancing and said, "Yes, who are you?"

"I'm Darwin. You were my baby sister's mentor for the AKA debutante program last year," he said. "Wait till I tell my mom and sister that I danced with you at Luckie Lounge!"

Whitney offered a stiff smile and said, "I wish you wouldn't. Okay, I have to go."

She spun around and bolted, but not before hearing, "Darwin got the young and old ladies wantin' him."

● ● ●

"That was quick," Senalda said, once Whitney got into earshot.

"It was a complete disaster, just like my marriage right now." She slid back into the booth, took a sip of her drink and sighed.

"What happened?" Jarena asked.

"That boy's *mother* knows me," Whitney said. "I'm so embarrassed! What are my sorority sisters going to think whey they find out?"

"Find out what?" Senalda asked.

"His mother is one of the officers of my chapter. He's going to tell her that I looked like a hooker and dirty danced with him! The horror!"

"And why are you wearing that getup tonight?" Senalda said. "And the truth this time."

Whitney told them that CC diagnosed Richie with a pornography addiction.

"And he admitted he is also watching pornography at the hospital," Whitney said. "And he says he can't stop. I'm so mad I could spit."

"But CC is going to help, right?" Senalda said. "That is what you are paying her to do!"

"Yes, she says she can help him and us," Whitney said, "but between being a mother of twins and getting back to work, I don't want to have to deal with this too."

"I went to see CC too," Mimi chimed in. "But I went in April after my ass was fired."

"You were what?" Senalda screeched. "What happened?"

"I haven't been on the air in two months," Mimi said. "I guess you weren't one of my listeners."

"And I guess you didn't see her mug shot with the accompanying story in the AJC either?" Jarena said.

"Is this a joke?" Senalda said. "You were fired and you have a mug shot?!"

Mimi and Jarena recounted the ordeal for their friends.

"It's all good, dough," Mimi said. "I've been seeing CC every two weeks since then, and I'm not even mad at what happened. I was tired of being a deejay anyway, so she's helping me think about other thangs I can do. Plus I got savings so I'm straight for a while."

"And what about Jovan?" Senalda asked. "That's one good thing that came from that mess. I know you're done with him now."

"I'm just taking it one day a time," Mimi said.

Senalda was about say something more to Mimi when she saw a group of men pass by her and sit in a booth a few feet away.

"I think Dexter was with those guys," Senalda said. "Excuse me, I'll be right back."

• • •

As Senalda was approaching Dexter from the left to where he sat, another woman beat her to him. He got up, hugged the woman and whispered something in her ear. Senalda briefly considered turning back toward her booth before he saw her, but she continued her stride, determined to not go home wondering whether Dexter was seeing this woman.

"Hey Dexter," Senalda said just as the two loosened their embrace.

"Hey Senalda," he said. "I didn't know you were here."

"I thought you and your boys were at J.R. Crickets every Friday night," she countered.

"Yeah, we decided to change it up tonight," he said, shrugging his shoulders with nonchalance. "This is one of my high school buddies, Felicia. And these are my boys. This is Senalda."

They all waved toward her, and Felicia walked away from the group.

"Can I talk to you over there for a second?" Senalda said, pointing away from the men.

"Okay," Dexter said.

He followed her to the club lobby where the music wasn't as loud.

"I thought Friday night was guys night out at a sports bar, but it looks like Friday night is really get together with the guys and look for new women night." She mentally prepared herself to go off while waiting for Dexter's response.

"What are you talking about? This is my first time here, and I haven't seen Felicia since I graduated from Mays High."

"Is our relationship exclusive?" Senalda demanded.

"You are the only woman I'm seeing," he said, getting closer to her. "But I do need time to hang with the fellas, okay? You are here with your friends!"

Senalda's scowl lasted for a few more seconds, the residual effect of thinking he was playing her. But after looking into his eyes, her scowl dissolved.

"Okay, I guess." She reached up and kissed him. "I guess I will head back to my girls, and you can head back to the fellas with my permission."

He laughed and hugged her.

As Senalda returned to her friends, she realized she had just scored a major victory in their Destination Wedding project—even if she was a bit uncomfortable with how it happened. She was in an exclusive relationship with six more months to secure a proposal and plan a wedding to spare.

CHAPTER 8

July

Senalda

IT WAS NOT LOST on me that I had two similar goals for the day: successfully running the Peachtree Road Race course for the first time, and determining the course of my relationship with Dexter. But first I would focus on the former, and the latter would be addressed later in the day.

I checked myself out in the bathroom mirror one last time after lacing up my sneakers and attaching my timing tag. To rep my sorority, I was wearing the perfect jazzy outfit, a fire-engine-red and stark-white running tank top and shorts that fitted enough to show my newly toned shape but were loose enough for easy movement. I bought the outfit at Phidippides, a running store in Ansley Mall. And since my hair had just been cut, I decided I could smooth my curls to my scalp after I started to sweat, and it wouldn't look so bad. *I look damn good.*

At 5 a.m., it was still dark and quiet as I backed out of my garage and onto the street. I turned on WBB, the news station, on my drive to the College Park MARTA train station. The broadcaster was already talking about the streets that were blocked off for the race. Dexter and I were meeting at the Lenox MARTA station near the start of the race. Most of the people who boarded the train seemed to be headed to the race as well.

I tried my best to be laid back, but I got squeezed more and more because crowds of runners got on at nearly every stop. I held my breath as long as I could because the armpit hair of a shaggy-haired white man hung like a furry umbrella over my head. I finally said, "Your armpit is in my face." The man laughed like I had told him a joke and then moved.

I found Dexter at Lenox station, waiting in front of the brochure area near the top of the escalator. I smiled because I could picture him in the same pose at an altar on the beach waiting for me as I walked down the aisle to meet him.

"Sen," Dexter called, waving to me.

"Hey, Dexy!" I ran up to him, and he bent down and hugged me. I never got tired of feeling his muscles, and they were on display today in the fitted green running singlet that he wore.

"So I know you're faster than me, but you won't leave me, right? I don't want to get lost with all of these people," I said, spotting two white fleshy-but-slim men in tiny shorts checking out Dexter. I couldn't blame them, because Dexter was fine.

"I've done this race about every year since I was nineteen, so I'm not worried about how fast I run," he said.

"That's a lie and you know it. I know you can run faster, but that won't stop me from trying to catch up to you or beat you!"

"So you don't mind if I run ahead?"

"That's motivation," I replied, trying to act like I was confident. I wasn't.

• • •

Once my feet hit the street about an hour later, I wondered why I had signed up to do this race in the first place. All of 6.2 miles for my first race! *That's what I get for being competitive.* For the first two, I kept up with Dexter, although I was breathing hard.

"You okay?"

"Yeah, yeah, I'm okay," I said, struggling to talk and run at the same time.

"Let me know if you want me to slow down."

"I'm good for right now," I released, still trying to breathe. "Go ahead."

"Okay," he said as his pace got faster, and I began walking.

After a couple of minutes I picked up my pace, although my legs wanted to crumble like pretzels. Maybe the "holy water" sprinkled on me and other racers by a white-collared reverend gave me some supernatural energy as I got to The Cathedral of St. Philip, Cathedral of Christ the King and Second Ponce de Leon Baptist Church, the three churches on Peachtree that made up "Jesus Junction." I slowed down again as I approached Cardiac Hill, trying to keep my pace steady while still moving forward.

"Water?" a race volunteer called with an annoying smile as she raised a paper cup in the air. She had come over to me from the left side of the street.

I shook my head to say no and tried to run faster, but my legs wouldn't cooperate. *At least I'm not walking.* As I passed the High Museum, I saw Dexter again and pumped my arms to help my feet get moving.

"Hey," I said, finally arriving at his side.

I reached up to feel my hair. Just as I thought, my bouncy curls were gone. Now my hair was just wet, and I could even smell my perm. But there was nothing I could do about it.

"Sen, just push through. When we do this again next year, it will be so much easier," he said as he grabbed my hand and started dragging me.

Next year? He plans for us to be together next year!

"You must have read my mind," I said out loud feeling a burst of energy brought on by his words, "because I was thinking this is my first and last time doing this race."

He laughed while he ran. *How did he do that?*

I looked up and saw that we were close to 10th Street. I dug deep, mustering up some extra energy since the race was going to end after another 1.2 miles. I was surprised to see that I was still keeping up with Dexter.

"Let's finish this race together!" Dexter said.

As we turned left to run down 10th Street, the crowd had multiplied, and everyone had their hands in the air and cheered for us. Their encouragement made me tap the last bit of energy I had to keep up with Dexter.

"Lift your arms in the air," he shouted over everyone. "See the photographers up there?"

I looked up and saw a line of photographers on a bridge contraption above the runners. I lifted my arms in the air as we got to them.

"Here we go," Dexter said. But then he picked up his pace, and his long legs passed me just like that.

I tried to run faster, but he was too far ahead to catch up.

"You did it," he said as he kissed me on the cheek once I got to him on the side of the street just beyond the finish line.

What happened to, 'Let's finish this race together'? This had to be payback for beating him in the election. He may have won the race, but I kept my eyes on my second but most important goal for the day—determining the course of our relationship.

• • •

Although Dexter's townhouse in Alpharetta was fine with its two bedrooms and two-and-a-half bathrooms, I wondered if he would mind living in my house once we got married. My home was bigger, after all.

"You can shower in my guest room bathroom," he said while pulling into his garage. "While you're doing that, I will look for something for you to put on. You're so small, I don't think I will have anything."

"Yeah, I must be musty, since you're practically pushing me into the shower," I said.

"You're not the only one," Dexter said with a laugh.

• • •

As I stuck my head under the shower nozzle, I was glad my mother was Puerto Rican. My hair would be wavy after I got the sweat out. A few minutes later, I dried myself off and walked into Dexter's room. A T-shirt and some sweatpants were on his bed. I only put on the T-shirt and went into his bathroom where he was showering.

"Hey, Dexy," I said as I walked through the steam. "You want me to get in there with you?"

"That depends. Are you starting something you can't finish?" he said, turning to look at me.

"Who says I can't finish?" I felt like working up a sweat again, but this time in his bed.

"I just want to relax and eat after that run," he said.

I frowned. Dexter was the moodiest guy I had ever dated when it came to sex. He had so many other things going for him, I didn't make a big deal about it. Other things I couldn't ignore.

"So where is this relationship going, anyway?" I said. "We've been seeing each other for almost six months."

"That came out of nowhere. Can we discuss this AFTER I get out of the shower?"

"Okay," I said with a laugh. "I will leave you alone FOR NOW."

It was already July. If I wanted to get engaged and married by the end of the year, we had to get moving. By the time he took me home tonight, I would know the answer to my question.

A few minutes later, he walked out of the bathroom, a black towel wrapped around his waist.

"So what do you want to do for the rest of the day?" he said to me as I lounged on his bed watching him.

I looked at him, gave him a sly smile, and finally said, "You said you wanted to relax and eat, but we could do other stuff too."

He laughed. "I got some hamburger meat in the fridge so I'm going to grill some burgers. And I bought some baked beans and potato salad from Publix yesterday."

"Sounds good," I said. "So we can have our own little July 4th barbecue!"

An hour later, Dexter and I relaxed on his brown leather sofa as we sipped Heinekens from the bottle and ate our food.

"So do you have some DVDs?" I said. "I feel like watching movies."

"Yeah," he said. "Look under the television."

I got on the carpet and searched through the television stand. "You've got *Coming to America*! That is one of my favorite movies," I shouted.

"*Boomerang, The Nutty Professor, Dreamgirls.* So obviously you're an Eddie Murphy fan."

"Yeah, he is one of my favorite actors," Dexter explained. "I saw *Eddie Murphy Raw* when I was ten years old, I think. I was hooked after that."

"Let's just watch Eddie Murphy movies all day," I said.

"Sounds good to me."

By 10 p.m., I realized that I needed to get home to get to work on Monday although I officially had the day off. And Dexter still hadn't told me where our relationship was going.

Jarena

In June, I made the biggest decision I've made since I said "PEACE OUT" to my last job and started my own business. I had been feeling like God was calling me to be a minister, of all things, in the months I'd been attending Hidden United Methodist. But I scheduled a meeting with Pastor Kirby to make sure I wasn't going crazy.

After church, I went to his office and waited for him to finish greeting members as they passed by him in the vestibule. Although Hidden United Methodist was old timey, his angular office furniture was actually contemporary. What surprised me the most was his office chair. It was one of those ergonomic chairs that looked modern enough to take flight. I was so used to seeing him sit in the burgundy velvet-covered pastor's chair behind the pulpit.

"Do you like my office?" he said as he walked in and looked around. "My wife spent months working so that it would look modern instead of how the sanctuary looks."

I laughed.

"She did a good job," I said. "I wasn't expecting it with rest of the church's décor for sure."

"So what can I do for you today?" Pastor Kirby sat down in his chair and leaned forward so that his arms rested on the glass shelf.

"Ever since I've been going here, I've been reminiscing about my grandmother. She used to take me to a country church that reminds me of this church," I said. "She was always saying that she believed I was 'anointed' and I would be a minister one day. That it was the 'highest calling' you can have on earth. I never really thought about what she said then because she said a whole lot of stuff to me.

"But lately her words have been coming back to me almost every day. And another thing. I used to read the Bible before, well at least on Sundays, and now I cannot live without reading the word of God every single day. So I started to pray about it, and I think God is telling me that I should be a minister. Is this what happened to you? Or am I going crazy?"

Pastor Kirby leaned back in his chair.

"Sorry for flooding you with all of that information," I said with a nervous laugh.

He chuckled and then paused before saying, "So I guess you're the one who God has been calling."

"Huh?" I said, forgetting I was speaking to a pastor.

"At the beginning of the year, God told me that someone in my church was going to be a new minister here."

I remembered the sermon from the first Sunday I visited the church. "You think God was talking about me?" I said, placing my hand on my chest.

"It is June and no one else has told me what you just said."

It was my turn to be quiet. Had this been the reason that I found this little church, or rather why God led me here?

"Maybe you're right," I said, finally. "I've been researching seminaries on the internet. Is that what I'm supposed to do now? Go back to school? What happens next?"

"Let's pray. That's the first thing. In fact, let's pray about it now."

Pastor Kirby came over to the chair next to me and grabbed my hands. He bowed his head and began. "Lord, you told me at the beginning of the year that someone in our congregation needed to be a minister, and here is Jarena today confirming what you said. But we need to be sure, Lord. Show Jarena clearly in a way she can understand and not deny what is your will for her. If you want her to be a minister, show her, Lord. In the blessed name of your son Jesus Christ, we pray. Amen."

"Amen," I repeated, feeling a warmth overtake me like a wave. "Thank you, Pastor Kirby."

"Would you like to be a certified lay minister here at the church?"

"What is that?"

"A lay minister is someone who serves in the capacity of a minister but is supervised by an ordained clergyperson." Pastor Kirby walked back to his chair behind his desk. "You can start a Bible study, start your own ministry at the church like a prayer ministry, visit the sick. You can be involved in any area that you feel led to be involved in. There is a two-day training session for lay ministers coming up in July in Charlotte.

"Also, after this session, there will be several courses offered by the North Georgia United Methodist Conference that you would need to take over a two-year period. During this time, I can mentor you and help you discern God's call on your life."

"Do I still need to go to seminary?"

"If you want to be an ordained minister, then yes, you have to go to seminary. But becoming an ordained minister can be a much longer process than the two years it takes to be a certified lay minister."

"I don't know if I want to be an ordained minister, but I do think I should go back to school. I just want to learn more. I already have a bachelor's degree."

"What about getting a master of divinity degree? I have some contacts at Candler School of Theology at Emory," he said. "Let's look at the website and see what you need to do to apply, if you're interested."

I walked behind his desk to look at what he had pulled up on his computer. I had until July 1 to submit my application materials to get into the school the next school year.

"That doesn't leave you much time," Pastor Kirby said, turning to me. "But you can count on my letter of recommendation."

"Yeah, a month isn't much time, but I think I want to do it," I said.

"That settles it, then. I will have my letter ready by next Sunday!"

"Wow! Well, thank you very much, Pastor Kirby," I said as I extended my arm to shake his hand. "I will see you next Sunday."

• • •

By July 1, my application materials had been turned in, only by the grace of God! I hoped I wouldn't have to wait too long to hear from the admissions committee to find out if I had gotten in Emory. In the meantime, I packed for my Charlotte trip.

It was almost as if Barry was telepathic. He sent me a Facebook message after I met with Pastor Kirby, and I told him that I would be in Charlotte on July 4th weekend for a ministry conference. He wanted to meet me for lunch on Friday. I thought I should probably decline, but I eventually concluded there would be no harm in two old friends meeting for a lunch, especially since I hadn't seen him in person since just after we graduated from college. Plus, we had changed since being the college sweethearts we once were, I told myself.

Barry remembered how much I loved soul food, so he suggested that we meet at Fat Daddy's Soul Food. Fat Daddy's was in a strip mall. It was easy to spot because the enormous blue-and-white sign featured a huge, jowled, pot-bellied black man. From my car, I looked through the glass storefront into the one-room restaurant, noting its bright fluorescent lighting and retro—or just plain old—blue Formica laminate tables and matching chairs. The stark ambience solidified it would be a friendly lunch, not a romantic reconnection. But I was also glad the restaurant looked like nothing special because I was suspicious of any soul food restaurant that placed too much emphasis on the décor. It wasn't easy to put "soul" into food, in my opinion, so that trumped décor all day every day for me.

I wondered what Barry would say about my huge curly Afro in person, especially in contrast to the simple black pantsuit with a white blouse I was wearing to be as conservative as possible at the training session. And then I saw Barry. For a second I wanted to drive off, but I was intrigued by what I saw. He was still rocking a medium-length curly Afro, but he had put on man weight. And then he looked at me. It only took him three steps to be in front of me as I opened the restaurant door. I wondered if his lips felt hot, because mine did. And then I was encircled in his arms. We still fit perfectly.

"Are you still wearing Drakkar Noir?" I said with a laugh.

"Hey, when you find a brand that works, stick with it."

"I guess you would know, Mr. Senior Brand Manager for Coca-Cola."

"And you have your own company," Barry said. "We've come a long way from eating ramen noodles in my grungy apartment!"

"Speaking of ramen, I want to try this North Cackalacky soul food," I said.

"Oh, so you finally can admit that you like a good piece of fatback," Barry shot back. "You're not hiding your love of soul food anymore, huh? Ms. Vidalia, born and bred."

"Uh excuse me, I was born in Vidalia but raised in the progressive city of Atlanta."

"Aww, whatever Jay, let's eat," he said while leading me to a table. One of my flats refused to budge, like it was my guilty conscience made tangible, and I nearly tripped over it, I was so nervous. But I steadied myself before he noticed.

A skinny white waitress with a pockmarked face and stringy blond hair wandered over to take our orders after we sat down. I wanted to try the ribs, but since I was notorious for spilling food on myself, I got the pulled pork with macaroni and cheese bowl instead.

"You've really changed," Barry said as he chose the barbecue steak. "You're even ordering swine!"

"Now that I'm older, I guess I don't care as much what people think about me."

"And I love your new hair too," he said with a smile.

"So how did you meet your wife? When you called to tell me you were getting married, you didn't tell me how y'all met."

I immediately wished I could eat my words. I hadn't intended on asking the question I wanted answered the most without any buildup, but he didn't seem to be fazed.

"I met Naomi in Nashville. You know I went to Vanderbilt for my MBA, and Naomi was at Tennessee State. We met in an Applebee's in downtown Nashville, and we've been together ever since."

"How sweet," I said before quickly grabbing my glass to take a prolonged sip of water. My face suddenly felt like it was on fire when I realized I had said his wife's maiden name. I silently prayed he wouldn't realize I knew her maiden name.

"That's funny you said that because her maiden name is Sweet, and that is why I fell in love with her. She was so sweet and easygoing. You hurt my heart so bad after you turned down my marriage proposal, I needed someone sweet," he said with a laugh.

"Wow, what am I supposed to say after that?" I said with relief. "But I guess it was meant to be. Y'all are happily married with two children."

Barry drank from his glass of Coke.

"Yes, little Barry and Amber make everything worth it. Barry just turned seven years old, and Amber is five. Do you want to see pictures of them? I have some on my phone," he said as he pulled out his phone.

I wondered if they were photos from his Facebook page. I had looked at them so much over the past few months I probably memorized them. I moved my chair closer to his to look at his phone. He did take me to his Facebook page to show me some of the photos of his children—opening Christmas gifts, at the grocery store, outside their home, and finally, a family portrait they had just taken that he hadn't had a chance to post yet.

I started to feel hollow. Barry was a great guy who wanted to do all of that for *me* years ago. And it was July, and I wasn't any closer to accomplishing my goal to meet another great guy, get engaged and marry, all by the end of the year.

"Barry, you have achieved the American dream— a beautiful wife and children, a nice home in the burbs, and a successful career," I concluded, trying to sound chipper.

"I guess I have," he said as if it just occurred to him. "So are you still breaking hearts? Who are you seeing, if you don't mind me asking?"

"Just my career," I said with a laugh that ended up being caught in my throat. I gulped down more water to stop myself from choking.

"Are you okay?" Barry said.

"Yeah, I guess the spices are getting to me."

"Jay, you're a beautiful woman," he said. "I bet there is someone in your life who is checking you out right now but you're so driven, you don't notice. When you're really ready to get married, it will just happen."

"I'm really ready now," I said, looking at him directly in his sky-blue eyes. "I've been really ready for a while, and nothing is happening. I'm just in this world alone. My mother is dead. My grandmother is dead. My father could be dead, but I wouldn't know since I've never met him. I don't have any brothers or sisters that I know of. And no man."

I didn't mean to blurt out all of that, but as I said it, I realized then I had been wanting to tell my old friend that for months. Thankfully, just as Barry opened his mouth to say something that I wasn't sure I wanted to hear, the waitress laid the check on the table, interrupting the moment. I changed the subject and started chattering about my famous clients while Barry paid for our meal. As we hugged before we left the restaurant, Barry said, "You're not alone in this world. You've got me, friend."

That night in my hotel room, as I was reading my Bible, I realized that I really didn't have faith that getting married would "just happen" for me, at least not anymore. My grandfather died before I was born, and my grandmother never remarried. My mother was obviously involved with my father at some point, but I never met him. And she never married or was involved with anyone else as far I could tell. Barry had asked to marry me, but I turned him down. And since then, every "involvement" I had just disintegrated like it never existed. I was starting to think that Barry was my one and only chance to get married, and I had blown it years ago.

Destination Wedding Meeting #7

Mimi and Jarena arrived at Senalda's home at the same time, and she opened her door to welcome her friends.

"I'm so glad we're getting together today," Jarena said as she went inside.

"Is everything okay?" Senalda asked, leading them to her living room where they positioned themselves on her couches.

"I guess I'm just sad that I haven't met anyone," Jarena admitted. She thought about telling her friends about Barry, but that would only lead to questions she couldn't answer for herself, much less for anyone else.

"At least yo man didn't kick you to da curb and cost you yo job," Mimi countered.

"She's got you there," Senalda said.

"I guess so," Jarena agreed. "How are you doing, Mimi?"

"Chillin' I guess," Mimi said. "In my counseling, I've been learning a lot about myself, and it's helping me figure out my relationship with Jovan."

"So do you still want to get married by the end of the year?" Jarena asked.

"Yeah," Mimi said before pausing. "But I'm focusing on me rat now, and I'm not accepting Jovan's calls either."

"Jovan still calls you?" Jarena said.

"A couple of times," Mimi answered.

"He's crazy," Senalda said.

"Yeah, I think you need to leave him alone, even if he is contacting you," Jarena advised. "Y'all are not good together."

Mimi didn't say anything at first.

"I know its crazy y'all, but I still think it can work between us," Mimi finally said. "I know I can't make y'all understand. I love Jovan, and I know he loves me. I know he's always been scared of commitment. Shit, I've always been scared of commitment too. But I'm ready now. And he just needs some time to get ready too. That chick—I refuse to say her name—is just hangin' around, hopin' that he'll be with her, but he still tryin' to get with me. Y'all gon see."

"You're right. You can't make us understand," Jarena said. "I've told you time and time again, he is not your man and you refuse to listen—"

Mimi put her hand in Jarena's face to stop her from continuing. "I do refuse to listen. I shoulda never said anythang, but I'm done now."

Senalda parted her lips to speak, but Jarena spoke first as she moved away from Mimi's hand. "So is Whitney coming over today?" she asked, choosing to defuse the situation by changing the subject.

"No, the marrieds have plans today, so it's just the three of us," Senalda said.

"So what are we doing today?" Jarena said.

"Oooh okay, after I ran the Peachtree Road Race with Dexter earlier this month, I Googled 'how to make a man marry you research,' and I found this great book," Senalda said as she held up a small blue-and-white book.

"What?" Mimi said.

"Okay, so I spent the whole day with Dexter, and I was trying to figure out how to get him to tell me where our relationship was going, and by the end of the day, zilch, nada, he said nothing. So I since I'm a numbers person, I decided to see if I could come up with some research-based advice or statistical data, and voilà! Check out it!" Senalda said, still holding the book in the air.

Jarena took the book and read the title and author's name out loud. "*Why Men Marry Some Women and Not Others: The Fascinating Research That Can Land You the Husband of Your Dreams* by John T. Molloy. Have you read it yet?"

"Of course," Senalda said as she disappeared into her office. "And I have created handouts for each of you, based on the research in the book." She returned to the living room with sheets of paper and gave them to Mimi and Jarena.

"Girl, with you on our team, we just ought to be married by the end of the year," Jarena said.

"Fa real dough!" Mimi agreed.

"I don't know about you guys, but I'm very serious about Destination Wedding," Senalda said, shaking her head. "One of the researchers in the book said the main reason why she didn't get married before she started the research was that she did not *insist* on being married. If Dexter doesn't propose by October 1, I'm moving on."

"Are you fa real?" Mimi said. "You gon let that good man go because he don't meet a deadline?"

"Yes and won't look back," Senalda said. "If Dexter asks me to marry him by October, we still have two months to get married before the end of the year. The second key point in the research is that women who want to get married don't stay in relationships that aren't going anywhere. You should think about that, Mimi. As for me, I'm not playing anymore. I deserve to be happily married."

"Can't argue with that!" Jarena said, waving her hand over her head.

Jarena and Mimi moved from the furniture to the floor, spreading out the handouts to read them. As the three women dissected and discussed the research, each one secretly pictured what happily ever after looked like. For Senalda, the perfect marriage was the interplay of position and pleasure and prowess and passion. Commitment, no matter how crazy or calm she was or could be, was what Mimi wanted most of all. Whether she lived up to her heavenly ideals or made her bed in hell, a haven huge enough for both was Jarena's hope.

CHAPTER 9

August

Whitney

EVER SINCE MY HUSBAND started attending Sex and Love Addicts Anonymous meetings, I wasn't seeing him very much. So when I did, I tried to make every second count.

"Hey, sweetiekins." I grabbed him from behind as he put on his shirt and tie in his bathroom. I attempted to wrap my right leg around his pants, but it slid down on the soft material until my foot touched the floor. "I can't believe it's Monday already. Now that we have the twins, our weekends go by so fast. Do you want me to get your jacket for you?"

"Nah, not wearing my jacket today," Richie replied while staring in the mirror and straightening his tie. He flexed his muscles underneath his shirt and zeroed in on his eyes as if he was trying to seduce himself. "I always have to take it off when I put on my lab coat."

"Oh, okay," I said, stepping back and admiring my conceited husband in the mirror. "What time will you be home tonight?"

"I have a meeting to go to after work so probably about 8:30 or so."

"You and these meetings!" I said in a sigh as I put my hand on my forehead.

"I explained to you that my sponsor said I had to attend ninety meetings in ninety days," Richie said, turning to me. "I'm almost done. Actually, I'm getting my three-month chip on Saturday, and I want you to come."

"I don't want to be around a bunch of weirdo addicts," I said. "I keep thinking you're hanging out with serial rapists and child molesters. Are you sure that no one at Grady knows you're going to these meetings?"

"We're supposed to be anonymous, remember? No one tells on anybody. So are you going to come?"

"Okay, okay, I guess I will, but I will not talk to anybody, and you can't make me, either," I said with laugh.

• • •

After the twins were settled with Gwenaëlle, I walked to the front of our home and looked out of our bay window. Richie was waiting for me in his Range Rover in the circular driveway. Ordinarily, I was either dressed in a sexy suit for work or a sexy but more casual outfit when I was out and about. I reasoned that women only had a small window to show off their figures, and I had a couple or so more years before I would be forced to transition into a more mature wardrobe.

However, tonight I did not want to be recognized, so I attempted to be as plain as I could. I had pulled my hair into a ponytail and slipped on some raggedy blue jeans and a T-shirt. Although I never wore flip-flops, I had a pair that I put on after I got pedicures at the nail salon. I didn't really need makeup, but I usually made myself up before leaving my home. Today, I was makeup free with only lip gloss on to moisturize my lips. My ponytail bounced against the back of my neck as I strode to his SUV.

"You look really pretty tonight," Richie said with a smile while pushing the passenger door open for me.

"I do?" I activated the passenger mirror to see if he saw something I had not seen. "I look like a slob! What are you talking about, Richie?"

"Not to me," he said, leaning in to kiss my cheek.

As he drove to DeKalb County, I thought about our marriage. The counseling had certainly helped. It wasn't like it was before we became parents, but things had improved. I hadn't noticed Richie going to the basement as much, and we made love about once a week; still not as often as before, but an improvement. But I also noticed that Richie seemed happier—actually the happiest I had ever known him to be.

"We'll be there in a few more minutes," he said before he started to hum.

"Are we on Memorial Drive?" I looked from side to side and pulled off my shades, eyeing the street that was nothing but check-cashing locations, fast-food restaurants, abandoned shopping centers, and MARTA bus stops. "We are in the hood. Where are we going, anyway? Are we going to be safe?"

"Yes, we meet in the basement of this historic church in the neighborhood."

"Is historic a code word for decrepit?" I asked. "Because if I don't feel safe, you're going to have to take me home."

"Whit, chill," he said, swinging into the parking lot of Sacred Heart Catholic Church. Once Richie parked and checked his appearance in the rearview mirror, an old white man who resembled Wolf Blitzer came over to the car next to us. He waved to Richie before getting a book from the car and turning back to walk into the church.

"Who was that?"

"Oh, that was Paul," Richie said.

"I mean. I thought this was an anonymous program?" I said. "Do I have to tell everyone my name?"

"We only know each by our first names, but you don't have to say anything because you're a visitor. Relax Whit, it will be okay. Really."

I found it ironic that although the church was a stunning work of Gothic architecture, these people were meeting in a tiny room with fluorescent lighting in the church's basement, like they were banished there. At the front was a large circle of metal folding chairs, and a 1980s coffee machine was brewing coffee on a chipped folding table in the back of the hovel. The silver-framed sayings on the walls like "Easy Does It," "First Things First," and "Live and Let Live" did soften the space. I was surprised by the diversity of the thirty or so people cramped in the room. I saw old people and younger people. Black people. White people. Chubby people. Slim people. And one very attractive, bald-headed, muscular, light-skinned man who apparently knew my husband.

"Richie, hey. What's up, man?" the light-skinned man said loudly as he bounded over to us and gave Richie the black-man hug when one man pulls the other man into his chest by holding the other man's hand with his hand. I could tell he came from New York because he had that aggressive, urban tone that reminded me of Senalda's voice, which I found distasteful until I got to know her. "By the time you leave this room tonight, you're going to have your ninety-day chip! You went to ninety meetings in ninety days! How does it feel, man?"

"I'm just thankful to my Higher Power and to you that I'm recovering," Richie answered.

Higher Power?

"Hey Victor, this is my wife Whitney," Richie said gesturing to me. "She's kind of nervous about being here, but she wanted to watch me get my ninety-day chip."

I almost snickered, but I chose to smile instead before speaking. "Nice to meet you, Victor," I said, extending my hand.

"I understand, ma," he said, taking my hand in his and covering it with the other instead of shaking it. "No need to worry. We don't bite. Can I get you anything? Some water or coffee?"

I shook my head and sat down in the chair closest to the door as Richie and Victor moved away from me to discuss something. Minutes later, the meeting started. Even though I was actually sitting among these people, I started to feel like I was watching a movie. I almost wished I had popcorn. Every person who spoke in the meeting had a crazy story to tell. They called it "sharing" but it seemed more like confessing, which was kind of funny since we were in a Catholic church.

Growing up, my family went to mass about once a month, but when I moved out and lived on my own in Atlanta, it seemed easier and easier to sleep in on Sunday. Richie's parents were Baptist, but he didn't make a big deal of going to church either, so we didn't include religion in our lives. And now we were in a Catholic church's basement, and he was literally sharing the most intimate details of our lives. I pasted a smile on my face as Richie finally stood up at the end of the meeting and received a coin the people called a chip from Victor, who was apparently his sponsor. Everyone cheered and clapped when Richie received his chip, but I wanted to disappear. I would be mortified if anyone found out that we were here.

Mimi

I'm the most "bout it bout it" person I know. I zip-lined in Costa Rica. I dove off cliffs in Jamaica. And instead of growing out my perm a lil bit at a time, I shaved all my hair off to grow dreads the day after graduating from college. But going to twelve-step meetings for sex and love addicts had me feelin' like I was a geek. I thought that running Jovan and his chick on the side off the road was gangsta, but the stories I heard in the meetings made me glad I started going when I did.

My sponsor Victor told me that his stripper troupe used to organize orgies with the women who attended their shows. One woman said she couldn't stop having unprotected sex with men although she was HIV-positive. A man admitted that he used to be a Peeping Tom and kidnapped a kid from her bedroom. All of them were trying to recover. Every meeting I went to felt like an adventure, not only because of what I heard, but because I knew that in a crazy way I was like these people I now called my "fellows." That was one of the program words I was learning. No, I had never gotten down in an orgy, given someone an STD or been a child molester, but I did act hella crazy when it came to sex and love. Victor helped me to see that. And he said it would only get worse until I did something about it.

I was going to ninety meetings in ninety days. That wasn't a problem because I wasn't working, although driving to Ashford Dunwoody every day from downtown wasn't always easy. But I liked the convenience of going to one place for my counseling with CC and for recovery meetings. By Friday, I would be getting my ninety-day chip.

I was runnin' late because of an accident on I-285 so I sneaked in as quietly as I could and sat near the back of the room. All the chairs were lined up side by side like in a classroom, and if you wanted to speak, you had to go to the podium in the front. I was leaning down to make sure my phone was off in my bag when I heard a voice I recognized, and not from a meeting. I looked up.

Damn. It was Richie, Whitney's husband. I put my head back down so that we wouldn't make eye contact.

"Up until three months ago, I was watching porn at least three hours a day. And I was thinking of hiring a prostitute. My disease had gotten out of control. But one day at a time I've stopped watching porn, and I'm starting to desire my wife again too."

You never know who somebody is just by lookin' at em. Richie looked like he could be on the cover of Country Club Magazine if there was one. Every time I saw him he had on some pastel Polo shirt with some too-snug khaki pants. But he sounded as sick as anyone else in the meeting. I thought about leaving to avoid seeing him, but I needed to get in a meeting today to get ninety meetings in ninety days.

Victor came up to me just after we finished saying the Serenity Prayer.

"Hey Richie, you need to meet Mimi. She is a newcomer too," Victor said loudly.

I spun around and there was Whitney's husband right in front of me. His eyes got all big.

"Mimi, I didn't expect to see you here," Richie said with a nervous laugh.

"Uh, me either... I mean, I mean, I didn't expect to see you here either."

"Oh, you met already?" Victor said, putting one hand on my back and the other on Richie's.

"Yeah. We know each other outside of the meetings," I said, looking at both of them.

"Oh snap," he said with a laugh. "I hope y'all are good because this probably won't be the last time you guys will run into each other in meetings."

"Probably not," I said, shaking my head.

"You guys look like you need to talk, so I'm going to excuse myself now," Victor said, backing away.

Once he was out of earshot, Richie spoke again. "Whatever you do, don't tell Whitney. She would kill herself if she found out that you know I'm coming to these meetings."

"Hey, if you keep my secret, I'll keep yours," I shot back. "I been making headlines all year behind my relationship drama. I don need to add dis too."

"Yeah, I heard about you losing your job at the radio station," Richie said. "Sorry that happened."

"Yeah, me too. On the other hand, I'm glad it happened when it did."

"What do you mean?... Hey, I was going to stop at a McCormick & Schmick's to eat lunch before I head back home. You want to join me? Maybe you can be my 'program buddy.'"

I laughed. "Oh, so you learnin the new recovery lingo too?"

"Yeah, I learn a new word at every meeting, it seems," he said with a laugh.

He stared at me like he was trying to read me. It's not that Whitney's husband was unfriendly, but he had barely said more than a few sentences to me. And now dude was asking me to lunch? He must be too scared I'm gonna tell Whitney what he shared in the meeting.

"Me too. Sure, I'm hungry," I said.

We walked to the parking lot together, and I followed his silver Range Rover to the restaurant. After we were seated, Richie started up again.

"So what did you mean when you said that you are glad you got fired?"

"I'm not glad, but I been working in radio ever since I graduated from college and I never even wanted to be a deejay. I mean I'm good at it so I did it, but I always wanted to sing."

"You went to Clark Atlanta, right?"

"Yeah, and I majored in music. I sang around town a few times like at Yin Yang or the Cotton Club, but I aine want to be no starving artist. So I got a radio deejay job and that's what I've been doing ever since. So now maybe I'll be forced to take my music seriously again."

"That's funny you're telling me this today." Richie looked down as he stabbed the ice with his straw in his glass of water.

"How you figure?"

"I had a photography business when I was at Morehouse," he said. "I used to take pictures at different parties around town. I would email them to friends, and people started asking for me to take pictures at all kinds of events. Then some girls who wanted to be models hired me to take pictures for their portfolios."

"So what happened?"

"During my senior year, I figured that I would be going away to medical school and I wouldn't have time for photography anymore, so I stopped. Plus, my dad told me that photography wasn't a profession, it was a hobby. Anyway, I've been thinking lately that I want to start my business again."

"Really?"

"Yeah. I don't know what step you're on yet, but when I was writing out my fourth step, I realized that I was mad at myself for not following through with photography."

"So you gon be a doctor *and* a photographer?" I asked with a laugh.

"I know it sounds crazy. I just thought I would take some photographs on the weekends or when I have time."

"Well, I have all the time in the world now, so I have no excuse to not work on my singing career."

"Want to know something funny?" Richie asked.

"What?" I said, wondering what other secrets I would find out about Whitney's husband today.

"You're not the only one who has been in the newspaper for something crazy."

I scrunched up my face in disbelief. "Oh yeah? Not you?!"

"I was arrested in a poker bust when I was in medical school. Since my father is a big deal in town, my name was mentioned in the AJC. Plus, I almost got a DUI in college. I think I have addictive personality. So I don't gamble or drink anymore. And now porn..."

"Does Whitney know all of this?" I asked, thinking Richie was more of a regular dude than Whitney made him seem.

"Yeah, she almost broke up with me after I was arrested, but when I asked her to marry me a few weeks later, she forgave me for my 'indiscretion,' as she put it. Plus my dad said I needed her stabilizing influence in my life."

"Well, thanks for sharing," I said like we were still in a meeting.

"I just thought I would tell you that so you know you're not the only one," he said before changing the subject. "So if you don't mind me asking, how are you going to pay your bills while you're out of work?"

I laughed. "I know you probably think I'm a dingbat because of my dreads or maybe cuz of whatever Whitney told you about me, but I know how to save my money. Remember I told you I aine want to be no starving artist. I got some coins saved up, so I'm straight for a while."

"I wish I could quit my job."

"Bwoi stop," I said as I chuckled. "You know Whitney aine having that! You probably need to get back to work right now."

The more I listened to him, the cooler he seemed. Maybe he wasn't the stick-up-the-ass dude he seemed to be. He always looked like he was either frowning, about to frown, or had just stopped frowning.

"I do have a late shift tonight," Richie said.

"So what you doin' all the way over here?"

"There's a photography store on this side of town that I wanted to check out, so I thought I would check out this meeting afterward," Richie said. "I usually go to meetings on Memorial Drive."

"Yeah, I just go to this meeting," I said. "So if you don't mind me asking, is Victor is your sponsor too?"

"Yes, he is," Richie said.

"Does he have you goin' to ninety in ninety?"

"Yeah, I just finished mine last week. So you're doing ninety in ninety too?" Richie said.

"Yep, and I'll be done this Friday."

"That's cool," he said. "I have another late shift on Friday so I'll come watch you get your chip, unless you don't want me to or have someone else coming. Whit came to my meeting last week to see me get my chip."

"Whitney Duvernay-Brannon was at a Sex and Love Addicts Anonymous meeting?" I hollered in disbelief. "I guess this program does make miracles happen. I hadn't thought about inviting anyone, but even if I did, no one I know knows I come to the meetings. I'm not ashamed or anything, but I wanted to wait until I had some recovery before I started telling people. Plus, it is an anonymous program."

"I know—'What you hear here, what you say here, when you leave here, let it stay here.'"

"Hear, hear," I said, reciting the end of the recovery slogan.

"So I will see you on Friday?"

"Okay, that would be cool," I said. "You know, when I saw you in the meeting, I was thinkin' 'bout leaving because I aine want to make you feel uncomfortable, but I'm glad I stayed."

"Me too. You know Victor has me making three calls a day to program people. You think it would be okay if I added you to my list of people who I call?"

"I have to call people too," I said. "Why not?"

We programmed our numbers into each other's cell phones.

"Okay, Miss Gayle, I need to get on the road now," Richie said, as he pulled the bill toward him and slid out of the booth where we sat. "See you on Friday."

"Cool," I said. "See you then."

❧ Destination Wedding Meeting #8

As Jarena pulled into the circular driveway in front of Whitney's house after driving for nearly a half mile on the gated Brannon property, she marveled at the virtual palace that a two-income household could afford. Their home was an imposing, European-styled fortress of windows, stucco, and stone. A lawyer and a doctor. They were the modern-day Huxtables, except in the lush green suburbs of metro Atlanta instead of the brownstone-laden Brooklyn.

They just need three more kids, Jarena said to herself but laughed out loud.

She maneuvered her Acura to park behind her friends' vehicles. As she stepped out of her car, Senalda opened the door and waved.

"Hey, Jarena."

"One of the good things about these meetings is that we are guaranteed to see each other every month," Jarena said, walking over to her friend and hugging her.

"I know," Senalda said. "So congratulations on getting into the ministry program at Emory! I can't believe I'm going to have a minister as a friend!"

Whitney came over then. "Hey, welcome back to Henry County."

"I know, right, with your OTP self," Jarena said. "You know I must love you to go outside the perimeter."

"OTP is for me," Whitney said with a laugh.

"I've got to admit, y'all wannabe-Huxtables are living good outchea," Jarena said.

"You're crazy," Whitney said.

"Okay, enough with all of the sentimentalities, let's get down to business," Senalda said. "We're in the kitchen today."

"In the kitchen?" Jarena said. "I know you didn't cook anything."

"No, I didn't, but Whitney did, and she is going to teach us."

Jarena waved to Mimi, who was slurping down a smoothie while sitting on a stool at the island of the huge kitchen, a granite-countertop and custom cabinet showpiece.

"Okay, well, let's get to business. Whitney told me that one of the ways she believes she got Richie to propose was to cook for him. I know that I don't cook very much, probably because I don't have to. So I thought it would be educational for Whitney to make one of Richie's favorite dishes for us," Senalda said, as if she were conducting an official meeting at Wachovia Bank.

"So do you girls remember when Richie proposed to me on Christmas Eve?" Whitney said.

"How we could forget the 'most romantic proposal in the world'?" Jarena said as she rolled her eyes. "You've told us the story a thousand times plus ten! He proposed to you on Christmas Eve at Anis Bistro in Buckhead in front of the whole restaurant."

"Romance, schmomance," Mimi said looking down, in between obnoxiously loud slurps of her smoothie. She couldn't help but think of what

Richie shared in and after meetings and how their marriage wasn't what Whitney wanted everyone to believe.

"Careful Mimi, your bitterness is showing," Jarena said with a laugh. "I still believe in love."

"Ladies, we are veering off topic again," Senalda said as she clapped her hands together. "You were saying, Whitney?"

"I know I've told y'all about my engagement story, but I've never told the back story to how I got engaged."

Whitney recounted reading the *Glamour* magazine article about engagement chicken and how she made the dish shortly afterward.

"Seriously Whitney, you think Richie asked you to marry him cuz you cooked some chicken for him?" Mimi said as she got up and threw her Styrofoam cup away.

"I'm sure he was probably already thinking about it. I am irresistible, as you can see," Whitney said with a straight face. "But y'all have got to admit it was a wonderful coincidence, and he has told me that it's his favorite meal that I make. I mean, shrimp scampi is his favorite food, but engagement chicken is his favorite of all the foods that I cook for him. Whenever I make it, it's like I cast a spell on him or something."

"Isn't that wild?" Senalda said. "So we have got to learn how to make this chicken! I'm definitely going to make it for Dexter ASAP. So show us how!"

The four women laughed as they prepared the meal, and later three of them sipped wine as the baking chicken filled the kitchen with its aroma. The sound of a slamming door interrupted the drunken laughter.

"Whit," Richie called out with force.

"We're in the kitchen," Whitney called, sliding off of one of the stools near the island. With her wine glass in her hand, she walked over to meet him as he arrived at the kitchen door.

"Hey Whit," he said before kissing her on the cheek. "Ladies."

"Hey Richie," the women said in unison.

"The chicken is almost ready," Whitney said. "I can bring you some when it's finally done baking."

"Oh I forgot you said you were making your special chicken," Richie said, his face pinched. "I picked up some shrimp scampi from McCormick & Schmick's on the way home. Can you fix a plate for me, and I will take it to the hospital for lunch tomorrow?"

Mimi raised her eyebrows as she sipped her wine.

"Oh, okay," Whitney said, the tone of her voice changing. "Well, it's been a long time since you've had your absolute favorite dish in the world."

"Yeah?" Richie said, looking as if he wanted to ask a question. "Alright ladies, I will let you all get back to your meeting. Whit, I'm going to check on the twins. They're upstairs, right?"

"Yes," Whitney said to him as he walked away.

"Are you sho we shouldn't be learning how to make shrimp scampi?" Mimi said. She put her wine glass down on the island countertop before releasing a hearty burp.

"Yuck, Mimi, and hush!" Jarena said, looking at her.

"If Whitney had made shrimp scampi a few weeks before Richie proposed to her, that is what we would be making. Who cares what he wants to eat tonight? She's already got the man," Senalda said, the overreaching defiance in her voice only highlighting Whitney's silent embarrassment.

Whitney continued saying nothing, pulling the chicken from the stove and putting it down on the table for her friends to see the finished dish.

CHAPTER 10
September
....

Mimi

IT WAS A MONTH later, and I was still thinking 'bout what happened the Friday night after I received my ninety-day chip earlier in the day. After coming inside of my place with groceries, I put them down on the floor to dig my chip out of my wallet. I held the chip, which looked like a plain white gambling chip, in my hands. I hadn't expected it to mean so much, but it represented that I took a gamble that cutting off all contact with Jovan and focusing on myself would make me feel better. And I did. And I was starting to feel that even if for some crazy-ass reason we never got back together, I would be alright.

That's why my heart felt like it fell out of my chest when I saw Jovan's text: "Are u at home? Can I come over? I got something 2 tell u." I stopped putting away the groceries and just stood in my kitchen. Was this my Higher Power's way of saying I was ready for him, and he was finally ready for me? Victor would probably disagree, but he wasn't my Higher Power. I hadn't heard from Jovan in a month. I read his text two more times, trying to decide what I should text back. I finally decided it was time we made up. All these months without me had finally taught him a lesson.

"I'm at home. Yeah, u can. When u coming over?" I texted.

"I can be there in 30 mins," he texted back.

In that time, I put up the rest of the groceries, washed my face, put on eyeliner and mascara, ran my fingers through my locs, smoothed on shea butter, and slipped on a pair of dark blue stretch jeans and a half sweater that showed my stomach. When the security desk told me that Jovan was downstairs, Victor's face flashed in my head, but I decided to let Jovan in anyway. I felt my heart pumping again.

"Hey," I breathed out as I cracked open the door and leaned on the doorframe.

"Hey," he said, standing still like he was afraid of me. I wanted to touch his smooth curly hair under his baseball cap.

"I guess I should invite you in," I said, without moving. "Are you gonna have me arrested if I do?"

"You know I wouldn't," he said as he got closer to me without coming inside. "Chula convinced me to do that, but I knew you wouldn't hurt me."

"You need to tell dat heffa that," I responded. *But I would hurt her*, I said to myself as I fully opened my door, walked back in my home and plopped down on my couch. Jovan followed me in and sat down across from me.

"So what do you wanna tell me?" I arched my back so he could see my sexy flat stomach. He had to miss my body as much as I missed his.

"I wanted you to know something before you find out on some blog or from somebody else."

"What?" I said, looking at him directly in his eyes.

"I'm going to ask Chula to marry me."

"Are you serious?" I screamed as I got up and charged at him. "After all of these months, you come over and tell me that you want to fucking marry this chick? Did your ass ever care about me?"

Jovan moved before I got to him. I stared at him as he walked over to the door and closed it before he turned back to face me.

"I care about you a lot, which is why I wanted you to hear it from me," he said, sitting back down. "I love her, Mimi... I do... I never really thought about marrying anyone before I met her."

"All dis time we been together, I was hoping you would feel dat way bout me, and a few months after meeting this youngun, you want to marry her?" I screamed back. I hurled a picture of us from an end table at him and began pounding him. Mostly I was shadow boxing, since he moved back to get away from my blows.

"I'm sorry, I'm so sorry," he finally said as he came closer to me and held my arms behind my back. "I never, ever wanted to hurt you. I always told you I didn't want to be in a relationship. You can't say I didn't, either."

I fell back on my couch and started sobbing into one of the cushions, not even caring that snot glazed my face. Then I felt Jovan behind me.

"I didn't mean to make you cry," he said, stroking my locs. "I can't stand to see a woman cry. Please stop."

I turned and cried into his chest. And since I wasn't sure if we would ever be alone again, I kissed him.

"That was a goodbye kiss," I said in between sobs.

I was surprised when he kissed me back. We kissed back and forth like it was a game of tag. And then he moved to the edge of my locs, my ears, my neck, my arms, my fingertips and to my stomach. I kissed him everywhere I saw skin too. My tears dried, and our clothes seemed to melt away in the heat.

• • •

The next morning I snuggled into Jovan's side as he lay on my bed. During the night, I heard his phone beep and I wondered if it was Chula trying to figure out where he was. I had been so tempted to text her and say, "U lost heffa. He's ALL MINE." The way we had been together throughout the night and in the morning proved that Jovan loved all of me. His words may have said one thing, but his body had said another over and over again. He stirred beside me before opening his eyes.

"Oh snap, what time is it?"

"Almost 10," I replied. "I can make some breakfast for us."

"Naw, I gotta be somewhere soon." He sat up, picked up his phone and looked at his messages.

"So what are we going to do now?" I said as I moved across the bed to lean my head on his shoulder.

"What are you talking about?" he said, giving me a full dose of his hot morning breath. I actually missed it.

"Me and you," I said, hoping my morning breath didn't turn him off.

"I told you last night," he said softly.

"But what about what happened after that and early this morning?"

"We've always been good together, but I love Chula."

"You know what?" I said, jumping up from my bed and clutching the sheets around me. "Just get out! Erase my number! I don't want to see you ever again!"

Jovan threw on his wrinkled clothes and hurried out of my bedroom.

"And you betta not slam my shit, punk-ass nigga!" I growled.

I heard my front door close. My stomach was so queasy I ran into my bathroom and puked in the toilet. Victor was right. I got dressed and made myself go to a noon meeting.

❦ Destination Wedding Meeting #9

Since the women couldn't coordinate their schedules to meet in person for their September meeting, they instead opted to have a conference call on Senalda's birthday. Usually Senalda celebrated her birthday with her girls, but Dexter said he wanted to take her out for her big day. He told her to be ready by 6 and to wear a party dress. She hoped her birthday present would be an engagement ring!

"So are we all here?" Senalda said while sitting on her bed.

"Present," Jarena said.

"Wazzup," Mimi said.

"Happy birthday!" Jarena and Mimi shouted together.

"Awww, thank you! I'm older but better," Senalda said with a curt laugh before changing her tone. "So have we made any progress on our individual goals? Jarena, have you started reading that book I gave you?"

"If you mean *How to Get a Date Worth Keeping*, I have." Jarena answered. "But as of today, I haven't had any dates. If only my new pastor was single, I would ask him out." She laughed.

She couldn't admit to her friends that the real reason that she likely wasn't meeting anyone new was that she had fallen back in love with her married college sweetheart. By September, their communication had evolved from chatting on Facebook and texting to speaking on the phone at least once a day. She told herself their friendship was still harmless, that it was only happening because they happened to be in the same city for the first time since they graduated from college.

"I'm going to act like I didn't hear that last comment," Senalda said. "No one likes a homewrecker. Do you still want to be married by the end of the year?"

"Yes," Jarena said slowly, pondering her answer, "but I don't know how that is possible anymore since we're nine months into it."

"Aren't you the one enrolled at Emory's school of theology?" Senalda said. "What about faith? I'm not even enrolled in theology school, and I have faith."

"Okay, you're right," Jarena said, although inwardly she remained unconvinced.

"Mimi, what's up with you?" Senalda said. "Is Jovan still calling you?"

"Naw, he stopped calling a while ago since I stopped answering his calls and texts," Mimi replied in a monotone. She wasn't ready to tell her friends what happened with Jovan yet. Especially since Jarena had been right about his feelings for her, which got on her nerves because Jarena thought she was right about everything.

"Good girl," Senalda concluded. "So Miss Thang Mimi, have you caught someone else's eye yet? Why don't you give that doctor a call? The one that we met at The Veronique Experience."

"Didn't I tell y'all that I went out with him and I was bored to def? He is jus not my type, okay?"

"In that book I gave to Jarena, the author says you shouldn't limit yourself to your type and you should go out on more than one date with someone to really tell if you like them or not," Senalda said.

"I don't wanna see him again," Mimi said, rolling her neck as if her friends could see her.

"So I guess you're not serious about our goal then," Senalda said.

"I think Senalda is right," Jarena interjected. "Give that man another chance! You could be passing up your blessing! In fact, you probably are."

"I am serious 'bout our goal," Mimi said. "I just have a different approach to this whole thang than y'all do. And how do you know I'm passing up a blessing, Jarena? Don't get all holier than thou with me!"

"No one asked, but I'm hoping to get an engagement ring tonight for my birthday," Senalda said as the excitement in her voice temporarily elevated its tone. "I miss spending my birthday with my girls though."

"Oh whatever," Jarena said. "You could care less about kicking us to the curb now that you have a man."

"That's not true," Senalda said. "What are the two of you doing tonight?"

"It's a Netflix night for me," Jarena said.

"I aine sho yet," Mimi said, "I'm thinkin' bout going to an album release party for this new artist. Hey y'all, I gotta take this other call. Happy birthday again Senalda!" She quickly hung up the phone.

"Well, I guess the meeting is over," Senalda said. "So what are you watching tonight?"

"I don't know. Some 'we're-in-love-but-can't-be-together' romance movie," Jarena said, followed by an uncomfortable combination of a giggle and a sigh.

"Maybe you shouldn't stay at home alone tonight," Senalda said, sensing Jarena's offhanded remark was masking her true feelings. "Maybe you should hang with Mimi at the album release party."

"Yeah, I may hang with her... We'll see," Jarena said. "I hope you get your heart's desire tonight, birthday girl."

"I can't believe I'm thirty-three," Senalda said. "I remember when I turned thirteen!"

"I know, right?" Jarena said. "Well, you've got it going on in every way."

"Everything but a ring, and I will have that too by tonight, hopefully," Senalda said.

"Well, let me know what happens tomorrow," Jarena said.

"I will!"

"And happiest of birthdays again!"

• • •

Senalda hoped her friends concentrated on their collective goal, whatever they decided to do for the evening. For her evening, she chose a fuchsia one-shoulder sequined dress. She also put on the diamond stud earrings she bought herself for her thirty-second birthday—hoping that the sparklers wouldn't be the only diamonds she wore home that evening.

When Dexter arrived at her door, she was so excited she kissed him for at least twenty seconds before he even stepped all the way in.

"Happy birthday to me," he said in a husky tone as they pulled apart. "I hope I can make you feel as good tonight as you just made me feel. With a kiss like that, maybe we can just stay right here."

"Maybe we can come back here later," Senalda said, nudging him toward the door. "So where is my birthday gift? I know you didn't come here empty-handed!"

"Oh, it's in the car," Dexter said. "You ready?"

"Of course," Senalda said.

The outside motion lights activated as they walked to Dexter's car. She quickly scanned the front passenger seat for a little box, but there was nothing.

After they got in his car, he turned, looked around and said, "Sen, please don't be mad, but I forgot your gift at my house. Do you mind if we go back to my house to get it?"

"All the way to Alpharetta?" Senalda said. "Do we have reservations any-where? I don't want to be late."

"Where we are going tonight doesn't need reservations, but I do want to give you your gift," Dexter replied.

"Okay," Senalda said, trying to keep a pleasant expression on her face. Her inner control freak, however, wanted to regulate.

As Dexter drove, he tried to tell her about his day and anything else he could think of, but Senalda gave him one-word answers or just nodded. Nearly an hour later, they pulled into his driveway.

"I will be right back, okay?"

"Okay," Senalda said, giving him her best feminine-not-bossy smile.

Minutes later, he returned. "Can you come inside for a second?" Dexter said. "I want to show you something before I give you your gift."

"Dexy, what's going on?"

"Woman, be quiet and follow me, okay?"

"Okay," she said quietly while following him into the front entrance of his home. "Can you turn on the lights? I can't see."

The lights came on then as people appeared from everywhere and yelled "Surprise!!!"

For a moment, Senalda was silent, momentarily rattled by the wall of people. And then she saw people she recognized. Whitney and Richie. Jarena. Mimi. Her assistant Nashaun. She saw an older woman and man who appeared to be Dexter's parents.

"Happy birthday, Senalda," Dexter said. "Are you surprised?"

"Is this a surprise birthday party for me?"

"All for you." Dexter handed her thirty-three fuchsia roses before kissing her on her quivering lips. "I want to thank your friends for helping me to coordinate this surprise."

He turned and faced the crowd. Senalda wasn't a crier, but she felt pressure around her eyes before she blinked while waving her hands in her face. Her girls circled around, hugging her as Dexter stepped to the side. She was glad for the support of their arms as the realization of what was happening made her lightheaded with joy and expectation. It would only make sense for the proposal to be next.

"You guys are some good liars," she said to her girls. "I had no clue."

"So what's a party without some music?" Mimi shouted, stepping out of the circle. "I need the deejay to get it poppin' up in here."

A deejay stationed near Dexter's patio doors stroked his turntables, emitting a jam that ignited spontaneous dancing. "Thank you so much, Dexter," Senalda said, standing on her toes, speaking directly into his ear.

"I told you we didn't need reservations," Dexter said with a cocky grin.

She laughed. He introduced her to his parents, co-workers, and friends before she felt a vibration in her purse. She reached in it to retrieve her cell phone.

"Hi Mommy," Senalda said while walking into Dexter's kitchen.

"How is the surprise party?" said Gloria Maria Warner.

"You knew, Mommy, and you didn't even tell me!" Senalda said. "Did you plan this party with Dexter? You haven't even met him yet!"

"Nashaun put him in touch with me so I got to know him a little bit. I wish I could be there to see it. It sounds like you are surprised, no?"

"I am," Senalda said.

"So have you cut your cake yet? I made a rum cake for you and shipped it to Nashaun."

"Mommy, my favorite," Senalda said while opening the kitchen door to walk back into the party and look for the cake.

As if on cue, Nashaun flicked the lights on and off and yelled, "Time for the birthday cake!"

On Dexter's dining room table was a colossal white sheet cake next to a smaller Puerto Rican rum cake, a golden-brown Bundt cake.

"You called at the right time," Senalda said. "I'm going to put you on speaker so you can hear everything, okay?"

"I hope I can hear," Gloria Maria said.

"Y'all come on over here because we need to cut this birthday cake for my boss and my friend, the one and only Mizz Senalda Warner," Nashaun yelled as a trail of sweat moistened the shimmering makeup she had applied to her pushed-up already large cleavage. "But y'all know we can't cut this cake without singing 'Happy Birthday' to her first." Leaning back in her tight gold lame minidress, Nashaun began singing like she was in church, moving her billowing arms as if she was directing the choir and motioning for everyone to join in with her.

"Mizz Warner, are you ready to cut your cake?" Nashaun said to her once the group finished singing. "And this cake right here is the main birthday cake for everyone but this one over here is a special Puerto Rican rum cake aaaall the way from the Bronx. Mizz Warner will let y'all know if you can have some of her special birthday cake so y'all betta not try to get some of this cake right here."

"Thank you, Nashaun," Senalda said in a steady tone, attempting to soften the spectacle of her gold-toothed assistant.

"You know I got you," Nashaun said as Senalda hugged her. "Blow out your candles, but make a wish first!"

Senalda was glad to only see three instead of thirty-three. She crossed her fingers as she blew them out. Then, she took a large cake knife from Nashaun to cut slices for people nearby the table before cutting rum cake slices for herself and Dexter. She hoped a proposal from Dexter was coming next, but two hours later, the crowd had thinned out without anything happening. Although Senalda loved Dexter for making her birthday the most special one she remembered having since she was a little girl, she wondered if it would come and go without her getting the one birthday gift she wanted. Nashaun was the last person to leave.

Before leaving, she whispered into Senalda's ear at the door. "Mizz Warner, you got a good ole man! You better hold on that man too. And he fine. And he got a good job. And he got this big ole house. Ummm ummm." She backed away and said loudly, "See you on Monday if you can make it in."

"You know your assistant is crazy, right?" Dexter said after he locked the door.

"Yeah, she's fun at work though," Senalda said.

"So the only detail I think I missed is packing an overnight bag for you to stay over," Dexter said, pulling Senalda to him.

Senalda seriously considered going home at that point. But then she thought maybe Dexter wanted to propose to her when they were by themselves since he did invite her to stay the night. One iota of hope was left within her, and she clung to it with all she had.

"In case you didn't know, I love you, Senalda Esperanza Warner. I wanted to show you that by planning this party for you. And in case you didn't know this either, I hope this is the first of many birthdays we spend together."

Senalda said nothing, but the tears forming in her eyes said what she wanted to say. This time she let them fall.

• • •

The next morning, Senalda was still speechless and unengaged. Had this exact same relationship unfolded in her twenties, she wouldn't have felt as pressed. But now that another year of her life was beginning, she didn't know what to think. For most of the car ride back to her home, she remained silent, and Dexter seemed not to notice. As he pulled in the driveway, she decided to just say whatever she felt like saying.

"Where is this relationship going?" Senalda squawked. "You said you love me. You threw a surprise party for me. We get along well. We have everything in common. We are grown. What's next for us?"

Dexter drove all the way in her driveway. "We've only been dating for seven months."

"Yes, but it's not like we didn't already know each other," Senalda retorted. "Do you see us being together long-term?"

"Yes," Dexter said quietly. "I told you that last night."

"What you said is that you wanted to spend more birthdays with me," Senalda said. "My girls and I have been spending our birthdays together for years, but I'm not marrying them."

"I can see us getting married one day," Dexter explained, "but I'm not ready to make that commitment right now. I hope my answer is enough for you. And the fact that I love you, and I don't plan on going anywhere."

He reached toward her to hug her, but she flinched, moving away from him.

"I'm planning on going inside my house because I'm committed to that," Senalda said as she slammed his car door and walked to her house without looking back.

CHAPTER 11

October

Jarena

I HOPED THAT PASTOR KIRBY had a word for me this Sunday because I couldn't get away from my feelings about my business any longer. My friends always found it hilarious that in spite of the raunchier artists I promoted throughout the week, I praised the Lord every Sunday. Sometimes I thought it was funny too, but I reasoned that the Lord wanted me to make a living, and it wasn't like I or many of the artists that I promoted even were living the degenerate lives portrayed in some of their songs.

So while I drove to church, I listened to Rich the Rapper's album, hoping its redemptive quality would be evident. Rich was my latest client, and his first song, "Make Money Not Love," off of his debut album, *Moolah*, was already a chart-topper. "Money is my rula, love gets no nigga. If you wanna rule this nigga, betta make dat money," was the first lyric on the song. The lyrics were jarring, but the beat was banging. And although I would be in church within minutes, my head moved in tandem with my shoulders so much so that I felt like pulling over and getting out to allow my whole body to pulsate.

I had fallen in love with Southern hip hop in middle school. Atlanta rappers like Kilo Ali, Raheem the Dream, and Kris Kross, and deejays like DJ Smurf, DJ Kizzy Rock and DJ Toomp started to get Atlanta noticed. And then when LaFace Records moved to town and OutKast came out, I watched Atlanta become the rap capital of the world. In 1995, the year that

I graduated from high school, OutKast won the Best New Artist award at the Source Awards. Dre said, "The South got something to say," in his acceptance speech, even though the East Coast and West Coast artists and their fans were booing them. And his words were like a prophecy. Then there was Goodie Mob, Lil Jon & the East Side Boyz, and the Ying Yang Twins. I couldn't believe it when one of my high school classmates, Chris Bridges, who was the radio deejay Chris Lova Lova, became the rapper Ludacris and blew up! Even when I moved hours away to go to college in Tuscaloosa, I drove home to Atlanta as many weekends as I could so Mimi and I could party at XS, Club Kaya, and Club 112 and all over the city, seeing the rap artists and deejays who were making our city famous.

I got to church a few minutes early, using the time to pray silently and ask God what to do. Once the service started, I didn't pay much attention to anything until finally it was Pastor Kirby's turn to speak.

"Church, you know I'm a big football fan. On Saturdays and Sundays after church, you can find me either watching a football game on television or at the actual game. As I watched a game last week, I realized the Christian faith is like a football game. After this particular game, the coach of the losing team was interviewed, and he admitted that some of the members of the team had been distracted. He said, 'We have to be all in to win.' And church, that's what I want to tell you today. You have to be all in this Christian faith to win at it."

"Speak on it!" a slight man with a curiously booming voice commanded from the back of the church.

Pastor Kirby gripped the sides of the wooden pulpit and leaned forward, the man's imperative emboldening him.

"In fact, God says in Revelation 3:15-17, you can't do this thing halfway. He compares being a halfway Christian to being lukewarm water. When you have cold water on a hot day, it quenches your thirst. And when you take a hot shower on a cold day, it prepares you to meet the cold. But what does lukewarm do? Nothing. And God said He will spit halfway Christians out of His mouth like they are lukewarm water. So I want to ask you today, are you all the way in or are you halfway in? Because whether you are halfway in or all the way out, the result is the same. You lose."

That was all I needed to hear. I had asked a question of God, and He had answered. In that moment, I knew I would be selling my business. After the church service was over, I rushed up to Pastor Kirby as he greeted church members.

"Pastor Kirby, I don't know if you're heading to see a football game after church, but if you have a few minutes to spare, I would like to speak with you in your office, please."

"Ha, glad you were listening," Pastor Kirby said with a laugh. "But as I said, God comes first. I'll be in my office in about fifteen minutes if you want to talk."

As I waited, I leaned against the wall outside of his office as if the wall would steady my flailing emotions. *Did I really just decide to sell my business?* I considered dashing to my car and skipping out on my impromptu meeting. Just as I was about to leave, Pastor Kirby appeared in front of me. After he held his office door open for me, I sat down in the chair in front of his desk.

"So what's going on?"

"A lot, Pastor Kirby," I said, trying to organize my thoughts. "I think I want to sell my business. As I drove to church today, I was listening to an album by one of the artists that I represent. I don't know if you've heard of Rich the Rapper? But anyway, I was listening to his lyrics, and I realized that although I didn't write the lyrics or believe in what he was saying, I am part of the reason why his music is so successful. And I was thinking that maybe God doesn't approve of that."

I sighed, the weight of my admission making me lethargic, before I finished my explanation.

"I never really thought about it before because in the past, going to church was just something I did on Sundays. But now that I am studying to be a minister, I'm starting to be uncomfortable with what I do. So I prayed before church started that God would speak through you to me about what I should do. And then you preached about being all in, and I realized that

I'm half in. And I feel like God wants me to sell my business so that I can be all the way in."

"I see why you were leaning against the wall," Pastor Kirby said. "You were carrying a load for sure."

"So what should I do?" I said, interrupting him.

"I think what you're talking about is a very serious decision," he began. "When I decided to go back to school instead of launching my career in business, I was worried about how that would affect my wife, who was my fiancée at the time. Thankfully, she supported my decision. Through some financial aid and her getting her first job as an attorney, I was able to get my master of ministry degree at United Theological Seminary.

"Long story short, I eventually got called here at Hidden after getting that degree, and I'm happier than I ever would have been, had I pursued business. And God provided for us financially the whole time. I'm not going to tell you what to do, but hopefully, my story will give you something to think about as you're seeking God's face about this decision."

I sighed again, knowing what I should do but wondering if I had the faith to do it.

"Thank you, Pastor Kirby," I said finally. "I'm going to pray about it some more."

I rose from my chair, shook his hand over his desk and walked out of his office.

• • •

I drove in silence on the way home from church until my cell phone rang as I turned off the freeway at Cumberland Boulevard.

"Hello?" I said, somewhat startled at the sound of my own voice.

"Hey Jay," a familiar deep and sexy baritone voice said.

"Oh hey, Bama," I replied.

"What's wrong, girl?"

"Nothing. Just sleepy and hungry. How are you?"

"I've got something crazy to tell you," Barry said.

"What?" I asked, hearing the excitement in his words as I pulled into a takeout parking space for This Is It! to get my Sunday dinner.

"I'm moving to Atlanta in December."

"Wha what whaaat? You, Naomi and the kids are moving here?" I stammered.

"No," Barry said. "Coke is launching a new product in Atlanta and they want to me to help launch it, so I'll be there for a year. My family is staying in North Carolina, so I'll go home every other weekend."

"Congratulations," I said when I could finally speak coherently. "Is this a promotion?"

"Yep!" Barry said.

"Cool!" I said. "Congratulations again!"

"Thanks."

"I cannot believe that you and I will be living in the same city after all of these years."

"I know. You've got to show me around when I get there."

"Where are you going to live?" I said.

"In Midtown Atlanta in one of those high rises," he said. "I can't remember the name of the building right now."

"Oh, you'll be right in the heart of things," I explained.

"Yes, very close to work. Do you live nearby?"

"I'm not downtown, but I'm not that far away, if you know how to get around in Atlanta," I said with a laugh.

"I'm counting on you to help me get to know the Black Mecca."

"That we are," I said, putting my hand on my stomach. "Hey Barry, my belly is rumbling so I probably need to get something to eat."

"Oh, I'm sorry, you did say you were hungry and sleepy," he said. "I just wanted to let you know."

"Thanks for letting me know," I said.

I didn't move for at least five minutes. *God wants me to sell my business, and the love of my life, who happens to be married, is moving to Atlanta. Why did it seem like I had an angel on one shoulder and a devil on the other?*

Senalda

Since Dexter didn't propose on my birthday, I had been seriously considering breaking up with him. That would be the end of my Destination Wedding goal. But I was beginning to think that maybe Destination Wedding would be a two-year instead of one-year project. That wouldn't mean that I would give Dexter a longer window to propose though. According to my relationship-book reading, I had to allocate my time wisely.

We made up since the day after my birthday in September, and Dexter asked me to go salsa dancing with him on a Saturday night in October. While he was living in Miami, he had taken dancing lessons and had even been in some salsa competitions, he said. Although my mother is Puerto Rican, I had never been salsa dancing, so I was looking forward to our date.

I wore a red, ruffled, short dress with high heels. Large gold hoop earrings completed my mamacita look. I texted a photo of myself to my girls, and they couldn't believe it! As I finished my makeup, I knew that Dexter and I would have a great time together. We always did. There was no drama between us, we liked the same things, I had an MBA, he had an MBA, we were in the same field, he respected me, and I respected him. He was everything I had always dreamed about in a husband. AND we had known each other since college. That's why I couldn't explain why we weren't moving along faster. I was starting to have that feeling in my gut that I had to either make a decision or stop obsessing about it.

I opened the door when the doorbell rang, and there was Dexter with a single rose in his teeth, dressed in all black. His shirt was unbuttoned to almost the middle of his chest. His pants were a little too tight, but I reasoned they were probably his salsa dancing pants or something.

"Look at you," I said with a laugh.

He took the rose out of his mouth and grinned.

"Are you okay? I hope you didn't get cut by any thorns," I said, taking the rose from him and examining it. "Is this your salsa dancing outfit?"

"Not really," he said. "Do you find me sexy, baby?"

He took the rose back from me and lightly grazed it down his chest.

"Ay papi!" I replied.

He laughed. "Let's go," he said as he put his hand on the small of my back.

We drove to Buckhead where Lupita's was located, on the top floor of a shopping plaza. The club was mostly filled with Hispanic people, but there were lots of black and white people as well as Asian people sprinkled in, a rare mixture in nearly race-segregated Atlanta. Within minutes of arriving, the instructors began teaching all of the salsa virgins like me the basics as experienced dancers watched. Dexter gave me a "thumbs up" sign during the lesson. After the hour was up, experienced dancers got on the dance floor and Dexter came up to me.

"So, are we going to be the hottest couple on the dance floor tonight?" he whispered in my ear and began moving his hips and feet in time to the music.

"I'm the best at everything I do, even if I am a beginner," I said to him.

As we danced, I couldn't believe Dexter hadn't taken me dancing before. Although I only barely knew basic steps, I managed to keep on beat with him as he twirled, dipped, and pulled me to him. Periodically, I reached up in my hair to find out if it had turned into curls, but after a while, I didn't care. We danced until I almost forgot that I was still frustrated with him. When the music finally stopped a few hours later, my body kept humming as if the beats had been injected into my blood. *Even if Dexter and I break up, I will definitely be back.*

Mimi

My period aine never been regular, but this time it was late fa real. I sat on the closed toilet seat in my bathroom, staring at the pregnancy test I bought at CVS. I wasn't the praying type, but since I joined SLAA I got more spiritual than I had ever been. *Please, please, please, don't let me be pregnant, Higher Power*, I said before getting the courage to pull down my jeans, open the toilet and pee on the test. Then, I waited for a $15.99 test to tell me what the rest of my life would be like.

"No, no, no," I said to my reflection when the second line started showing minutes later. I fell down on the floor, not sure what to do next. I decided to call Jarena, so I reached up to get my cell phone from the counter, trying not to get twisted up in my pants since they were still around my ankles. Jarena was a know-it-all, but did she know what to do most of the time.

"Hey, Mimi," Jarena said so nonchalantly I wanted to smack her. "What's up?"

"My blood pressure," I spat back.

"Why, what's going on?"

"I'm pregnant, Jarena."

"You're what?" she said with a laugh. "Who is the baby daddy?"

"I'm serious," I said. "And the baby daddy aine none other than your favorite client Mr. Jovan Parker, the last guy I got down wit."

"Are you sure?"

"I'm on the bathroom floor, nekkid from the waist down because I just took a pregnancy test," I hollered.

"How did this happen? I thought you hadn't seen Jovan in months, and the last time I saw you, you didn't look pregnant!" Jarena said.

Finally, I told her what happened in August, expecting her to say, "I told you so." But she didn't.

"You need to have a professional test with an actual doctor," she said quickly, as if she was trying to calm me down.

"Yeah, yeah, I'll do that," I said, relieved she told me what to do next without judging me. "Okay, I'll call you back. I'm gonna make an appointment with my doctor rat now."

"Okay, call me back."

"Okay," I repeated, ending the call.

• • •

I called Jarena as I drove home from the doctor the next day. It felt like only what was inside my Jeep was real, and everythang and ereone outside, the road, the buildings, the trees, the other cars, the people in them, were fake.

But I felt like I needed to connect with something or someone outside my Jeep or I was gonna suffocate.

"Mimi."

After hearing her voice, I could breathe again.

"Yup, I'm preggers."

"How do you feel?" Jarena asked, all of the nonchalance in her voice from the day before gone.

"Not pregnant," was all I could think of to say.

"How far along are you?

"Two months."

"So what are you going to do?"

And that was the question that kept a nigga up all night. It was probably the question that made my mama give up going to Clark College before it was Clark Atlanta University and marry my dad, a Jamaican who was lucky enough to come to America. A man who dreamed 'bout being a famous guitarist and almost soon as he arrived got a good gig at the Royal Peacock where he met James Brown and Gladys Knight. But he had to give all dat up to be a husband and father to my big brother first and then to me. Neither one of them seemed to ever get over what they had to give up until they finally divorced. So as much as I wanted to give Jovan a reason to be with me, forcing him to be a father and maybe a husband wasn't the way I wanted it to go down.

"I thought about dis all night, and I hope you don judge me now that you're a minister, but I don wanna have Jovan's baby. Not this way."

"So you're thinking about an abortion?"

"Yeah," I said, my voice quivering.

"My religious beliefs aside, and I definitely won't judge you for any decision you make, but why?" she questioned.

"I don want to force a man to marry me cuz I'm pregnant, and I don wanna be a single parent."

"Oh. Well, how about adoption?" Her voice was still hopeful.

"I could never give a child of mine up and not be a part of his or her life, so the only real option for me is abortion," I said, more decisively than I felt.

I paused before continuing. "So will you go wit me? I don wanna do this by myself."

"Of course, I got you girl. You're not alone in this," she said with a sigh. "Do you want me to come over tonight?"

"Naw, I just wanna be by myself. I've already researched places so I'm just gonna make an appointment."

"Okay, well I will pick you up and take you wherever you're going. Just tell me when and where."

"Cool," I said.

• • •

After I told them about being pregnant, Senalda and Whitney offered to take off work to go with me and Jarena to the clinic the next day, but I only wanted my oldest best friend with me. I waved to Jarena as she pulled up in front of my building. I got in the car and looked at her.

"So do you still want to do this?" she said. I could tell she wanted to say more.

I only nodded, scared that I would start crying if I opened my mouth.

She sighed and said, "So the clinic is located across from Grady Hospital, right? Peachtree Reproductive Services. Okay, let's go."

I hoped we wouldn't run into Richie or anyone else we knew. Within twenty minutes, Jarena pulled into the parking deck. Once she parked, I opened the car door, but Jarena stopped me, putting her hand on my leg.

"Would you mind if I prayed for you?"

"Alright," I said. "I hope God doesn't strike you down or anything."

"Oh Mimi," she said as she took both of my hands in hers.

I just stared at her as she closed her eyes and bowed her head.

"Dear God, I pray that you would be with my friend Mimi throughout this process. Please keep her in your care. Amen."

"Dat was short," I said, managing to laugh.

"So, are you ready?"

"I guess so," I nearly whispered.

Four hours later, I was done and woozy. Jarena's nose was red like she had been crying. She held my hand as we left the clinic and crossed the street. As she helped me into the car, I saw a figure walking toward me.

"Hey, Mimi. Remember me? Ian?"

"How could I get forget you, Dr. Ian?" I said, hoping that I didn't sound sarcastic. But I was too weak to really try to be cordial.

"How are you? You look like you're not feeling well," he said.

"Thanks," I said. "I know I look like crap."

"Oh, I didn't mean it like that."

"I know," I said. "Dr. Ian, you're right, though. I'm not feeling well. I hate to be rude, but I don wanna keep my girl Jarena waiting. She's taking me home."

"Oh, I understand," he said. "If you don't mind, I will give you a call to check on you since I am a doctor and all."

"Fa sho," I said while getting into the car.

"Thanks, Dr. Ian," Jarena said as she shut my door.

"Okay Jarena, take good care of her," he said.

"I will."

As Jarena drove, I leaned my head back on the seat, closing my eyes to sleep a lil bit before we got to my place.

• • •

Later that night, when I was all by myself in bed, I didn't try to stop the tears anymore. I halfway wished I was one of those crazy chicks who trapped a man into being with her because she was having his baby. But I knew what it was like to grow up knowing your father didn't really want to be there and tryin' to keep him around. And I just couldn't do that to a child.

I took some pain medication and got on Twitter on my cell to pass some time before I fell asleep. I checked Jovan's feed, and all of a sudden, like a bomb dropped in the middle of the night—I saw a picture of Jovan and Chula on a beach. They had gotten married in Puerto Rico earlier in the day, her birthday, Jovan tweeted. They both were wearing white. He was in a linen suit without any athletic gear for once. Like the trick bitch that she was even on her wedding day, she was wearing a too-tight ruffled minidress. They looked so fuckin' happy it made me even more miserable. I curled myself up on my bed and sobbed.

❧ Destination Wedding Meeting #10

The Saturday after Mimi had an abortion, the girls agreed to meet at her home for their monthly meeting. But this time, instead of working on their Destination Wedding goals, their real focus was cheering up their friend. She lived on the twentieth floor of the pricey Mayfair Tower Condominiums on 14th Street. While she was bohemian in her appearance and attitude toward life, she still appreciated luxurious living.

Whitney brought homemade chicken noodle soup. Jarena brought lasagna and a salad. And Senalda brought desserts. As they assembled the food in Mimi's small kitchen, they whispered furiously to each other. Her locs nearly shrouding her face, Mimi was on her couch, cocooned in her blanket, clicking her remote and staring straight ahead at her television.

"I want to know how Chula got a destination wedding in Puerto Rico before I did!" Senalda hissed.

"I think you're focusing on the wrong thing," Jarena said, as her eyebrows creased.

"You're right," Senalda said before pausing. "Can you believe that dude married someone else? I always thought he was a jerk, but I thought he was a non-marrying jerk."

"I knew he was going to marry Chula even before he told Mimi," Jarena admitted. "I kept trying to warn Mimi, but she wasn't trying to hear it."

"I don't believe in abortion, but I can't see raising a man's child after that man married some other woman," Whitney said.

"I can hear y'all," Mimi belted out.

The women momentarily stopped their conversation.

"Let's discuss this later," Senalda whispered before raising her voice so that Mimi could hear.

"Mimi, I hope you're hungry because there is plenty to eat."

"I aine hungry," she said in a monotone, still staring straight ahead.

The women looked at each other and then gathered around her in the living room. Jarena sat at her feet on the hardwood floor while Whitney and Senalda sat on either side.

Mimi's phone rang. "I bet it's that doctor guy again," she said.

"Huh?" Jarena said.

"Dr. Ian been calling me ere day since we saw him on Wednesday."

"Answer it, and put him on speaker phone," Senalda directed.

Mimi obliged. "Hi, Dr. Ian," Mimi said. "I have you on speaker phone."

"How are you today? Are you feeling any better?" he said in the caring tone of a health care professional.

"A little better I guess," Mimi replied. "Thanks for checking on me again."

"No problem," he said. "I don't have to go to the hospital today. Maybe I can swing by and check on you in person this time."

"Actually, my girlfriends are here with me."

"Hi, Dr. Ian," Jarena, Senalda and Whitney sang out.

"Hey, ladies," Dr. Ian said.

"We can leave if you want to make a house call, Dr. Ian," Senalda said to the laughter of her friends.

"Thank you for checking on Mimi," Jarena said.

"Dr. Ian, I'll call you back later, okay?" Mimi declared, shifting in her blanket, trying to get comfortable with her friends encircling her. "I don wanna ignore my friends."

"Okay, I understand." he said. "Goodbye."

"Bye."

"Dr. Ian from Veronique's store!" Senalda said. "What a cutie! You guys went out once, right?"

"Yeah, it was boring too," Mimi said, as she stopped moving, finally finding a comfortable position.

"But maybe you should give him a chance on a second date," Jarena suggested, putting her hands on top of the blanket over Mimi's hands underneath. "You said he has been calling every day since we saw him across from the clinic. Did you tell him what happened?"

"Naw, just told him I was feelin' sick that day and you took me to Grady."

"Oh, does Dr. Ian work at Grady?" Whitney asked.

"Yeah," Mimi said.

"I wonder if he knows Richie?" Whitney said. "I'll have to get the scoop on him so that you can be fully informed about this man beforehand."

"We already know that he's a doctor who is caring and willing to make house calls," Senalda said sweetly, stroking Mimi's locs. "You should definitely give him a second chance."

"Definitely," Jarena agreed. "He's really into you."

"Maybe," Mimi said. "I don know."

Her friends looked at each other, silently hoping Mimi would get out of her funk soon enough to realize Dr. Ian was already treating her better than Jovan ever did.

CHAPTER 12
November

. . . .

Destination Wedding Meeting #11

IT WAS 8 A.M. on Thanksgiving and Mimi was feeling lonesome. Now that Atlanta's temperate weather was finally starting to get colder, it was getting harder to ignore that she didn't have anyone to keep her warm.

"You said to make a call if I felt like doin' somethin' crazy," Mimi said without apology when Victor picked up the phone.

"That I did, ma," Victor confirmed. "What's up?"

"So would it be wrong for me to drive by Jovan's house?"

"He's married now," Victor said. "Remember?"

"I know, I know," Mimi agreed.

"See that's that stinking thinking," Victor said. "So what triggered this?"

"Today is Thanksgiving and just the idea of being at my grandmother's house makes me want to sleep da whole day," she started. "I'm going over there in a couple of hours. It aine cool being in a divorced family during the holidays; it will just be me, my mama and my grandmother. My mama and my grandmother are divorced, and my older brother will be at his girl-friend's house so... At least I'm going to Richie's house tonight, so I don't have to stay there all day."

"I feel you, ma," Victor said in sympathy. "Hey, I'll be at Richie's house tonight too!"

Mimi paused, momentarily shocked. "Richie invited you to Thanksgiving dinner?"

"Yeah, last week. I told him that I didn't have my daughter for Thanksgiving so I really didn't have any plans."

"Does Whitney know who you are?" Mimi said hesitantly.

"Yeah, I've met her before," Victor said.

"Today gon be interesting after all," Mimi said, a sly smile spreading across her face.

"Whaddya mean?"

"Whitney invited me—not Richie," Mimi said.

"Yeah?"

"I bet she don't like the type of people in twelve-step recovery meetings, so I'm surprised that she don't mind you coming over. Then again, you are high yaller, and Whitney and I both like light-skinned men," Mimi said with a cackle.

"I don't know about all that, but she was very nice to me when we met," Victor said.

"That's good. Hey Victor, don't take this the wrong way, but I haven't told my friends I go to SLAA meetings. I'm not ashamed, and I do plan to tell em, but not yet."

"Hey, we're an anonymous program," Victor said, "I wouldn't drop a dime on you like that."

"I'm not ashamed that I know you because I knew you back in your stripper days. I just don't want people to know I'm in program yet."

"No one will know that I know you and Richie from program," Victor said.

• • •

Senalda helped Whitney arrange a smorgasbord of dishes on the island.

"Did you make all of this?" Senalda said, surveying the spread which included a turkey, fried chicken, a green bean casserole, candied yams, dressing, mashed potatoes and gravy, corn, cranberry sauce, and rolls.

"I started yesterday, but yes, I made everything," Whitney said proudly. "Jarena is bringing some macaroni and cheese and collard greens from This Is It!, but other than that, I slaved over this Thanksgiving dinner. But save the applause until after we eat!"

The two women laughed.

"So where is that scrumptious man of yours? I thought for sure that y'all would be together today," Whitney said, using the pad of her index finger to wipe away moisture from her hairline.

"Dexter did invite me to his parents' home for Thanksgiving, but I told him I already had plans."

"You did what?" Whitney questioned, her voice rising. "What's going on? Did you break up with him? He's too good of a catch to toss him back in the sea!"

"Not officially; I'm just giving him the slow diss and hopefully he will get the message," Senalda said in the logical, unwilling-to-be-questioned tone she used at work.

"Not the slow diss!" Whitney said. "So basically you're not answering all of his calls and not responding to all of his invitations until he stops calling and asking. Girl, we're not in college anymore. Just break up with him if that is what you want to do. But you're not going to find another gainfully employed, well-connected, fine man without children and ex-wives easily."

"I want to break up because he hasn't asked me to marry him yet, but I don't have the heart to do it. I'm hoping this way he will see that I'm slipping away and try to get me back."

A ringing doorbell interrupted their conversation. Jarena and Mimi smiled in the doorway with the on-demand joy of Christmas carolers as they held containers of food.

"I can't believe that we are having a Destination Wedding meeting before Thanksgiving dinner," Jarena said as she set the macaroni and cheese down on the island.

"I know, I know, but since it's a holiday, let's just do a quick status update," Senalda said charitably.

"Still single," Jarena said.

"Me too," Mimi said, while folding back the foil cover over the collard greens to peek in. "These smell so good. When we gon eat?"

"When Richie's friend gets here, we can sit down to eat," Whitney said quickly, trying to not to scold Mimi for putting her nose near the food.

"A male friend?" Senalda inquired.

Whitney nodded.

"Is he single?"

"I haven't seen a wedding ring on his finger, but that doesn't mean much nowadays," Whitney replied.

"Is he cute?" Senalda said, her enthusiasm permeating the air as much as the steaming food.

"I thought we were having a Destination Wedding meeting," Whitney said, turning up her nose. "Jarena and Mimi may not have anything to share but you sure do."

"Really, what?" Mimi said, sidling up to Senalda.

"I finally broke up with Dexter."

"You did?" Jarena and Mimi said in unison.

"Not officially," Senalda explained. "I'm doing the slow diss."

"Has it worked?" Jarena asked.

"Maybe," Senalda said. "He is calling me more, but that's about it."

Whitney ignored the ringing doorbell this time, and minutes later, Richie walked in the kitchen.

"Whit, Victor is here. Are we just about ready to eat? It smells so good," Richie said while rubbing his stomach.

"Hey Richie," Senalda said as she walked up to him. "I thought your hair looked a little long at my birthday party in September, but I didn't realize you were growing dreadlocks."

"Yeah, just trying something new," he said as he reached up and pulled a baby loc.

"Oh," Senalda said, a befuddled expression on her face.

"That's what I said when he told me, girl," Whitney said, shaking her head.

"They look cute ta me," Mimi said, looking at Richie.

Richie smiled at Mimi, their eyes locking for a moment.

"You can get away with a mop on your head because you're a woman, but not a doctor at Grady," Whitney said.

"Whit, everyone doesn't have to have a perfect image like you," Richie said icily before turning and walking out of the kitchen.

Whitney pressed a smile on her face as her friends looked away, trying to act like they hadn't witnessed the contemptuous exchange.

"So girls, will you help me get the meal on the table?" Whitney started picking up containers of food. Wordlessly, her friends helped her take the platters to the formal dining room. A short time later, at the dinner table, Richie blessed the food with a quick prayer. The table was silent for a few uncomfortable minutes. Senalda broke the silence first.

"So Richie, why haven't you brought Victor around before?"

She took in the man who sat across from Mimi. Even in a long-sleeved shirt, she could see the outline of his muscled chest and arms. She didn't like the diamond studs he wore in his ears, but she was willing to overlook them since all of Richie's friends had serious credentials. *I bet he has tattoos too.* Final assessment: He was too street-looking for her taste, even if she was available. But he would probably be perfect for Mimi.

"We just met a few months ago," Richie answered.

"He's cute, right Mimi?" Senalda said, looking at Mimi. "He looks like just your type."

"Senalda, you don't even know this man. Don't embarrass him," Whitney said.

"I know if he's a friend of Richie's, he's got to be a catch."

"I agree with my wife," Richie said with too hearty of a laugh. "Back off, Senalda! Mimi may be seeing someone."

"She's not. She's very single," Senalda said, as if Mimi couldn't speak for herself.

"Will you stop tellin' my bizness?" Mimi finally said as loudly as she should at a dinner table. "I thought this was Thanksgiving dinner, not 'Hook Up Mimi Night'!"

"I'm sorry Victor," Whitney said. "Please excuse my friends. They forget to be on their best behavior when there are new people around."

"That's okay, ma. Just glad to be in the company of good people on Thanksgiving Day," Victor said in his heavy Brooklyn accent with a smile.

Senalda raised an eyebrow and looked at Whitney.

"So you're from New York?" Senalda said.

"Brooklyn baby," Victor confirmed.

"I'm from the Bronx," Senalda said.

"I knew you were a home girl," Victor said with a laugh.

"So Victor, I've been trying to figure out where I know you from because you look so familiar," Jarena said with her fork in the air.

Mimi looked down.

"Are you? Oh yeah, you're... Oh, forget it." Jarena said. She put her fork back on her plate, preparing to fill her mouth with food.

"Yeah, I used to be an erotic dancer with the Hot Boyz, but I'm an addictions counselor now," Victor said looking directly at Jarena.

"What?" Senalda and Whitney said at the same time. Richie told Whitney Victor was an addictions counselor, but he neglected to tell her about Victor's previous profession.

"I apologize, Victor," Jarena said, "I wasn't trying to make you feel uncomfortable."

"I'm not ashamed of my past, ma," he said. "My past is helping me to become the man I am today."

"Well, that is why you are so fine," Senalda ultimately said with a laugh after recovering from her surprise.

• • •

As soon as the women were alone cleaning up the kitchen, Senalda pounced. "Okay, so why is Richie hanging out with a former-stripper-slash-addictions counselor?"

Mimi discreetly slipped out of the room and headed for the bathroom. As she walked down the hall, Richie pulled her to him.

"Hey, come to my darkroom downstairs," he said, her hand in his. "I got some photographs I wanted to show you."

Mimi followed Richie into the basement where he showed her photographs he had taken of people at different Atlanta locales. Photographs of homeless people. Children. At Dr. Martin Luther King Jr.'s last home on Sunset Avenue. MARTA stations. The DeKalb Farmers Market.

"Richie, you really talented," she said. She looked through the pictures, taking time to study each one.

"Thanks," he said. "I hope so, because I'm going to tell Whitney that I want to start my photography business."

"I don see why she would have a problem with dat," Mimi said.

"I don't want to be a doctor anymore, either," Richie also revealed, staring at her.

"Oh," Mimi said. It was suddenly clear that Whitney was not, in fact, going to like that. She also suddenly realized that she was alone with her friend's husband in their basement. "Hmmm... Hey Richie, I'm gonna head back upstairs before the girls miss me."

"Okay, I guess I will see you at a meeting then, program buddy," Richie said brightly, not noticing her discomfort.

When Mimi got back to the kitchen, it seemed she hadn't missed a beat.

"I'm still trying to figure out how Richie knows Victor," Senalda said as soon as she walked in the door. "Richie's hanging out with a former stripper, and he's growing dreads. What's next?"

For the third time that evening, Mimi kept uncharacteristically quiet while helping the women put the food away.

Mimi

The Saturday after Thanksgiving, I finally I took my girls' advice and let Dr. Ian take me out again. I was tired of being alone at home when I wasn't at meetings. Richie was walking with me to my car after a meeting when my cell phone rang.

"Hey, Dr. Ian," I said.

"I'm off on a Saturday night finally, and I thought I would ask you out," he said. "Are you doing anything later?"

"I got a date with my couch." I laughed at my joke.

"Could you break your date and come out with me instead?"

"Alrighty." I smiled as if he could see me.

"Pick you up at 7?"

"See you then."

"Are you dating?" Richie said, studying me as he leaned against my Jeep next to me.

"Not sho yet."

"But you're going out on a date with a Dr. Ian?" he continued.

"I know."

"I thought program suggests that newcomers don't date for a year."

"I aine dating this guy," I said. "I went out with him once a few months ago, and I didn't even like him. So we just hangin' out tonight. What do you care? You're worse than Victor."

"I couldn't be that bad," he said with a grin. "Okay, tell me how your 'hanging out' goes!"

"You know I will," I said, hitting him in the shoulder.

• • •

Unlike Jovan, Dr. Ian got to my place exactly when he said he would. Jovan had the worst habit of underestimating what time he could get anywhere in the city. *Stop comparing every other man who tries to holla at you to Jovan*, I said to myself as I walked to the door and opened it.

"You look beautiful," Dr. Ian said.

"Really?" I asked, looking down at my fitted white T-shirt under a knit poncho and jeans. I felt underdressed. We scheduled the date so quick I forgot to ask where we were going. Dr. Ian was dressed in a brown tweed blazer, a crème button-down shirt, and brown slacks. For a second I wondered what he looked like without his glasses. Even with them he looked cute, if geeks were yo thang.

"So where we going?" I figured his answer was gon be boring so maybe it was good that I was wearing a T-shirt and jeans. *Least I'll be comfortable when I fall asleep this time.*

"I thought we could stop by Apache Café and hear some live music and maybe stop by The Varsity and get some greasy food."

"I haven't been there since it was Yin Yang," I said. "What does a doctor know 'bout Apache Café and The Varsity?"

"Let's get this straight first: I'm just Ian right now, not Dr. Ian," he said. "And just because I'm a doctor doesn't mean I don't have a life outside of a hospital."

"My bad," I said. "That's cool that you like live music. But you know you're overdressed to go to Apache Café unless it's different than the Yin Yang used to be."

"I know." He laughed as he pushed up his glasses on his nose. "I need some regular clothes. I'm just always working, so I really haven't had time to shop."

"The buttoned-down look fits you though, and I love your glasses," I said, trying to be nice.

Ian held all the doors open for me and helped me into his black Volvo as if I was delicate as one of my locs. I still didn't feel any chemistry with him, but I had to admit it felt good to know he was into me. And since I thought he was just cool, there was no chance for him to hurt me, even if he tried.

Although the name was now Apache Café, it still had the Yin Yang flavor. Since it was a hole-in-the-wall type spot, the size of the club made the artistic vibe real strong because everyone was so close. With all of the industry parties I had to attend at the slickest and the largest clubs for various appearances, I didn't have time to check out more arty spots. I didn't know how much I missed the vibe until the band started playing and I was nearly close enough to see my reflection in the instruments. And as the band kept playing, I started hearing my own melodies in my head. I closed my eyes to focus.

"Having a good time?" Ian's breath flooded my ear.

I nodded with my eyes still closed. *I miss singing.*

"You know I used to sing before I was a deejay," I said, opening my eyes and looking at Ian.

"For real?" he said. "I used to be a drummer in a band in college before I went to medical school."

"Yeah, right," I said with a chuckle.

"I'm not lying," he said. "I was the drummer for a band called Danger when I was in undergrad at FAMU."

"I was a singer when I was going to Clark Atlanta, but I couldn't make anything happen so I got into radio instead," I said. "It was all good before I got fired from KISS earlier this year."

"Yeah, I heard about that," he said. "I thought about calling you but I didn't know if you wanted to hear from me then."

"I'm glad we ran into each other again," I said, and I was, actually. "Yeah, I got fired over some mess, but you probably know all of the details since they were in the paper."

"Don't even worry about that," he said, putting his hand on mine. I tensed up, preparing to move my hand, but then I didn't.

"So what's your next move?" he asked.

"I've been thinking about trying to write some songs. I used to write my own music, and now that I have some industry contacts, I might give it a try."

"You should," he said with an encouraging smile.

In all of the time I spent with Jovan, I never mentioned my songwriting to him, even though he knew some of the hottest songwriters in the industry. I was cool with being physically naked around him, but I didn't feel comfortable sharing some of what was going on inside of me. It was easier to be myself around Ian because I didn't have that thang for him, I told myself.

• • •

As Ian drove me home later that night, I dozed, but not because I was bored. My belly was full of chili dogs slathered with mustard and onions from The

Varsity. Once we got into the driveway in front of my building, he woke me up.

"We're back at your place," he said gently.

"Thanks," I said, fluffing out my locs and reaching for the door handle to let myself out.

"I'll get your door, Mimi, but I want to tell you something first," he said, reaching over me to stop me from getting out.

"Okay," I said, my eyebrows scrunching together.

"I don't want to scare you away, but I believe this my second chance to get you to be mine," he said. "And I do want you to be mine, Mimi. I'm going to do everything I can to make that happen. You don't have to say anything about it tonight. I just wanted you to know."

I'm glad he aine want me to say anything because I aine have nothin' to say after that.

He got out of the car and opened the door for me. Then, he walked me up to my condo and hugged me at the door.

"Call you tomorrow," he said. I half-smiled at him and closed the door. I still couldn't think of anythang to say, even to myself.

CHAPTER 13

December

. . . .

Senalda

NASHAUN GIGGLED AS I walked by her desk.

"What's up with you? You've been acting weird all day." I crossed my arms, staring down at her.

"What do you mean, Mizz Warner?" Nashaun said, looking up at me as her eyes got bigger. "It's just a regular ole Wednesday. Just happy to be working for the bestest boss in the whole world!"

"If you say so, but I'm watching you," I said with a laugh outside of my office.

Nashaun giggled again. I opened the door to find my office was dark, except for lit candles on my desk, the floor, and everywhere I turned, and soft music was playing too. My desk chair swung around suddenly and Dexter was sitting there.

"Dexter, what are you doing here?" I closed my door behind me.

"I wanted to surprise you, Sen." He got up and hugged me. "I've been missing you. And since you've been dodging me, I figured I'd show up here. You can't dodge me at work."

"What's this all about?" I sat down on my couch. And then it hit me. *The slow diss has worked. This is his grand gesture.* I leaned back and folded my arms across my chest to take it all in. And then he dropped to his knees in front of me. I uncrossed my arms, sat up straight and put my hands on the couch, squeezing the cushions.

"I don't want to spend another holiday without you, Sen," he said as he kissed my cheek. "You're right. We should get married. But I've got to tell you something first."

"YES!" I put my arms around his neck. "My answer is YES!"

"Wait, wait, hold up." He pulled my arms from around his neck and leaned back. His eyes stared straight into mine.

"This is hard for me," Dexter said before taking a long breath. "When I moved back home from Miami, I decided that I wanted to meet the woman I would marry. I had no idea it would be a woman I already knew. It happened so fast... But I need to tell you something first..."

"What is it?" I leaned forward.

"I'm trying to tell you... I've... I've... had a situation with a man before... But I've put all that behind me because I want to be with you."

"A situation? What do you mean by that?"

Dexter said nothing.

"Do you mean you've been with a man before? Tell me that's not what you mean!"

He still said nothing, so I continued.

"All this time, I thought I was getting a ladies' man but you're a ladies' man and gentlemen's man too!" I spat.

"I didn't deserve that," Dexter said quietly, looking down.

"Like I deserve this!"

"I've only been with one man, but I've never felt this way about anyone else," Dexter said, lifting his head. "And I've been faithful to you the whole time, and I will be faithful to you for the rest of our lives. I want start a family with you... I know I should have said something in the beginning, but it all so happened so fast, and you wanted it to go even faster."

I stood up to walk away but stopped when Dexter reached in his pocket, pulled out a ring box and opened it. Although it was dark, I could see the sparkle of the square solitaire diamond and platinum ring. I could have probably picked out the ring myself. *Figures.*

"What the what?" I sat down again. "You're gay, but you're proposing to me?"

"You don't love me?" He took my hands and put them on his soft lips.

"Yes, I do." I commanded my tears away and continued. "But I don't want to marry a gay man. I can't do that. I'm sorry."

"But I'm not gay. Bisexual maybe. But not gay." Dexter sighed, got up off of his knees, turned on the lights, and blew out the candles before he came back to where I sat. The soft music continued to play. I finally realized it was "Take Off the Blues" by The Foreign Exchange. I remembered the name of the song because Mimi used to talk about it all of the time when it came out. She said it was the best slow jam since Keith Sweat's "Make It Last Forever."

"I thought I should be honest with you." His voice got deeper, as if he was going to lecture me. "Women always say they want an honest man, but when they get one, they can't handle the truth. I love you enough to be completely honest with you."

He kissed me hard, like his lips could erase what he just told me. "Baby, we could be great together," he said, his forehead still touching mine, "a powerful couple in our city. Don't mess it up because of something in the past."

His words stoked something in me, but I couldn't reconcile the two sides of him, at least right then. Competing with women for a man didn't intimidate me, but even I, who prided myself on never backing down from a competition, knew I wasn't equipped to compete with men for a man. Theoretically, that could happen. I just didn't want to acquire new rules of engagement to get engaged and married.

As if he could read my mind, Dexter placed the ring box on my desk. "After you think things through, call me," he said, while opening the door, letting cool air in. "I'm not an average brother. I think you know that."

The door opened to reveal Nashaun and other assistants holding up a banner with the word "Congratulations!" which they began to yell as Dexter exited, walking past them without saying a word.

"Y'all, put down that banner," Nashaun screamed.

I didn't even bother to close the door. I just sat there for a few minutes, staring at nothing. Finally, I picked up my purse and the ring box and walked out of my office.

"Nashaun, clean up those candles and everything else. I'm taking the rest of the day off," I said as I passed by her desk, not looking back.

As hot as if I had a fever, I drove straight home, put on my pajamas and got in bed. I went to sleep, hoping I would wake up hours later and realize what happened had just been a nightmare. But when I woke up that evening in the dark, I realized had I said yes to Dexter, I would have been able to marry him in a quickie wedding before the New Year and my Destination Wedding dream could have been a reality. Instead, I shivered alone in the dark.

Jarena

From the moment I knew Barry was in town, I felt on guard but also pulled to him, like Atlanta had become a magnetic field. For the first week he was here, he was, thankfully, tied up in meetings and getting his living arrangements together. I was busy too, studying to take final exams.

And then, in the middle of the second week he was in Atlanta, he asked if we could meet after work. I said yes, but as I drove to meet him at Café Intermezzo in Buckhead, I contemplated making up an excuse and bailing. Barry was wearing a double-breasted black leather coat that swung from his basketball-player build. He made winter look good. His summer tan had faded, and the contrast between his light skin and sky-blue eyes made them sparkle. I detected the beginning of a few slight wrinkles around his eyes, but they only confirmed Barry was no longer the cute boy I met in college. He could now easily qualify for any of those misnomer "grown and sexy" parties folk were always having in the A nowadays, except he was actually "grown and sexy" instead of grown and fat.

I hoped he thought I looked nice too. I had plaited my hair the night before and didn't pull them out until just before I left my house to meet him. My Afro was huge and wavy. I wore a red sweater-dress with black tights and patent leather Mary Jane pumps. As he hugged me, I remembered how nice it was to feel small in the arms of a six-foot-two man.

As he released me, he looked me up and down and said, "Beautiful."

"Thank you," I said quietly, all of a sudden feeling shy.

"I'm sorry I'm late," Barry said, pulling out my chair for me. "I heard about Atlanta rush-hour traffic, but now I know for myself. I've been on Peachtree Street the whole time. It's crazy!"

"As an 'ATLien,' I will fill a brotha in on the back streets to get everywhere!"

"Cool. Well, I hope they have man-sized portions here," Barry said, surveying the small coffeehouse's décor. "You never know with these European-type places."

As we ordered and ate, I noticed Dr. Ian eating alone on the other side of the restaurant. I tried to catch his eye to wave but never could, and when I looked at his table again, he was gone.

"So, you have anything to do tonight?" Barry asked after paying for our dinner.

"Not really," I replied. "I will probably just watch some reality TV before I go to sleep."

"Y'all women and that garbage!" he said. "You know, you can watch TV at my condo. I guess I can watch the 'Real Housewives of Atlanta' or whatever comes on Wednesday night for a few hours."

Sensing my trepidation, Barry kept on talking.

"Just for a little while," he coaxed. "I'm in Atlanta all by myself, so I could use the company."

"I guess you're pretty lonely without your family, huh?"

"During the day, I'm cool, but at night, it's so quiet."

So I followed him in my car down Peachtree, silently praying that everything would be alright. After we got into his condo, Barry left the living room and came up back wearing a T-shirt and basketball shorts. For a second, I was transported back to his college apartment.

"Why don't you take off your shoes?" He dropped himself on the other end of the couch where I sat. "You look so tense. I won't bite. I've already had dinner."

I smiled at him, pretending I didn't hear his flirty words.

"If I get too comfortable, I'll get sleepy, and I still have to drive home."

"Can I get you something to drink?" he said, heading toward the kitchen. "I'm gonna get a beer."

"Some water would be cool."

I turned on his television, flipping through channels. Then I remembered that none of my shows were on tonight. I saw the rapper Juvenile and stopped channel surfing. "Back That Thang Up" filled the room. In spite of myself, I got up and starting gyrating my backside. I wanted to get it in quick before Barry came back with our drinks, but he caught me.

"You still know how to back that thang up?" he said, putting our drinks on the table.

He came up behind me and started dancing. For the rest of the video, we danced and laughed.

"For obvious reasons, I used to love that song," he said with a sly smile. "I think I even broke a sweat. I haven't watched videos in forever."

"Me either," I said as we sat down on the couch. For the next hour, we watched old school rap videos and hopped up and danced if we felt like it. During our impromptu dance party, I couldn't help but think being single was starting to feel like a ruthless game of musical chairs. Except it wasn't just that the chairs were disappearing. The music was getting younger too, and I didn't want to be the oldest woman without a chair. We collapsed after the show's final video. Almost like it was choreographed, Barry leaned over and pecked me on my mouth. It happened so quickly, I didn't even taste his lips.

"Lips just as sweet as they used to be," he said, grinning.

"What are you doing?" I sat straight up and moved away from him in one fluid motion.

"Since we were watching old school rap videos," he said, still leaning against the couch, "I thought it would be okay to kiss my old school girl-friend...That didn't come out right."

He was quiet then. "I apologize if I offended you."

"I probably need to go now." I looked around for my purse and shoes.

"I don't want you to go," he said as he grabbed my face and closed the space between us. I said nothing else as he anointed my face with wet kisses.

I tried to silently ask God for help, but the truth was I hoped He wasn't listening.

Mimi

"Damn, damn, damn," I cussed while balancing my checkbook on my bed. I was proud of myself for stretching my savings for so long, but with what I had left in my bank account, I didn't have enough for my December mortgage payment. My cell phone rang.

"Ian," I said with a grateful smile. He had been the best distraction since we started going out three weeks ago. He came along at just the right time to help me forget Jovan, his man-stealing hoe of a wife Chula, and the baby we could have had. I thought of all three of them the most when I was alone at night, but that hadn't been very much lately since Ian practically declared himself my man on our second date.

"I want you to go to this medical conference with me," he said. "The one in Vegas I told you about."

"But I won't distract you from erethang?"

"Not at all," he said. "I'm going to have to be around doctors all day, but I want to be around you all night and maybe during the day if I can sneak away."

I had to admit, his answer make me kinda hot. *I will balance my checkbook when I get back from Vegas!*

"So do you want me to come over tonight?" I said, thinking 'bout what clothes I could pack.

"You know I do," he replied. A tingle went through my chest. Within an hour I had packed and driven over to the West End where he lived. As soon as I pulled into his driveway, Ian opened his door. And by the time I turned off my car, he was on the other side of my door and opened it for me. It was nice to have a dude feelin' me like that.

"You're going to have to live with me because I want to see you every day, baby," he said, pressing his body up on me before kissing me on the lips.

"I haven't been to Vegas in years," I said. "Where are we staying?"

"The Hilton where the convention is, but we can find the more exciting hotels to go to after my classes are over," he said as he got my suitcase from the back seat.

"Fa sho," I replied.

That night as Ian went through his conference materials, I entertained myself by watching television in his bedroom. I was dozing most of the time until I saw Jovan on the screen with Chula. They were being interviewed about being a couple in business and in their personal life. The interviewer was saying they were the next Beyoncé and Jay Z! I turned up the volume, hoping Ian couldn't hear in his office. After the interview was over, I strolled over to Ian's office, swaying my hips like the dime that I am.

"I'm so glad we going to Vegas tomorrow," I said, sliding my tongue up and down his ear as he faced the computer.

"Me too, baby," he said, lifting me from the floor and putting me on his lap.

• • •

On the flight, the visual of Jovan and Chula being interviewed kept popping up in my head. But the closer we got to our destination, the better I was able to distract myself. We got there 'bout noon. While Ian took a nap to counteract jet lag, I went down to the lobby to make program calls.

"Hey Victor."

"Mimi, are you on the way to tonight's meeting?"

"I'm in Vegas!" I yelled.

"With your new boyfriend?"

"Yup," I said.

"What's going on there?"

"A conference for doctors," I said.

"And you decided to tag along."

"Why not?"

"I'm not going give you my opinion this time, but if you can, try to get to a meeting out there."

"You aine neva sugarcoated anything else, so why start now?" I said. "What you thinkin'?"

"I already told you, ma, but I will tell you again since you asked. You living real dangerously. Using one man to get over another."

"I care a lot about Ian."

"But he's in love with you," Victor said. "You in love with him?"

"I'm getting there."

"Like I said, if you can, get to a meeting out there, okay?" he said.

"Okay, Victor," I said. "Alright, I'm gonna get somethin' to eat. I'll call you back."

I wasn't hungry. I just wanted to get off of the phone. I thought about calling Richie, but he had been acting all weird with me for the last few weeks. I knew he had some issues going on with Whitney so I forgave him for being moody, but I aine want to deal with dat on the phone. So I wandered down the strip for a while. Vegas was my kind of city. Spontaneous, over-the-top, and teeming with money. After a few hours, though, all the neon blinking lights made it seem like I was supposed to be happy when I wasn't. I was so lonesome I headed back to our hotel room and chilled for the rest of the day while Ian was in the conference opening session.

• • •

Ian woke me up early, since he had to get to the conference by 7. Once he left, I lollygagged in the room till around noon. It was a warm winter day in Vegas, and after seeing people splashing in the hotel swimming pool from the window, I figured that would be fun. I bought a swimsuit in the hotel gift shop and headed to the pool. The last time I had been in a hotel pool was almost two years ago when I was in Miami with Jovan. Although we hadn't come there together, it was a music convention and we both knew we would be there so we hooked up. After hours one night, we skinny-dipped in the dark pool. But that wasn't all we did. We were in that pool for a long, long time.

As I swam in this hotel's pool, I let all of the sadness I had been feeling for months flood over me. The pool water hid my tears. An hour later, I decided to put my tears and loneliness behind me once and for all. When Ian walked back in the room at 7, I was wearing a sequined black dress and sitting on the bed, waiting for him.

"Hey baby," Ian said. "I won some tickets for the Ultimate Fighter Finale mixed martial arts event at the conference. It's going to be held at the Palm Casino Resort. Do you want to go?"

"You know I'm down for just 'bout anythang!"

"Give me a half hour and I will be ready to hit the strip," he said while he hugged me. "All the other women are going to be jealous of you tonight."

While he showered, I watched videos. I couldn't believe what I saw. There was Chula singing and Jovan was behind her, standing there like he was Diddy to her Cassie. I couldn't get away from them. I turned off the television and waited for Ian to finish getting ready.

I had never seen a mixed martial arts competition before and neither had Ian. While the fans were getting crunk around us before the fight started, I leaned over and yelled, "Since we in Vegas, let's make a bet. I bet you I will marry you here in Vegas if that Gomez guy wins tonight."

"Are you serious?" Ian pushed his glasses on his nose and looked at me.

"Dead," I said turning back to the action in front of us. "Get it Gomez!"

As we watched the fight, I snuck a look at him. He even looked like a nicer guy than Jovan with his squinty-eyed self. Ian's bigger, wide-set eyes seemed kind. Plus I liked the way I looked in them. My mama told me that when you're ready to settle down, pick a man who loves you more than you love him. I didn't know what she meant then, but now it made sense. *Shit, that's probably where the phrase 'settle down' came from! If you gon settle down, you may as well be the one on top.*

I wasn't surprised when Gomez won, since he was a bigger dude and had a bunch of tats.

"So I guess I gotta marry you, huh?" I said with a big grin.

"There's nothing I want more, but why don't you think about it tonight and let me know how you feel tomorrow?"

After the fight, we hit the Bellagio and gambled. We hotel-hopped until about 5 a.m. before taking a cab back to the hotel Sunday morning. We didn't get up till noon. When I woke up, Ian was spooning me. I had never felt so loved.

"So will you marry me today?" I wasn't sure if he heard me since my mouth was in his hair.

With his eyes still closed, he said, "Yes."

"What?" I squawked, jumping up in the bed. "Did you hear what I said?'"

"Yes and yes," he said groggily.

"You really want to do it?" I said.

"Yes, I will marry you."

If Jovan can elope in Puerto Rico after he knocked me up, I can get married because of a bet in Vegas.

An hour later, we bought souvenir rings in the gift shop, planning to buy the real rings in Atlanta. We printed a marriage license application from the Clark County Marriage Bureau's website and took a cab over to the bureau to fill it out. I bought a white dress at the mall, and we were married at a chapel by 5 p.m. and back at the airport by 9 p.m. for a red-eye flight. The next day, after I left Ian's house to go home and get some things, my checkbook was the first thing I noticed on my bed. Instead of worrying about paying the mortgage, I had to figure out how to sell my condo because I was moving in with Ian!

Whitney

It was Christmas morning, and I was a little sad because it would just be Richie, the twins and me celebrating the holiday together. Gwenaëlle had the holiday off. My parents were in California visiting my sister and her husband, and Richie's family was traveling overseas. Richie was in the living room taking pictures of the twins in their Christmas outfits. Blane was dressed in a black-and-white tuxedo with a red velvet bow tie, while Blythe wore a red velvet dress with a white baby-doll collar and black buttons down the front. They were taking turns yelling, "Da da" and laughing hysterically like they were telling each other jokes. I peeked in on them periodically and scolded myself for feeling sad. *I have a beautiful family.*

And then I got annoyed when I saw Richie fiddling with those snakes on his head. He was always twisting or patting them or scratching his scalp. *Gross.* I could see why the Jamaican people called them dreadlocks. They looked dreadful. And since Richie's hair was so soft, his looked messy. I couldn't figure it out. We were too young for a midlife crisis. Still, I made a conscious decision to focus on the holiday instead of his hair.

"Richie, do you want to open up our gifts?" I asked, surveying our magnificent, twelve-foot Christmas tree. I had painstakingly decorated it with white balls and silver tinsel with twinkling white lights. Most of the gifts were for the twins even if they couldn't fully appreciate them, but it had been a joy to shop for them.

We attempted to show the twins how to open their gifts but they just tossed them to one another and laughed as Richie took pictures. We couldn't tell if the twins were more excited by the gifts or our exaggerated responses to them.

We saved our gifts for each other until last. This year's big Christmas gift for him was a crisp black suit I had custom-made from Ozwald Boateng's store in London. I also gave him cuff links engraved with his initials. I wasn't sure how his new suit and monogrammed cuff links would look alongside his unkempt hair, but I hoped the gift would remind him that he looked good dressed up. It had been a few months since I had seen him willingly dress in a suit. Lately, he was reluctant to go anywhere that required one. He complained the whole night about going to the Mayor's Masked Ball just a few days ago.

"Remind me why this is necessary again," he said while assembling his bow tie in the mirror.

"It is necessary because you may as well be black royalty in Atlanta," I said to his reflection. "Everyone is expecting us to be there, and they will wonder what's going on if we don't show up. Your father, your stepmother, your colleagues, my colleagues."

"I don't even like most of the people at these types of things," Richie complained. "I bet I can find more genuine people at a twelve-step meeting than at this ball tonight."

I was annoyed again, thinking about it. I realized then I had bought him the perfect Christmas present. I had to remind him who he is, who we are. He is Dr. Richard Bradley Brannon III, the grandson of the first black doctor at Grady Hospital and the son of the chief of staff at Grady Hospital. And I am the youngest daughter of the first black district attorney in the Orleans parish of Louisiana. A power couple descended from powerful people.

"Thank you," Richie said, holding out the suit in front of him before putting it down on the couch. He walked over to the Christmas tree, where he picked up a large gift box, beautifully wrapped in red gift-wrapping paper with a gold bow, and handed it to me. I tore off the gift-wrap. It was a large leather mounted photo album. The whole album was pictures of me that Richie had taken when we were in college. A picture of me in front of the Cosby Center on Spelman's campus, at a Morehouse football game, at the Sun Dial, in Piedmont Park. The last was a picture of me the night we got engaged. I kissed him without saying anything at first.

"Richie, this is so beautiful," I said. "Your gift beat mine this year."

"It's not a competition," he said while hugging me. "I just wanted to show you how beautiful you are to me. And there's something I've been wanting to tell you for a while now."

"What, sweetiekins?" I said, looking into his eyes.

"I know you're probably not going to approve, but I want to start a photography business."

"I don't have a problem with that. You obviously take beautiful photographs when you are inspired." I smiled at him while pointing at myself. "All of this beauty would inspire anyone. But with all of the hours you work at the hospital, are you sure that your photography doesn't need to be a hobby and not a business?"

"Well, that's just it," Richie said, "I don't think I can practice medicine and be a photographer at the same time and be good at both. And I don't want to, anyway."

"What are you saying?"

"We have money in the bank. I want to quit Grady and work on my photography business full-time."

"Have you lost your mind, Richie? You spend almost a decade in school and you want to turn your back on that? And we have children now! Who does that?"

I remembered the twins when they began crying.

"I had hoped you wouldn't react like this, but you've always been about our image instead of who we really are," he said before stomping out of the room.

"Where are you going?" I screamed at him. "It's Christmas!"

"To a meeting if I can find one!" he yelled. The front door slammed behind him.

I seriously considered stomping on the suit I bought him, but it cost me too much to damage it.

Destination Wedding Meeting #12

After Jarena, Mimi, and Whitney realized none of them had heard from Senalda all month, the feisty search party corralled on her driveway on New Year's Eve. Like a haunted house in a horror movie, they noticed one lone light was on upstairs but the rest of her home was eerily dark, as they noisily unloaded their belongings from their cars and headed to the front door.

"I hope she here," Mimi said to the women as they stood together waiting.

Whitney rang the doorbell three times to no avail before finally calling Senalda's number.

"You better let us in or we're going to call your parents and then we're calling the police. I know you're inside," she said with an attitude on Senalda's voicemail.

They waited a couple of minutes more before seeing another light come on in the front hallway. Senalda halfway opened the door and stood there. Her bone-straight pixie cut had reverted back to her natural curls. Her lips looked leathery, as if she hadn't moisturized them in weeks. She wore a dingy white terry-cloth robe that was pulled tightly around her but didn't hide her ashy legs.

"So I guess you guys can't take a hint," she uttered finally. The smell of days-old pizza wafted toward her friends.

"Not when we haven't heard from you in a month," Whitney declared, holding her nose with one hand and pushing the door all of the way open with the other. "When was the last time you had a shower, sweetie?"

"You always looked like a munchkin, but now you look like a po munchkin," Mimi said, holding a box of cupcakes. "We need to fatten you back up."

"I know, right?!" Jarena agreed, while walking behind Mimi to the kitchen with containers of food.

"What's going on?" Senalda said, trudging to her couch.

"We haven't met for our Destination Wedding meeting, and it's the last night of the year," Jarena said with the singsong cadence of a cheerleader.

"I don't know what happened to you, but you better tell us now," Whitney said as she sat down next to her friend. "And after you tell us, I'm running a bath for you because you stink. You're still my girl, though."

The corners of Senalda's lips turned up momentarily before they fell back down.

"You wouldn't believe it if I told you," she said. "Since you guys bumrushed my house, I hope you brought something stronger than water over here."

"A glass of wine coming up," Mimi said. "White or red?"

"Some vodka if you have it," Senalda commanded, holding her hand in the air like she expected a glass to magically appear in it.

"So what's been up with you all month long, Bossy?" Jarena said. "I'm assuming Dexter has something to do with what's going on."

"Dexter proposed," Senalda said, smoothing her robe over her legs.

"He did what?" her friends squawked in unison from different corners of the room.

"I refuse to say anything else before I've had a sip of something," Senalda said. "My house. My rules."

"Well, she's still bossy," Jarena concluded as she took a glass of wine from Mimi, brought it to Senalda and sat down on the other side of her.

Senalda snatched the glass, sipped for a few moments, and continued with her story. "So the slow diss worked. It worked too well, actually. On December 1, Dexter surprised me at my office. He said he didn't want to spend another holiday without me and then he proposed in my office. But he also told me he was gay. Or bisexual? I don't know," she recounted matter-of-factly, her eyes listless.

Senalda guzzled the rest of the wine from her glass, setting it down on a table before releasing a loud and smelly burp.

"I mean... Are you serious?" Whitney asked in an incredulous tone. "For real?"

"Seriously real," Senalda said.

"Wow," Mimi said. "My gaydar's pretty good. I never even suspected. But if dude is gay then why did he ask you to marry him?"

"He said a woman never made him feel like he felt with me and that he wanted to get married and start a family," Senalda said.

"Sounds perfect. Except for the gay part," Jarena said.

"Yeah, that's what I thought," Senalda said. "Another glass of wine please."

"What did you say?" Jarena said, getting up to pour more wine for her friend.

"I told him I didn't want to be married to a gay man, of course!" Senalda said. "He even told me that he could be faithful."

"So what happened next?" Whitney asked.

"After I told him I wouldn't marry him, I took off the rest of the day and came home. I've been here ever since. We did have a few phone conversations and I asked him a few questions about his sexual fluidity. I think I understand better, but it's still over. I apologize for going underground, but I had to take some me time to process..."

"Well, I hope next year won't be the relationship disaster that this one was for us," Jarena said. With her elbows on her thighs, she held up her face with her fists.

"Oh excuse me, I didn't know you were in a relationship this year?" Senalda said with a snicker. "Unless there is something you're not telling us."

Senalda, Mimi, and Whitney howled while Jarena only smiled.

"So what should we do about our Destination Wedding project?" Jarena asked.

"I want to be optimistic, but our investment of time hasn't yielded much of anything except heartbreak," Senalda said. She picked up her glass of wine, holding it high in the air for a toast. "A year of meetings and zilch to show for it. Happy fucking New Year, ladies!"

"Hol up ladies—before we go toastin' to heartbreak, I got something to share at this last Destination Wedding meeting of the year," Mimi said before pausing. "I got married on December 19!"

"Stop the presses!" "Say what?" "You did what?" Jarena, Whitney and Senalda shouted simultaneously. It was then they noticed the simple platinum band on Mimi's ring finger as she held a wine glass.

"How did this happen?" Senalda asked. She wiped white crust from the corners of her mouth. "And why didn't you call one of us to tell us before now?"

Mimi recounted how her Vegas bet ended in a wedding.

"So y'all are really married?" Jarena questioned with a laugh. "Didn't y'all just start dating a few weeks ago? That was fast!"

"That's why I aine say nothin' before now. I wasn't sho how y'all was gonna react after erethang with Jovan," Mimi said.

"Why go slow if you have a good man and you know what you want?" Senalda said, feeling simultaneously admiration for and competitive with her flaky friend. It was the first time since her bombshell proposal that she thought their project could be extended another year after all, because if Mimi could do it, she could do it too. "I'm proud of you, girl."

CHAPTER 14

January

Senalda

AFTER A MONTH OF wearing pajamas and devouring pizza, I declared that I was all better, or at least I would be. First, I went back to work. And I took a chance and rocked my natural curls to work, since I hadn't seen my stylist since November.

When I stepped out of my office midmorning, everyone was there. As I walked to the break room, I could tell they were trying to not act like the last time they had seen me was the day that Dexter proposed. No one made eye contact, but I still felt their eyes on me. Only my girls knew exactly what happened, but Nashaun had called my home every morning and left a bright, cheery and funny message after realizing that I wouldn't be back for a month. I remember her first message was, "I know you blue but this office aine nothing without you!" I didn't want to, but I cracked a smile when I heard it. And although I was off, she also made sure that I was abreast of anything major going on. Making my way back from the break room with my second cup of coffee, I noticed there were still a few pairs of eyes on me above their computers.

Nashaun handled them, though. "I'm sure y'all have plenty work to do while y'all are eying Mizz Warner," she said, standing up and snapping her fingers. "And if you don't, she can make sure that you do."

My assistant knew me well.

I left work early to do the second thing I felt I needed to do to get myself back together. Both Whitney and Mimi said CC had really helped them. Since they met her through me, it was time that I give her services a try too. As this was my first time seeing a therapist, I had to tell myself that I wasn't crazy as I sat in her waiting area. At 5 on the dot, CC appeared in the white room.

Okay, she has a few points for punctuality.

"Senalda, welcome," she said as she stood in front of the door and waved her arm toward her office.

"So what can I do for you today, dear?" CC said in a calm tone that I wondered if she only used with crazy people. "How is Destination Wedding coming along?"

"That's a long story. Are you sure you want to hear the whole thing?" I laughed, trying to hide my nervousness.

CC nodded, so I told her about the project's progress since the conference call, ending with Dexter's proposal.

"So, was our project crazy?" I said, immediately regretting my choice of words.

"No, I think you are exactly where you need to be, dear," she said while jotting down notes.

"You're not writing a prescription for Prozac, are you?"

"No, I'm not. Just reflecting on what you told me," she said, putting her notes on the table next to her. "When you refer to Dexter, you describe him as the perfect man for you. What made him so perfect?"

I wondered what her point was, but I explained what I meant anyway.

"Other than him being fine, he graduated from Morehouse. I graduated from Spelman. Morehouse College and Spelman College are like brother and sister schools. He has an MBA. I have an MBA. I work as a client manager. He is a vice president at his company. We're on the same path. And we have a lot of the same interests and tastes too."

"All of that sounds good, and yet you had no idea he is gay or bisexual and ultimately not truly available to you," she said, taking off her glasses.

"Have you ever thought you could have some common ground with a man who may not seem perfect for you on the surface?"

"What do you mean?"

"Tell me about your parents' marriage," she said.

"My mother is a payroll clerk for a bakery in New York," I said. "Actually, she met my father at the bakery. He was the delivery driver, but he hasn't worked pretty much since I was born because he got into a car accident. He's in a wheelchair now and on disability."

"So that is what they do, but what about their marriage?"

"Hmmm... They seem to be happy, although my grandparents almost disowned my mother for marrying my father."

"Tell me about that," CC said.

"My mother is from Puerto Rico and she was supposed to go to college in New York and come back and work at the family bakery there. But she fell in love with my father, who got a divorce just before he met my mother, and she stayed. My grandparents accept their marriage now, but they were mad for a long time. I love my father, but my mother was the one who held the household down. We didn't have a lot of money for extras, just the basics."

"Okay," CC said, putting on her glasses again. "Did your experiences lead you to your career path?"

"Yes, I guess I get my math ability from my mother, but I also decided that I would never be in a situation where I didn't have everything I wanted and needed," I said, looking at her directly in her eyes.

"And so far, you have made your vision a reality except in the man department," CC said equally as straightforwardly. "Have you ever considered that you don't know everything you want and need when it comes to that department, dear?"

"No. I know I need a black man who is college educated and excelling in his chosen but very lucrative field," I said, not caring that my neck was rolling like I was a stereotypical black woman. "He needs to be a take-charge person who can handle a strong woman like me. Of course, he needs to respect me, love me, you know, all of that."

"Sounds like a male version of you, dear," CC said with a chuckle.

"And your point?" I said, not keeping the sarcasm out of my voice.

"Maybe Dexter came into your life to show you that your male equivalent may not be the best choice for you," she said, now serious. "Why not be open to whatever man comes into your life and see what happens."

"I told my friend that," I said to her.

"And yet you haven't taken your own advice?"

"Well, she used to date creative types, kind of like her, but she just married a doctor," I said, before realizing I proved her point. *So if Mimi married a doctor, did I have to marry a janitor? I still don't get how Mimi married before I did.*

I was quiet for a few moments while she looked at me. "Okay, CC, but I'm not dating losers."

"No one wants a loser, dear," she said with a laugh. "Just reflect on the idea that you may not even know all of your wants and needs when it comes to a mate and see what comes into your life."

By the time I left, I realized that Destination Wedding didn't have to be over, but I didn't know how to proceed this year. In my peripheral view, I saw two people laughing at the end of the hallway. I looked up to see Mimi standing there with Richie. After putting my head down, I nearly ran onto the elevator so they wouldn't see me. I dialed her cell number while driving home.

"What you know good?" Mimi said.

"What?"

"Sorry Yankee," she said with a laugh. "I mean what's up?"

"Why is my newly married best friend hanging out with the husband of another one of our best friends?"

"What you talkin' 'bout?" Mimi said.

"I saw you with Richie at the Perimeter Building earlier today," I said, accusingly. "What's going on with you two?"

"Oh," she said, her voice trailing off. "I can explain... I go to Sex and Love Addicts Anonymous meetings there."

"*What* meetings?"

"CC recommended that I go to these meetings because of the way I acted with Jovan and losing my job and all of dat," she said. "She also recommended that Richie go to the meetings too, but please don't tell him I told you."

"Why?"

"Sex and Love Addicts Anonymous is an anonymous program, and we don't tell who we see at meetings, to protect our anonymity. So me and Richie just program buddies."

"Does Whitney know?"

"I've told no one I go to meetings," she said. "I was tryin' to get some recovery or feel better before I tol anyone."

"Oh."

"So can you keep this to yoself? Richie and I are just friends. You know I'd never try to get with a friend's husband, especially since I got one!"

Mimi was wild and crazy, but she wasn't a man stealer and was definitely loyal to her friends.

"I won't tell, but I won't lie either. If someone asks me a direct question, I won't lie."

"Preciate that," she said.

"So you know Victor too, huh?"

"How you figure?" she said.

"There is no other way that Richie would know a guy like that," I said with a laugh.

"Yeah, I do," she admitted. "He's my sponsor. That's someone who helps you to learn about the program. So what were you doing at the Perimeter Building? You seeing CC too?"

"I have to do something to get back to normal."

"You will love her," Mimi said. "She's da truth."

While getting ready for bed, I realized that it wasn't Mimi being "program buddies" with Richie that bothered me, it was Richie being "program buddies" with Mimi. He was looking at her like he liked her, but then again, what did I know? The previous year proved that I couldn't trust my own instincts when it came to men.

❧ Destination Wedding Meeting #13

Senalda assembled snacks and wine on the multicolored paint-spotted table in the area she had reserved for their first Destination Wedding meeting of the New Year. Senalda had convinced Jarena to give their project another year. Mimi, who still wanted to come to the meetings when she could, out of solidarity with her single friends, arrived at Just Paint Parties in Virginia Highlands first.

"So I aine know you like to paint?" Mimi commented as she shed her coat and knit cap. "I thought I was the creative one in our group."

"You are," Senalda replied before taking a sip of wine. "I just thought painting would be a good way to physically create what we want to happen in our lives this year instead of doing the traditional vision board like we did last year."

"I'm down! So what we paintin'?"

"We are painting hearts like this one," Senalda said, pointing to a canvas of a huge heart.

Jarena arrived then. "I love paint parties," she said, coming toward them.

"Good, because the instructor told me she would be ready to start soon," Senalda said as a slim, pale white woman with white-blond hair, wearing a paint-spotted black apron, positioned herself in the center of the studio.

Senalda selected random colors that didn't necessarily go together to reflect what she had been learning from CC over the past month. Ultimately, she just wanted love to come into her life, and she hoped she could accept however that love came.

Mimi painted her heart red and other bold colors, demonstrating that she was finally ready to move past her "relationship" with Jovan and forward with Ian. Still, though she would never admit it, even to her sponsor, a small part of her still had love for Jovan. But instead of nurturing that hope like she had before, her plan in the New Year was to ignore it and hope it died. Eventually.

Jarena prayed to the Father, the Son and the Holy Spirit as she painted, pleading for the strength to stop seeing Barry. Since spending the night together the month before, they had seen each other twice more and it always ended the same way—wondering how it happened in Barry's bed. She prayed her trinity of mistakes would be forgiven and that she could pry herself away from the love of her life.

CHAPTER 15
February

···

Senalda

I TOOK MYSELF OUT TO dinner after work on Valentine's Day. Puerto Rican food was my favorite, but for some reason I was craving soul food. So I opted to head to Jackson's in East Atlanta. I remembered from my date with my girls there last year that the food was very good, and the restaurant was upscale, not a shack like some soul food spots.

I ordered everything I had been craving: fried chicken, macaroni and cheese, collard greens, sweet potato soufflé, corn bread, and pecan pie for dessert. I was thankful for my mom's naturally slender genes. I would probably weigh two more pounds in the morning, but it would be worth it.

I scrutinized the couples obviously out for Valentine's dates. I could tell which couples were married and which ones were dating by what the women were wearing. The single ladies wore something short and tight while the married women were dressed more conservatively, if not bordering on frumpy. *But at least they have men.* I looked down at my brown pantsuit and black blouse. *What is Dexter doing for Valentine's Day?*

I was startled by the arrival of a chef at my table. "How are you tonight?" He smiled, but his nice smile was canceled out by his country accent. And he looked like a Pillsbury Dough Boy that had been deflated.

"I'm well, thank you." I reached in my purse to pull out a copy of *Money* magazine. Either he didn't see the magazine or didn't care that I was attempting to look busy, because he kept on talking.

"I'm one of the chefs here. My name is Wendell." He reached out his slightly powdery hand to shake mine, but I kept my hands on the table. He wiped his hand off on his uniform before reaching out to me again.

"Wendell," I said with a sarcastic smile. "The name fits you."

Neither my magazine, nor keeping my hand to myself, nor my sarcasm worked.

"Oh really? Why? Because of my country accent? That's alright. I know I'm a country boy, purrrty," he said.

I laughed. "Hey, I remember you. I saw you the last time I was here, a year ago." I noticed that his skin was the color of a brown sugar crust, but then again, I was hungry.

"So our food was so good you came back a year later?" he offered. "So you remember me from last year? What was I doing?"

"You were breaking up a fight between two other chefs."

"Oh those chefs!" His stomach jiggled like custard when he laughed.

As the waitress placed my food down, I hoped Wendell would leave me alone to pig out in peace.

"So you haven't told me your name," Wendell said.

"It's Senalda, and since my food is now on the table, I want to eat."

"I don't think you should be without a man on another Valentine's Day, so here is my number," he said placing a slip of paper on the table. As his hand passed my face, I smelled nutmeg. "I remember you from a year ago, too. You were with your girlfriends then. I will let you enjoy your food, but give me a call when you get a chance, purrrty," he said with a wink.

"Okay, I will call you," I said, hoping that would get him to walk away.

I considered complaining to the hostess later that a chef was badgering customers, but since it was Valentine's Day, I decided to be tolerant. After devouring my meal, I picked up the paper. Obviously, he had written the information before he got to my table. And he obviously remembered me because he knew I was with my girls last year.

A month earlier I had vowed to be open to whatever kind of love came to me, and on Valentine's Day, a chef approached me. *I will give this chef a call only because CC told me that I may not know what I want or need in a man. At the very least, I will be eating good.*

Destination Wedding Meeting #14

Still surprised to be someone's wife, Mimi appraised her new living room where she was hosting February's meeting. She had mopped the hardwood floors and dusted earlier in the day. Ian wasn't a big television fan so the living room didn't have a TV. Admittedly, a television didn't fit with the eclectic African-American art and furniture. But today, he had moved their bedroom TV into the living room so the women could watch a movie there. Ian, who seemed to be wearing married contentment as a garment, left for the hospital at noon. She hoped the garment would eventually be stretched large enough to clothe and protect her from her own destructive longings. Many times, she had to talk herself out of texting Jovan or calling his voicemail just to hear his voice.

Ian had kissed her lips as he walked out of their home. "Our life couldn't be more perfect," he said as his lips lingered on hers, "that is unless we had a baby."

Mimi flinched, flashing back to the day he spotted her across the street from the abortion clinic. At some point, she wanted to tell him about her abortion, but she hadn't found the perfect time to do so. She relegated her thoughts to the back of her mind when she looked out of the window and saw Senalda stepping onto their porch. Mimi met her at the door.

"Bossy, welcome to my new home!" she said while lifting her arm in the air with a flourish.

"It's beautiful," Senalda said, surveying the refurbished nineteenth-century Eastlake Victorian home. "I can tell Ian put a lot of work in here or paid someone a lot to do it."

Within minutes, Jarena rang Mimi's doorbell.

"Great! All three of us are here!" Senalda said.

"So what's the game plan for today?" Jarena said after hugging her friends and finding a place on a couch. She felt something crumble beneath her.

"What's this?" she said, holding up a photograph.

"Wait a minute," Senalda said scrutinizing the image. "I remember that pic of you and Jovan at your condo. What is that doing here?"

"Gimme dat," Mimi said as she yanked it from Jarena. "I've been getting rid of stuff from my old place, and this must have dropped from one of my boxes."

"Yes, out with the old and in with the new," Senalda agreed.

Jarena wasn't entirely convinced that was why the picture was there, but she didn't say otherwise.

"Anyway, to answer Jarena's question, I thought it would be interesting to watch a movie about hopeless love," Senalda said. "Except in the movies you're always guaranteed a happy ending, and I need a happy ending more than ever."

"Amen and Hallelujah!" Jarena said. "So what's the movie?"

Just then, Mimi's phone, which was nestled in the cushions of another couch, buzzed. She fished it out and peered at the phone. It was Richie.

"Please call me when you get a chance," he had texted. She made a mental note to return his call later.

"I thought we should watch *Something's Gotta Give* with Jack Nicholson," Senalda said, holding up the DVD.

"Ooh, I love that movie," Jarena said, clapping her hands together.

"Lemme see dat," Mimi said, grabbing the DVD from Senalda and examining it. "Is dis a love story about old-ass fogies? It don't matter anyway because I'll be drunk in a minute."

She sprang up, heading to the kitchen. "Anyone else want some wine? It's Moscato. And I got some Jamaican food too."

"I love when you cook! You're so A-Town down I sometimes forget your father is Jamaican until you cook," Jarena said. "Did you make the fried dumplings?"

"You know I did," Mimi replied.

"Okay, so I want some," Jarena said.

The aroma of dumplings along with cocktail beef and vegetable patties and saltfish fritters surrounded Mimi as she arrayed the spread on the table.

Senalda brought back the wine glasses and Moscato for herself and Mimi and bottled water for Jarena before slipping in the DVD.

From the moment Mimi realized that Jack Nicholson portrayed a playboy music executive, Harry, who didn't realize that he mistakenly passed over the right woman, she was hooked. The right woman, Erica, who was played by Diane Keaton, didn't stand for Harry's playboy ways, however, and went on with her life. And she was glad the room was dark by the time Harry finally figured out that he was in love with Erica and came back to her, although Erica knew they were soul mates at the beginning of the film. Tears doused her face so she made her way to the bathroom to wash them off. While there, she texted Richie.

"Hey program buddy, are you alright? The girls are over so I couldn't respond earlier," she texted.

"I'm okay now," Richie texted back. "Was thinking of watching porn but thinking about you and my recovery stopped me."

"Glad I cld help," Mimi texted back.

"Are you okay?" Richie texted.

"Yeah," she texted back. She was afraid to text anything else in fear that Richie would realize she wasn't as over Jovan as she wanted to be.

"So did you like the movie?" Jarena asked when Mimi reappeared.

"Real love always wins," Mimi said with a wistful smile.

CHAPTER 16
March

. . . .

Jarena

IT WAS SATURDAY, AND Barry and I had been devouring basketball games all afternoon in his condo. Earlier, we had ordered in pizza for lunch and now it was time to order dinner.

"I'm just going to do it," Barry said, his eyes feasting on me. His head was in my lap, and I was playing with his golden-brown curls.

"You're going to do what?" I questioned, extending one curl as far as it would go. "You mean order dinner? What do you want to eat?" I wasn't hungry, but being in love and eating more seemed to go together, something about the relaxing of all of your boundaries.

"No, that's not what I mean," Barry stated, popping up, "I'm going to ask Naomi for a divorce."

"Come again?" I said. "What did you just say?"

"Being with you for the last few months has shown me what was missing from my marriage," he said. "I was unhappy even before we reconnected, but now that we're together again, I see it was a mistake to get married in the first place. I was on the rebound after you."

"Barry, we are not together." I shifted away from him on the couch. "We've been spending time together, but we are not together."

"Oh, we're not together?" he said. He moved toward me like he was lion, pulling me down underneath him for a long kiss. I struggled until I surrendered, allowing myself to be swept up in the moment, like my mind wasn't connected to my soul. To stop all thoughts capable of restoring reality, I closed my eyes and let waves of hope roll over me. I ventured to the place where nothing was capable of separating true love. "I don't feel any of this with Naomi. She's sweet. A very nice person. But we don't have this."

He slammed his mouth on mine again. My face was so hot I felt like we would spontaneously combust.

"I want a divorce," he said, our lips still pressed together. "The next time I go home I'm going to tell her that."

The word "divorce" unceremoniously dislodged me from my emotional getaway. "Barry, you're not making any sense." I stood up and pushed him off of me. "You have a wife and kids and a whole life you've created without me. I love you, okay. I do. But I've created a life without you, too. I'm studying to be a minister now. It couldn't work between us now even if we want it to!"

"Do you want it to?" He stood up before me, clutched my hands in his and said, "Because I love you too." In spite of myself, I suddenly envisioned what it would have been like if we were standing at an altar waiting for a minister to pronounce us husband and wife.

"I don't know what I want," I said, my heart churning. *That's a lie.* I released his hands, about to get something to drink when Barry maneuvered me back toward him.

"I do," Barry said. His lips dropped from my mouth, and it wasn't much longer until we fell into bed. The next morning as I put on my clothes, I thought about telling my girls what was happening with me and Barry for the first time since he reappeared in my life. *Hell, praying for strength wasn't working.* But my girls looked up to me as the godly one in the group and I didn't want to let them down. Plus, my mother always told me that you cannot depend on others to fix your problems. You have to do that on your own.

Senalda

It took me two weeks to call Wendell. Every time I thought about it, I recalled my entire relationship with Dexter and chickened out. But I had to have something to report at the next Destination Wedding meeting, so I put my fear aside and called him one Saturday while I was at my office.

"Talk to me," a loud voice commanded.

"Hi," I said, uncertain I had the right person. "Is this Wendell?"

"I am he. He is me."

"This is Senalda from Valentine's Day."

"Hey purrrty," he said even louder. "You sure took your time to call a brotha."

"I guess so," I said with a laugh. "And you're lucky I'm calling now."

"I love a woman with no filter," he countered.

"I don't want to keep you from your work." Food sizzled and pots and pans clanged in the background. "It sounds like you're in the kitchen."

"I am, but I got a minute." A moment later everything was quiet.

"Your boss just let you walk out of the kitchen?"

"Oh, he's cool," he said. "So when you gon let me take you out, purrrty?"

"Wow, no build up?"

"I told you I had a minute," he said with laugh.

"That you did."

"So I'm through with work at 11 tonight," he said. "How 'bout a midnight movie? Do you stay up that late?"

"How about we wait until you have a day off?"

"Naw, you not getting away again," he said. "What side of town do you live on?"

"Near Camp Creek," I said, hoping I wasn't giving away too much information.

"Do you mind meeting me at the movie theater at Atlantic Station?" he said. "I would come and pick you up after work but if I did that, I would still be in my chef uniform. But if I meet you there, I can go home and take a shower and get myself lookin' good for you."

"Okay," I said in spite of myself. *I'm getting out of my comfort zone like CC suggested.*

• • •

As I left my house at 11, I realized that I was dressed in all black everything. I hadn't thought about it as I was getting dressed, but I noticed my reflection in the glass outer door that I locked. But when I did think about it, it made sense that I had chosen my outfit according to my state of mind.

A year ago, I was hopeful when Dexter arrived at my home for our first date. And now, I was leaving my home at nearly midnight to meet a chef at a movie theater. *I probably could have worn sweatpants and a T-shirt.*

I was glad to see Wendell standing outside in front of the theater. If I had to search for him, I would have probably just have turned around, gotten back into my car and sped home.

"I wasn't sure you would show up, purrrty," he said as he strode up to me.

"I'm here," I said, shrugging.

"And looking sexy in all that black, too," he said with a laugh.

I secretly sniffed him to see if he smelled like a restaurant kitchen as we made our way to the ticket booth. But he actually smelled good. And he was cute, too. In a country boy kind of way.

"So what movie do you want to see tonight?" I said, looking up at the movie marquee.

"How 'bout *Big Mommas: Like Father, Like Son?*"

I inwardly cringed but decided to just go with it.

"You probably think you too classy for a movie like this, but you know Martin Lawrence is funny," he said, as if he read my thoughts.

"Yeah, I used to love Martin and Gina back in the day," I said with a weak smile. "Since you picked the movie, I can pay for our tickets."

"Why you tryin' to punk me like that?" Wendell said with a laugh. "I know I'm just an average brotha, but I can pay for movies. But if you wanna hook a brotha up another time I'll let you know."

I smiled but didn't say anything.

"So you do you want some popcorn or anything else?" He walked toward the concessions area and looked back at me.

"No, I'm not hungry," I said. Out of habit, I almost offered to pay for our food. "Are you hungry after working around food all day?"

"I can always eat," he said, rubbing his small potbelly like he was a Buddha.

He ordered a tub of popcorn slathered with butter and a large Coke. I was impressed that he held the door open for me as we walked into the theater. After we settled in, Wendell began chomping on his popcorn and sipping on his Coke so loudly I had no choice except to stare at him.

Wendell stopped chomping, looked at me and said, "I'm sorry. Do you want some? I don't mind feeding you." He held a piece of popcorn in front of my lips.

"No, thank you," I said, moving back from his fingers.

"People pay me top dollar to feed them, so let me feed you, purrrty," he said with a grin.

How many dollars?

"Okay, I guess so," I muttered.

He took the popcorn, maneuvering it like it was an airplane before directing it into my mouth.

"Ummm good," I said to appease him.

"You want more?"

"I'm good, thank you." I covered my mouth.

"Okay, purrrty." He began chomping as carefree as he did before.

I was surprised that I laughed along with everyone else as we watched the movie.

"See purrrty, I knew you would laugh." Wendall's lips barely grazed my ear, but it was enough to make me shiver. I hoped he hadn't seen that. "You look like you haven't laughed in a while."

After the movie was over, he walked me to my car. "So I noticed that black women in Atlanta do one of three things if they are still single in their mid-thirties," Wendell stated. "And if one of those doesn't work, they get depressed, bitter about men, and eat up erethang."

I started to unleash on him, but I did spend all of December depressed, feeling bitter about men, and eating fast food. So I opted to hear him out.

"What three things?" But I did start rolling my eyes and curling up my lips in preparation for his answer.

"Either they start working a bunch of overtime like it's the end of the world. Or start being a church lady up in church every time the doors open. They at Bible Study. Prayer Meeting. Feeding the homeless. Or they start running marathons here and in other cities and countries, and changing their diet. Which one of those describes you, purrrty?"

I couldn't help but laugh.

"You could be right," I replied, thinking about myself and my friends. "But I'm not going to tell you which category I could be in."

"That's cool, because you won't be single much longer anyway—"

"What?" I interrupted, but he kept on talking.

"So purrrty, I hope you had a good enough time to want to go out again. I'm off on Mondays and Tuesdays, but you look like you have a corporate job, so those days probably don't work for you. But I would be honored to take you to lunch on Monday if you could make the time," he said, stringing the words together like a rehearsed pitch.

"Sounds like I make you nervous," I said, finally getting a chance to speak. "I can meet you for lunch on Monday. Why don't you pick the place, since that's your specialty?"

"What kind of food do you like?"

"Puerto Rican food is my favorite," I said, figuring he wouldn't know of any Puerto Rican restaurants in town.

"Hey, one of my chef buddies owns a Puerto Rican restaurant in Norcross. Is that close to where you work?" he said.

"I can swing it," I said, surprised again that he knew of a Puerto Rican restaurant. "It's not too far away. What's the name of the restaurant?"

"Manolo's," he said. "Bet you didn't think a country boy like me knew about an international restaurant?"

"I guess I didn't," I said with a smile.

He hugged me then. "Alright purrrty, gotta head home. A long day at the restaurant tomorrow so I gotta say goodnight. Call me when you get home so that I know you made it."

"Okay," I said, keeping my arms at my side.

He wasn't suave and sophisticated like Dexter, but I had to admit he was a good guy. Not my type, though. But at least I had something to report to the girls.

🦋 *Destination Wedding Meeting #15*

Since Whitney offered to host their March meeting, Senalda, Mimi and Jarena ventured back to Henry County.

"Every time I come to your house, I feel like I'm taking a day trip," Senalda said as the women gathered their goodies to take to the den.

"It makes me feel like I'm about to drive to Vidalia," Jarena said.

"Country girl," Senalda said with a laugh.

"Boogie or Bougie Down Bronx, in your case," Jarena threw out with a faux New York accent. The women cackled as they placed the food on a table and sat down on the couches and floor.

"So Mimi, how is married life?" Senalda asked, her voice rising in anticipation.

"Great," Mimi replied, as she snacked on chips.

"I still can't believe Mimi is married to a doctor of all things!" Senalda said with enthusiasm. "And that you beat me to the altar!"

Mimi half-smiled while continuing to stuff chips into her mouth like the thoughts she wanted to push down. Richie stuck his head inside the room then, halting Senalda's interrogation. Mimi had never been happier to see her program buddy.

"I'm sorry to interrupt, ladies, but I want your opinion on something," he said. "Do you mind, Whit?"

Whitney grimaced before replying. "Sure Richie, I guess so if y'all don't mind."

"What's up, Richie?" Jarena said, looking in his direction.

"I don't know if Whit told you, but I'm getting ready for my first photography show next Friday," he announced.

"I knew you took pictures," Jarena said, "but I didn't know you were serious enough to have a show."

Senalda raised an eyebrow and locked eyes with Whitney.

"I didn't know I was that serious until recently," Richie admitted. "But some of my photographs are going to be displayed at an art gallery in Castleberry Hills."

"Congratulations!" Jarena said.

"Thank you," Richie said. "So would you ladies mind taking a few minutes to look at the photographs I'm thinking of displaying? I want to get your honest opinion."

In the basement, the women examined the framed photographs leaning against the walls.

"You have a great eye, Richie," Jarena noted. "You're probably the first artsy doctor I've ever met."

"Ian's artsy too," Mimi said. "So there's two of em."

His face aglow, Richie beamed at Mimi.

"So do you think I should go with these photographs? I have more."

"They all really nice," Mimi said. "I think you should use these ones."

"I agree," Senalda said.

Whitney was silent as the women praised Richie's work.

"Well, ladies, Whit is probably mad at me for keeping all of you down here this long, so I will let you get back to your meeting."

"Are we ready to head back upstairs?" Whitney said quickly without disagreeing with her husband.

"Sure," Jarena said. "Thanks again, Richie, for showing us your work. I want to come to the opening. Whitney, can you email the show info to all of us?"

She mumbled, "Yes," barely uttering anything else for the remainder of the meeting.

CHAPTER 17

April

Whitney

SINCE RICHIE WOULDN'T LISTEN to me, I decided to speak with his father about getting him to forget about his harebrained hobby. After his Christmas Day declaration that he was abandoning medicine to be a photographer, I managed to get him to agree to wait six months and really contemplate his decision before changing the course of the rest of our lives.

But after his photography show earlier in the month, I knew he was still set on switching careers, if you can call photography a career. *You can't.* In two months, our life was scheduled to implode if I didn't do anything about it. So in the middle of the day, a day that I knew Richie didn't have to be at the hospital until the evening shift, I met with Richie's father at Grady. I was grateful my very important father-in-law had a last-minute opening in his busy schedule.

I steadied myself in my navy Christian Louboutin pumps, took a quick look down at my pearls and Giorgio Armani business suit, shook my hair so that it cascaded straight down my back, and proceeded toward his office. But before I got there, the door opened and Dr. Brannon came toward me. He was one of the most handsome, distinguished gentlemen I had ever met, a caramel-brown older version of Richie, and his white hair only enhanced his coloring and features. I hoped Richie aged just like his father had.

"Whitney, how are you, dear?" He kissed my cheek then took my hands in his, holding them for moment.

"I'm well. How are you? Thank you for meeting with me."

"Anything for my beautiful daughter-in-law," he said, closing his door behind him and pointing toward a cashew-colored leather armchair.

"So what has got you so upset?" he said, as he sat down in the matching armchair next to it and observed me through rimless glasses.

"Dr. Brannon, I really respect you and Mrs. Brannon," I began. "The both of you have always been so nice to me and you welcomed me into your family since the day we met, but—"

"What is it, Whitney?" he said, interrupting me. "Just say it."

"Okaaay," I said, slowly at first before letting the words tumble out. I filled him in on what happened on Christmas and told him about Richie's showing.

"I wish you had told me about this sooner," he said, taking off his glasses with his right hand and placing his left on his now wrinkled forehead.

I didn't know what to say, so I remained silent.

"I guess my son really does take after his mother," he finally said, shifting in his seat and peering out of the bay window that gave a privileged panoramic view of the city.

"You mean his real mother?"

"How much has Richie told you about my first wife?" He turned back to face me.

"Richie told me his mother left the family when he was a little boy and moved to Costa Rica," I said. "I know he has seen her once since then. We invited her to the wedding, but she couldn't come because she was sick. He doesn't really talk about her."

"That is the abridged version of the story, my dear. Viola left us because she wanted to be a painter and no longer wanted to be a wife and mother. I tried to convince her to stay, but after a while, I realized that she couldn't be the woman I needed her to be, and we divorced."

"Richie never told me all that," I said softly.

"From the time he was a little boy, he has reminded me of Viola. The way he looks at life. How he thinks. He asked me for a pretty fancy camera when he was ten. He was always taking photographs of the family or at family gatherings. When he was a senior in high school, he told me he wanted to go to an art school in New York. I told him that he if went to art school, I wasn't going to pay for it, and he decided to go to Morehouse instead. After that, I never heard any more about it, and I thought he had outgrown all of that."

I still didn't say anything, and Dr. Brannon continued.

"I'll have a talk with him." He put his glasses back on and placed his hands on his knees.

"What are you going to say? Threatening to not pay for his education won't work now."

"Telling him how much it hurt when Viola left might," he said while getting up.

"He isn't leaving me and the twins," I said, wondering where he was going. He arrived at his desk and pulled out an old, tattered photograph from a drawer.

"See this photo?" he said as he handed it to me. I took it carefully, afraid it would disintegrate, it was so paper-thin. It was a yellowed photograph of Dr. Brannon dressed in a '70s outfit. He was hugging a very light-skinned woman with thigh-high boots, a dress that stopped at the top of her thighs, clunky hoop earrings and a huge Afro. A less curvy Pam Grier she was.

"That's Richie's mother," he said.

I had always assumed that Richie got his coloring from his mother, and I was right. And she was as gorgeous as Dr. Brannon was handsome. Something about how she pushed her hips out although she was in an embrace showed me her wild streak. I couldn't see her being Dr. Brannon's wife, though.

"That was the night we met," he said with a sentimental smile. "It was our junior year. She was at Spelman. I was at Morehouse. She was the finest woman I had ever seen. Our parents were disappointed when she got pregnant with Richie a few months later, but I knew from that first night I was going to marry her anyway. I'm not sure she really wanted to marry me so soon or at all, but that is what you did at the time."

"Did you see it coming?" I asked.

"You mean did I know she was going to leave me eventually?"

I nodded.

"I guess I did," he said, as tears glossed over his eyes. "You're the first person I ever admitted that to. Trying to make her stay was hard. One day, I came home from work and she was gone. She had left Richie at my sister's house."

"Dr. Brannon, Richie never said anything about wanting to leave me," I reassured myself as well as him. "He only wants to switch careers."

"Don't you worry about it," he said, wiping away tears with his hands and returning to his more controlled demeanor. "It's time I tell your husband the truth about his mother. He won't break your heart the way his mother did mine. I'll see to that."

I realized that I was the one who needed to threaten to leave this coddled trust-fund baby I called my husband. Maybe then he would realize what was at stake.

🌸 Destination Wedding Meeting #16

Senalda volunteered to host April's meeting at her home, but 45 minutes before her friends were scheduled to arrive, Wendell called with an urgent request.

"Hey purrrty," he said. "I really need your help. I thought I was gonna be able to stay at home with Kailen, but I got called into work because one of the other chefs got sick. Can I drop her off at your house and pick her up after work?"

She had only met his three-year-old daughter once, but she said yes anyway. Kailen was only with her dad Mondays and Tuesdays and the occasional weekends.

She looked around, wondering if she needed to childproof her home somehow. It occurred to her then that if she continued seeing Wendell, she could eventually become a stepmother.

Unlike with Dexter, who fit so perfectly in her life, dating Wendell was an adjustment. Based on his small apartment near Little Five Points where many of Atlanta's artists, healthy-eating advocates, and drug users hung out, Senalda concluded that she earned significantly more than he did. He had attended Bethune-Cookman College but dropped out when his grandmother, who raised him, passed away. He later graduated from a culinary school in Atlanta. He drove a black Honda Accord—a nice one, but still a Honda. And he had an ex-girlfriend, who was the mother of his child.

But Wendell did make her laugh unlike any man she had ever dated, including Dexter. And he adored her and didn't mind telling her so regularly. He took her to lunch twice a week, and if he wasn't too tired on Saturday night after he got off of work and didn't have Kailen, they saw each other again.

Since she had very little experience with children, she wondered what she would do with his child until at least 11 p.m. Luckily, she discovered she had the Cartoon Network, deciding to park the child in front of her living room television. She hoped her friends wouldn't mind the additional company. As she straightened her home, her doorbell rang.

"Hey purrrty," Wendell said, holding Kailen on his side. She looked just like him, a brown-skinned chubby girl with thick pigtails. "Kailen, you be good for Miss purrrty while Daddy is cooking, okay?"

She nodded, her eyelids lowering.

"Kailen, I'm so happy you've come to visit me," Senalda said, holding her arms out. "Do you want to watch TV with me?"

She just looked at Senalda for a moment before moving toward her. Senalda took her in her arms, straightening her pink T-shirt to fully cover the child's rotund belly. She also got Kailen's Princess Tiana backpack with her snacks and pajamas in it from Wendell.

"She'll be knocked out before you know it," Wendell said, reaching over and kissing Senalda on the cheek. "Thanks. When are your friends coming over?"

As if on cue, Jarena pulled into her driveway.

"I would love to speak to them, but I gotta get to the restaurant," he said.

"You better get there fast before your boss gets on you," Senalda said, giving him a hug.

"We look like a family," he said while touching her cheek. "Okay, gotta go. Bye bye Kailen. Bye purrrty baby."

He kissed Kailen and darted to his car.

"Who was that, and who is this little cutie?" Jarena said.

"That was Wendell the chef, and this is Wendell's daughter. Can you say hello, Kailen?"

Kailen laid her head on Senalda's shoulder and hugged her tighter.

"Awww, look at you looking like a mother," Jarena said.

"Really? Stop!" Senalda said with a smile. "So you don't mind that we have another girl for our meeting?"

"Of course not," she said, "Jarena loves the kids."

Senalda put Kailen and her backpack on the couch, sitting down next to her while Jarena sat on Senalda's other side.

"Obviously, things between you and Wendell are going well. He trusts you with his daughter. That's huge," Jarena said.

"Yeah, he's really sweet," Senalda said.

"So where is this going?"

"Let's talk in the kitchen," Senalda said, nodding her head toward the child.

The two sat at Senalda's island where she could watch Kailen while speaking privately.

"I like him a lot, but it's hard to think about us together long-term," Senalda said, glad for the chance to air out her thoughts. She explained her thoughts to Jarena.

"You are really trippin'," Jarena hissed. "Dexter was bisexual or gay, and he didn't even tell you until he had to... Senalda, take it from me, if someone demonstrates that he loves you and you love him back, don't walk away from it just because it's going to be an adjustment. Love is an adjustment."

During the time she had been seeing Barry again, it dawned on Jarena that part of the reason she didn't accept his proposal back then was that she didn't think she could go after her career and still have the time and energy to be married. Now that she was successfully balancing ministry, school, and a business, she realized it was a mistake in judgment she would probably regret for the rest of her life. The most successful women were able to pursue their careers and be happily married.

"Is this your minister talk or are you speaking from experience?" Senalda said, raising her eyebrows. "You're the only one of us that hasn't had a relationship disaster since we started doing this project. As far as we know, you haven't even been on a date!"

Jarena's phone beeped then. "It's Mimi."

"Where is she?"

"Sorry cldn't make the meeting. Ian and I are in NYC for the weekend. Last-minute romantic getaway!" Jarena read.

"Are you serious? She just keeps surprising me! And for the better, too!" Senalda said. "Maybe if things keep going the way they are going with Wendell, I can be the second to get married."

"Everything is a competition with you," Jarena said, shaking her head.

Senalda noticed then that Kailen had fallen asleep.

"I'm going to put her in the guest room," she said.

"Girl, that's my cue, too," Jarena said, standing up. "Since Mimi isn't here and you've got Kailen, I'm going to head home. I've got a paper due on Monday, and I have church in the morning, so I have a long day tomorrow."

"So any luck on selling your business?" Senalda inquired.

"Funny you're asking me that. I think I have someone finally, but I don't want to jinx it."

"I thought ministers didn't believe in jinxes," Senalda said with a laugh.

"I don't, but you know what I mean."

"I hope it goes through," Senalda said. "Okay, next time we meet, we're going to devote a whole meeting to YOUR love life because it's been over a year, and you haven't even been a date... unless there is something you're not telling us."

For a moment, Senalda wondered if Jarena had a secret dating relationship of some sort. Over the course of their friendship, Senalda noticed her friend had a curious habit of keeping secrets, as if she wanted to present a glossed-over image of herself like she did with her clients. But she dismissed the thought, figuring Jarena couldn't have kept a secret like that, with everything else going on in her life.

"Girl, bye," Jarena said as she opened Senalda's front door and hurried to her car.

"You can't marry Jesus," Senalda hollered, temporarily forgetting she had a sleeping child nearby.

CHAPTER 18

May

. . . .

🔔 Destination Wedding Meeting #17

FOR THEIR MAY MEETING, the women thought it was time to see how their men interacted with everyone else. Although Jarena would be the only uncoupled one, she assured them she would be alright. The Atlanta Jazz Festival, a must-do event for Black Atlanta held every Memorial Day weekend, was the perfect opportunity for this meeting. The Brannons opted to supply the meat and grill for the group at Piedmont Park, where the festival was held. They also brought a tent, lawn chairs, and blankets. Wendell was off of work for the entire weekend, so he made the side dishes. Senalda contributed desserts from Manolo's, now her favorite Puerto Rican spot in Atlanta. Mimi and Jarena provided the paper supplies, drinks, and coolers.

The weather was perfect. The sun was high in a cloudless blue sky so serene that any surprises that could transpire that day would be softened by its calming influence. A gentle breeze supplied natural air conditioning. Black people from all corners of metro Atlanta had swarmed to the park, collectively kickin' back and reveling in the food, music, and overall atmosphere.

Whitney, Richie and the twins arrived first. They worked side by side to set up their area and grill the meat while minding the twins, getting along without sarcastic comments and misunderstanding. Hand in hand, the

Goodmans arrived next. Instead of her usual bohemian style, Mimi wore a strapless baby-blue jumper with simple gold sandals. Her locs, which were usually here, there, and everywhere, were assembled in a large bun at the nape of her neck.

She actually looks presentable! "Over here," Whitney shouted, waving wildly at them.

Richie turned around just as Ian got close.

"Hey, Richie," Ian said.

"Ian, man, what are you doing here?" Richie said, his face contorting in surprised recognition.

"Richie, this is Mimi's hubby Ian," Whitney explained. "I kept forgetting to ask if the two of you know each other. Obviously you do."

"Oh, Mimi..." Richie said, before pausing and starting another statement. "Small world," he said instead.

"Hey man, if you need help on the grill, let me know," Ian said.

"Me and the wifey have got it right now, but thanks," he said, forcefully grabbing Whitney to him with his free hand while his other hand held tongs in the air. Mimi's phone rang then, dissipating the awkward tension.

"Hey Jarena," Mimi said. "Okay, I'ma get Ian and Richie to help you."

"Y'all," she said to the men. "Jarena has drinks and a cooler in her trunk, but she needs help gettin' it all ova here."

"Where is she parked?" Ian asked.

"She's ova there near Grady High School," Mimi said, pointing to the school across the street from the park.

As the men walked away, Senalda and Wendell made their way to the site.

"Hello ladies, remember Wendell?" Senalda said, pointing to the thickset man beside her.

"So glad to be seein' y'all again," he said a little too loudly. "Purrrty has told me all about you." He put his cooler down on the grass, charged over to Mimi and Whitney, and hugged them in a tight grip.

"Purrrty?" Whitney said, her eyebrows wrinkling as Wendell released them. She smoothed her white blouse and shorts.

"He means 'pretty,'" Senalda said with nervous laughter.

"That's sooo sweet!" Mimi said.

"So where is your husband?" Senalda asked Mimi.

Jarena, Richie, and Ian walked up then.

"Here he is," Richie said, hitting Ian on the back with so much power, he was thrust forward.

Thirty minutes later, the crew of friends were eating, drinking, and enjoying the day. Even amongst her friends, Jarena wondered what Barry was doing. He told her he was probably going home for the holiday weekend. She thought about texting him but decided to leave him alone with his family. As if she had conjured him up, she heard a voice that sounded like his getting closer to her group.

"Naomi," the voice said, "I see some vacant spots over there nearby the stage."

Barry was right in front of her. With his wife Naomi and their son and daughter. Before she could act like she hadn't seen him, Mimi's voice screeched from behind her.

"Is that Barry Simpson? Jarena, there's Barry! I tol y'all the jazz festival is Atlanta's black family reunion!"

"Oh hey, Barry," Jarena said, hoping she didn't look as guilty as she felt.

"How are you, Jarena?" Barry said, not moving from where he stood when he saw her. "This is my wife, Naomi, and Barry Jr. and Amber."

In a flash, Jarena assessed the woman Barry had chosen to salve his heart after she rejected his proposal. Her very being made her the type of woman that could cater to man's wounded ego with her short stature and small waist, hands, and feet. She was a delicate creature that a man could care for and contain. Jarena had grown taller than many boys when she was twelve. Coupled with the independence instilled in by her mother and grandmother, Jarena wasn't sure she could allow herself to be taken care of physically or emotionally. As if she were twelve, she wanted to shove Naomi to the ground, slap the smile from her face, and scrap with her rival.

While the encounter between Barry and Jarena was public, something about the way it unfolded made everyone in its vicinity feel like they had encroached upon a private moment. The mingled smell of intimacy, long-ing, and regret hung heavy in the air as detectable as the mingled smell of hundreds of moving bodies, assorted cookouts dotting the park, and the span of the outdoors.

"Wow, aine it funny y'all ran into each other after all of these years?" Mimi asked.

"Yeah," Barry said, his face oddly blank of any expression. "Well, it was nice seeing you and everyone."

Naomi opened her mouth to say something to the group, but Barry ush-ered his family away before she could get any intelligible words out.

"Nice meeting all of you," Jarena called to them as the family traveled in the opposite direction.

"Is that THE Barry you used to talk about all of the time after we met?" Senalda said.

"The one and only," Mimi confirmed. "Jarena's college sweetheart. The only one she's eva loved."

"Looks like the two of you still have some chemistry," Whitney said. "Too bad he's a married man."

"Yeah, too bad," Jarena said, trying to make her face look as void of rec-ognition as Barry's face had. "I guess I can finally stop thinking about him, since he's married with kids."

"You mean to tell me you've never looked him up on Facebook or any-thing?" Senalda asked slyly.

"Not really," Jarena said. "I think Incognito is getting ready to get on stage. I'm going to try to get as close as I can. Anyone want to go with me?"

As Mimi walked with her toward the stage, she said, "You know you're aine fooling nobody, acting like you haven't seen him since college. I saw how y'all looked at each other. That's why I started talking fast, so no one else would see what I saw. But lemme say this, girl. And I learned it the hard way. Don't keep thinking 'bout a man that's moved on."

"Oh, so now that you have been married for less than six months, you're giving relationship advice?" Jarena quipped. "Spare me. God will send the right man for me at the right time."

"Well, maybe God is trying to tell you something right now," Mimi said with a laugh, not realizing that a startled Jarena believed her incisive words, meant as a joke, were directly from God.

CHAPTER 19

June

· ·

Jarena

I CAN'T WAIT TO GET to church today, I said to myself a full ten minutes before my alarm clock sounded on Sunday morning. I had a testimony to share, and I couldn't wait to share it! I had been working on selling my business since November and on Friday, it finally happened. My attorney and broker had been negotiating with Urban PR, a public relations company based in New York, for months, and the deal went through! Urban PR wanted to open an Atlanta office with my clientele to jumpstart their business in the city. I made enough from the sale to keep me comfortable while I finished school and began working full-time as a minister. Plus, I was also excited because I received a check from Hidden United Methodist in the mail that same week since I conducted a three-month youth Bible study at church. The check made me feel like I had officially started my new career, although I was still in seminary.

The check reminded me of the checks my grandmother received from Redemption Baptist Church. A tall, skinny, dark-skinned man would stop by G-ma's house at the beginning of the month and hand her an envelope with the church's name on it. When I was ten, I asked her what was in the envelopes, but she always replied that was "grown folks' business" and shooed me away. When I was eleven, I just looked in her nightstand drawer where she always put the envelopes and peeked inside. I saw a check from the church. After she passed, the checks started coming to my mother. I asked her about them, but she wouldn't tell me, either.

Since I began taking courses to be a certified lay minister at Hidden United Methodist in December, I sat up closer to the front. I could barely contain myself as I took my seat in the second pew today. I managed to get through the prelude, call to worship, invocation, scripture lesson, and prayer hymn. But as soon as the word "testimony" left Pastor Kirby's lips, I jumped up.

"I have a testimony, Pastor Kirby," I said.

"It must be an awesome testimony, because I couldn't even get the word out," Pastor Kirby said with a laugh. "Please share with us, Sister Jarena."

I looked at him mostly as I shared, but I turned around a few times to make eye contact with the church.

"I'm so thankful for my church. I didn't know that when I came here over a year ago that God had ordained for me to be here. Since I've been here, I've started taking classes to be a certified lay minister, enrolled in theology school, and last fall I decided to sell my business so I can be in ministry full time. And on Friday, it finally happened. My business has been sold. Now I can fully dedicate myself to be what the Lord wants me to be."

"Amens" and applause erupted from the church until a woman dressed in a large black hat and black suit stood up.

"Does the Lord want you to be a mistress too? Because that is what you are!" the woman yelled.

Everything stopped. At first I couldn't see her face because of the netting over her hat. She lifted the netting and fixed her eyes on me. It was Naomi. *Oh My God.*

"Stop seeing my husband, Jarena," she said. Her lips quivered, and she swayed like she was about to fall. She grabbed a pew in front of her before continuing loudly. "He was yours in college, but he's mine now. And we are MARRIED, not boyfriend and girlfriend!"

Trembling, like an electric shock was running through my body, I just stood there, paralyzed, not knowing what to say. An usher ran to the woman's side and escorted her out through the swinging doors at the back of the church into the vestibule. I escaped through a side door and ran into the bathroom, locking the door behind me. Some members followed me and knocked on the door, but I ignored them.

The scene played out again in my mind as I hid in the bathroom for the rest of the service. In the replay, I rushed up to her and roared to her face, "Barry was never yours because his heart was and always has been mine. He only married you to replace me. You are a rebound wife!" If Naomi wanted a public reckoning, so be it.

An hour or so later, Pastor Kirby knocked on the door.

"Jarena, are you in there?"

I didn't say anything, wishing I could click my heels like Dorothy in the *Wizard of Oz* and be at home. "Yes, Pastor Kirby," I finally answered.

"Do you want me to come in there and speak with you, or do you want to come to my office?"

Neither. I didn't reply, but I unlocked the door. Although the service was over, most of the congregation was milling around in the hallway, probably waiting to see the mistress minister. I kept my head down as I followed him into his office.

"Jarena, I don't even know what to say," he said after sitting in his chair and gesturing for me to sit down too. "I've known you for over a year now, and I know you are a woman of integrity and character, and I'm excited about what you will do for the Lord. But is this woman telling the truth? Are you seeing a married man?"

I nodded without looking up.

"I'm so sorry, Pastor Kirby," I said. "He was someone I dated in college, and we reconnected on Facebook last year. I just can't seem to stop seeing him. I love him. And he loves me. He wants to divorce his wife and marry me."

Pastor Kirby sighed. "I'm sorry to hear that," he said. "I'm not discounting your feelings, but I just don't think that God would lead you into a relationship with a married man. And despite this mess, I still think God has a wonderful ministry for you, but you won't be able to walk into it until you leave this married man alone. The devil is always trying to sabotage God's plan. The greater the sabotage, the greater God's plan. Pray with me right now that you will allow God to end this relationship."

Pastor Kirby took my hand and prayed for me. I so wanted to feel repentant, but the only emotion I recognized within me was anger. But I knew the rational thing to do right then was cut off my relationship with Barry. According to God's law and human law, he was married to Naomi, no matter how it happened.

While I drove home, Barry blew my phone up, but I didn't answer his calls. I knew he had heard what happened. But being publicly humiliated was all the incentive I needed to resist him, I thought.

Two days later, I sent Barry a long Facebook message explaining why I could no longer be in any contact with him. I "unfriended" him once he received the message and blocked his number.

And then he showed up at my house on Friday night.

"You left me no choice," he said as he leaned against my doorframe. Tears shone in his bloodshot eyes. "What am I supposed to do without you in my life?"

I attempted to shove him out of my door, but I stopped resisting, letting him all the way in. Nothing was said as we reacquainted our bodies. Everything I wanted to say I communicated in moans as he kissed me from the tip-top of my Afro to the soles of my feet. During the night we spent together, I silently bargained over and over again with God, telling Him that I would do whatever He wanted me to do if He would only allow Barry to be my husband like he was supposed to be years earlier. I told God that I could not enter the ministry if Barry wasn't by my side. *He was mine first. Why do I have to be alone?*

But by dawn Saturday, I surrendered to God. I sent Barry back to his wife, although he told me that no matter what I decided, he planned on divorcing her.

• • •

I didn't go to church on Sunday, but Pastor Kirby called me to schedule a meeting with him and the church board for the following Sunday after service. I arrived after the service was over and went to the conference room. The board members sat silently around the table as Pastor Kirby spoke.

"Jarena, while we believe that you have already greatly impacted Hidden United Methodist's lay ministry even without being officially certified, due to your moral transgressions, we have decided that we no longer need your services in that capacity. Of course, you are free to continue being a member, but we don't feel comfortable with you being in leadership until you have sufficiently addressed the sin you allowed into your life."

I didn't protest. Instead I thanked them for their wisdom and walked out the door. I knew I would not be returning to the church. God obviously wasn't leading me to ministry there, I concluded. And now that my business had been sold and I cut off all contact with Barry, I knew that I could clearly hear from God about his next destination for me.

Destination Wedding Meeting #18

Senalda and Wendell were nearly finished preparing for the party they were hosting for Mimi and Ian. Senalda had convinced Mimi that her nuptials needed a more official celebration, particularly as it was the first bona fide victory for their Destination Wedding project. She was expecting about fifty people to attend. Wendell had cooked all of the food. She had decorated her expansive backyard and rented some furniture.

As Senalda placed vases of flowers on each of the tables, she heard the doorbell.

"Where's Richie?" Senalda asked Whitney, surprised to see her friend at the door solo.

"At home."

"What are we going to do about photos?" Senalda said. "What happened?"

"I don't know. We were all set to leave, and then he said he wasn't feeling well. He asked me to apologize for him," Whitney said, stepping inside.

"I guess you can't help if you feel sick," Senalda said. "I'm glad I have my digital camera, but it won't be the same." Whitney didn't say anything else, so Senalda changed the subject.

"So can you believe that Mimi has been married for six months?" Senalda said.

"Yeah, good luck to her with that," Whitney spat. "I thought my future was set when I married a doctor too, and now..." Her voice trailed off into a melancholy silence.

"Awww, you guys are the couple I look up to," Senalda said, "I'm sure you will work it out."

"We will see," Whitney said. "What is going on with your hair? It looks really thick!"

"I haven't had a perm since that disaster with Dexter last year. I'm just getting it pressed now. We'll see how I can long I can go without one!"

"That's not my favorite style on you," Whitney said, scrutinizing Senalda's wavy roots, "but it does look really healthy."

"Really, Whitney? Whatever." Senalda said, choosing to not check her friend.

Party guests began to arrive shortly, with the guests of honor arriving last. Channeling '90s Erykah Badu, Mimi was adorned in a multicolored African-print dress with a matching gele holding her locs, while Ian wore a white polo shirt and khakis. People flooded them with congratulations, hugs, and handshakes.

Once everyone had food and was mingling, Senalda approached Jarena.

"Hey girl, I haven't heard from you all month," she said. "Are you okay?"

"Why do you ask?" Jarena asked, her cheeks rounded as she swallowed whole chunks of macaroni and cheese.

"Because you're sitting here with your head buried in a plate of food," Senalda said, sitting down next to her. "Why don't you mingle? Somebody here may know a single man whom you need to be introduced to."

"You don't stop, even for a minute," Jarena snapped. "After I eat my food, I will talk to somebody, okay?"

"You better be glad I'm on my best behavior tonight or otherwise I would check your attitude," Senalda said through a clenched smile as she stood up and walked away. Between Whitney's marital issues and Jarena's blues for no good reason, she was excited that at least one of her friends was in love and happy! And since love and happiness were still her goals over a year into their nearly stalled Destination Wedding project, she believed Mimi would be her most formidable ally going forward. She asked Wendell to give champagne-filled flutes to everyone.

"When Mimi told me that she and Ian had eloped in Vegas last December, I couldn't believe it," Senalda said with a laugh, holding her flute in the air. "Everyone knows that Mimi is hard to pin down. She is the ultimate hippie chick, forty years too late. But Ian, Dr. Ian, I might add, won this girl's heart, and Mimi, of all people, asked him to marry her! Join me in celebrating their union."

"And we got next," Wendell yelled from the other side of her backyard as people raised their glasses and said, "Cheers!"

Senalda smiled, making a mental note to speak with Wendell after everyone left.

Jarena surveyed the smiling faces around her, wishing she felt happy too. She hadn't attempted to smile in two weeks. She wanted to tell her friends what happened, but then she would have to admit she was a mistress. She wasn't sure Mimi would be judgmental, but now that she was a married woman, she really wasn't sure how she would react. Plus, she was a little annoyed that Mimi and Senalda seemed to be getting closer without her.

Mimi was probably connecting with Senalda because she knew she could fool Senalda with her happily-ever-after fairytale, she reasoned. But Jarena knew better than to swallow her tale. She, however, swallowed the final crumbs of her second plate of food—eyeing Mimi and her new husband. It was obvious that Ian was in love with Mimi. He constantly gazed at her even when she was talking to other people, and when they stood next to each other, he found a way to touch her whenever he could. Mimi, on the other hand, was decidedly restrained. Jarena had known Mimi since they were teenagers. When Mimi was into a guy, she talked about him incessantly to anyone who would listen. Mimi spoke of Ian positively... but generally only if asked.

Whitney filled her glass with more champagne. She'd downed her first almost in one gulp during the toast. She thought about calling Richie to check on him, but she didn't feel like arguing. Every conversation they had now eventually turned into an argument. And the time between a calm conversation and a vicious argument was getting shorter and shorter. So she continued to guzzle champagne, hoping Mimi's doctor wouldn't turn on Mimi the way hers had turned on her.

CHAPTER 20

July

Whitney

IT WAS 9 P.M. and I was still in my office. I finished my work at 7, but I didn't want to go home. I sat at my desk, staring out of my floor-to-ceiling window. Then I padded over to it, watching the cars traveling up and down Peachtree Street several feet below.

Richie was done at the hospital. He was at home "developing his business." Every time I thought of the moment he told me that he was going through with his plan to quit medicine last month, I wanted to scream all over again.

We were finishing breakfast, and I was just about to eat my last spoonful of Greek yogurt when Richie had placed his empty cereal bowl in the sink. Even from across the room, I could see there was a flake of Raisin Bran left in his bowl. As I opened my mouth to tell him to rinse the bowl, he said, "Whit, I'm going through with it."

"You're going through with what?"

"I'm turning in my two-week notice today," he said. "RBIII Photography officially begins in two weeks."

"Come again?"

"I waited six months as you asked, and I've decided that I still want to start my business. And I'm glad I waited, because I was able to find more clients."

The calm way he delivered this news infuriated me. "Oh, so your photography business is going to pay for this house, the twins' private school when they get old enough, our retirement?" I yelled. "Have you thought about that, or do you expect my salary to pay for everything?"

"If you're going to yell, I don't want to talk about it," he said as he started to walk out of the kitchen, "but you know good and well that with all of the investments we have, we're okay. And my business will be successful."

I felt like saying more, but I had learned in seven years of marriage that some things should just remain unsaid because they couldn't be taken back. So I said nothing else, but that didn't stop me from worrying about it all day at work. When I got home that night, I went to the basement to look around.

As I studied the photographs, I had to admit he was a talented photographer. But photography was still just an expensive hobby, not a way to make a living. I tried to imagine I was at one of my firm's parties explaining that my husband, a former Grady doctor, now took pictures for a living. I definitely couldn't explain it to my parents. My father had worked nearly his whole life to be where he was while my husband had been virtually given a job. *That is the problem.*

"This just isn't going to work," I declared out loud.

"What isn't going to work?" Richie asked as he stood at the top of the stairs peering down at me. "What are you doing in here?"

I almost blurted out my ultimatum, but then I opted to appeal to his rational side—if he still had one.

"You know, Richie, you are a talented photographer," I said, holding up the photographs closest to me, "but do you think photography is as important as bringing new lives into this world? That is what you do every day. Can you really walk away from that?"

"I thought about that, Whit," he said calmly as he came down the stairs. *Maybe this new approach is working.*

"But the longer I work in medicine the unhappier I get, and nothing is worse than an unhappy doctor," he said. "A doctor is supposed to make you feel better, but I don't think I can do that anymore."

"I know what's worse," I snapped, no longer able to control my tone nor my words. "A broke photographer for a husband. If you don't stop this, I want a divorce." I dropped his photographs on the floor and rushed up the stairs.

He ran behind me, catching up with me at the start of the stairs. After grabbing my arm, his face was so close to mine, I felt the anger in his steamy breath. "If that's how you want to play this, Whit, that's how it's going to be. I won't put up with this." He let go of me then and moved away, leaving me motionless and alone in the hallway. After retracting my ultimatum, I hardly spoke a full sentence to him for weeks.

So I was still at work. After checking on the twins, I reserved a hotel room for the night. *If the silent treatment didn't work, maybe sleeping away from home would.*

Destination Wedding Meeting #19

Bonded by Mimi's realization of their original Destination Wedding goals, Senalda and Mimi hatched a plan for their nineteenth meeting. Since they were both devotees of CC's counseling, they invited her to come to Mimi's home for their meeting. CC could help Jarena get a date if neither of them could, they deduced. The women couldn't pinpoint what was going on with their friend. But it was a conundrum they finally had the luxury of fully focusing on, now that their own formerly prickly love lives had been pacified.

Senalda and Mimi noticed that Jarena and CC were walking up the wooden steps to the porch at the same time.

"Hi Jarena! Hi CC!" Mimi said, as she opened her front door.

"Nice to finally meet you in person, CC. I've heard a lot about you from Mimi, Senalda and Whitney," Jarena said, inwardly wondering why the psychologist had been invited. "Where is Whitney, by the way?"

"She's hanging out her with family today," Senalda answered.

"So why don't we all have a seat?" Mimi said, gesturing to the living room.

"First of all, CC," Senalda started, "I cannot thank you enough for helping us to identify some unhealthy behaviors that were keeping us unhappy in our love lives."

"You put that beautifully, dear," CC said. "I may have you write that down so that I can put it on my website as an endorsement."

"I would be happy to," Senalda said. "So Mimi, are you ready to get to the business at hand?"

Mimi nodded while Jarena stared at the two. They were partners in something, and it pissed her off. *Mimi is* my *best friend, not yours.*

"Last summer when I was seeing CC, she explained the Imago theory to me and asked me to read a book by Harville Hendrix. He is the one that came up with the theory. He believes that we are attracted to a combo of our parents. All their good and bad traits. But the bad traits are the ones that really attract us more than anythang. Aine that a trip?

"When I thought back on my relationship with my father, he was there physically, but not emotionally. I was always tryin' to get his attention. Acting up and erethang! That is one of the reasons why I couldn't leave that loser Jovan alone. He was there physically, if you know what I mean, but he could never commit to me emotionally. CC, thank you for helping me to see that Ian is not only here for me physically, but he is also down for me emotionally."

"Isn't that awesome, Jarena?" Senalda said, eyeing her friend who wasn't trying to hide that she was rolling her eyes. "CC helped me to understand what happened with Dexter and what I needed to do in the future. She helped me to understand that what I thought was my type may not necessarily be good for me. Everyone knows Wendell is not my usual type. But he is really sweet. And he helps me to relax. And I know for a fact that he wants to marry me. We still have a few details to work out, but he makes me very happy."

"So CC," Mimi said, "you think you could help our friend the way you helped us?"

"I can't believe it," Jarena interjected angrily. "Is this a dating intervention? I have told y'all again and again that I'm good."

"Why do you come to our meetings month after month with absolutely nothing to report if you're good?" Senalda spat back, her voice getting louder with each word. "And if you tell us that you're busy in school or at church or you've just sold your business again, I'm going to scream. Because we're all busy, at least I am anyway, and we have found time to date and even get married! What's really going on?"

The three women fixated on Jarena, waiting for an answer. Jarena thought about blurting out the whole scandal with Barry, but she just couldn't bring herself to admit what had happened. Instead, she opted to just allow the "dating intervention" to unfold even if she was humiliated. At least her affair wouldn't be exposed.

"I don't know," Jarena said of her conscious and subconscious subterfuge. "The truth is I really can't explain why I haven't met anybody. CC, since my friends think you have all of the answers, what do you think?"

"It's hard to say without knowing more about you, but I will ask one question," CC said, leaning forward on the loveseat where she sat. "Our past always provides clues to our present. If you don't mind me asking you this in front of your friends, what was your relationship like with your mother and father?"

Jarena sighed loudly and answered in a monotone. "My mother died from breast cancer when I was in college but before she died, we were very close. I never knew my father."

"You don't know the identity of your father?" CC probed.

"When I was a little girl up until I was about twelve, we lived in housing projects, and no one seemed to have a father. But when we moved to the suburbs, I noticed that other kids had two parents. So I asked my mother a lot about my father when we first moved, but she always changed the subject or put me off, so I stopped asking eventually.

"So no, I don't know the identity of my father. But it hasn't affected me. I owned a successful business which I sold earlier this year. I'm in school getting my master's degree at Emory University's Candler School of Theology. I paid my way through the University of Alabama where I got my bachelor's degree in public relations. I think I've done very well in spite of not having a father."

"Jarena, no one is saying that you're not successful, but you really don't see the connection between not knowing your father and not having even a date to speak of in the last nineteen months that we have actually been working on our love lives? I'm not a trained psychologist, but damn," Senalda said in exasperation.

"Yeah," Mimi said. "I've noticed either she aine dating anyone or she's dating a married man. What's up with that?"

Jarena opened her mouth to speak but closed it again without uttering a word. Out of everything that was said, Jarena realized her best friend's final words were most potent. The worst part was that she couldn't answer the question, even for herself.

CHAPTER 21

August

Jarena

I RELAXED ON THE GRASS outside of Emory University's theology school, a relief to feel the sun's warmth on my face after a full day inside going from class to class. I couldn't believe it was the start of my second year of my master's program. The first year had flown by. I wondered if this year would too. I thought of my grandmother then. She would be so proud. If she had been alive she would be the one hollering the loudest at my graduation, because she was the one who planted the idea about being a minister in me all those years ago. *Can I still be a minister after all that has happened?*

Before I could answer my question, a classmate, a white boy named Bryson, situated himself beside me.

"Hey Jarena," he said, looking at me.

"Oh, hey there, Bryson." I attempted to look back at him while shielding my eyes from the now glaring Georgia sun.

"Did you take good notes during Professor Odumosu's class?" he asked. "I tried my best, but I'm still in summer mode."

"I know," I said with a laugh. "She taught like we were ending the first semester instead of starting our first day."

"I watched you taking notes, and you seemed to be writing a lot," he said. "I have to get to work now, but maybe we can meet later tonight for dinner and compare notes."

"I wish I could," I said, "but I have plans tonight. Maybe we can meet before class tomorrow instead?"

"Okay, meet you twenty minutes before class?" Bryson asked. "We can meet right here."

His words were casual, but his eyes were intense, prodding me to agree.

"Okay, see you then."

He waved goodbye before he got on a bicycle and rode off. He was tall but had a solid frame with sandy blond hair and matching golden eyes. I could tell he was athletic, too, because I could see the definition of his muscles beneath his maroon T-shirt. He had made a point of speaking to me throughout last year, but I had never really paid attention to him. I wasn't sure if this white boy was trying to hit on me or not. Had he been black, I would have thought maybe so, but I just didn't know what white boys did when they were trying to holla at someone. Either way, I wasn't trying to holla at any man, white or black, at least for right now. I was still waiting on God to tell me what to do in that department. And after last month's Destination Wedding meeting disaster, a "dating intervention" on my behalf, I thought it was best to skip the next meeting.

Now that the sun had sufficiently warmed me up, I took out my laptop to look through my notes. *But first, let me scroll through Facebook and see what's going on with my friends.* I contemplated shutting down my page after what happened with Barry, but I decided "unfriending" him would be enough. I noticed I had a message from a Rev. Dr. David P. Baker. *Who is that?* I didn't recognize him as one of my Facebook friends, but I thought he might have something to do with Candler, since he was a reverend.

I clicked on the message.

```
Dear Jarena Johnson,

I am writing to you to confirm that you are the grand-
daughter of Minnie Jean Johnson of Vidalia. If you
are, I have something very important to discuss with
you. Please call me at (555) 912-1234 at your earliest
convenience.

Sincerely,

Rev. Dr. David P. Baker
```

I remembered then that Dr. Baker was the pastor of my grandmother's church in Vidalia. *I wonder why he's contacting me.* Since it was in the middle of the day, I called him back right then. My heart thumped as I dialed the number.

"Hello," an elderly male voice said.

"Hi," I said. "This is Jarena Johnson. May I speak with Rev. Dr. David P. Baker?"

"Oh Jarena," the voice said with excitement. "This is he. I'm so glad you called. And you are the granddaughter of Minnie Jean Johnson of Vidalia?"

"There was only one Minnie Jean Johnson, at least in Vidalia, as far as I know," I replied with a nervous laugh.

"Well, you are my daughter then," Dr. Baker said without any prelude or warning.

"Say what?" I said as I stood up.

"I'm sorry to tell you such news over the telephone, but this information has been kept from you long enough."

"You knew my mother, Priscilla Johnson?" I asked.

"Yes, I knew your mother very well," he said forcefully. "I haven't seen you since you were twelve years old and asking me what it is like to speak to people, but I would like to see you again and explain everything in person. I would drive up to Atlanta to meet you, but I've been sick lately so I don't travel as much. Can we meet in Vidalia?"

"I really need some time to think this through," I said, my thoughts jumbling in confusion. "I will have to call you back another time."

"I hope to hear from you before too long," he said.

"You've waited thirty-four years. A little while longer shouldn't be too difficult," I said before hanging up.

Senalda

Although I had just seen CC in July, I needed to see her again—this time one on one.

"Senalda, thank you for inviting me to your meeting last month. Your girlfriends are a hoot! How is your friend—is it Jackie?—doing?"

"Oh, Jarena," I said, shaking my head as I sat on my favorite couch in her office. "I guess she's okay. I haven't heard from her since then. I've called her a few times, but she hasn't called me back. I'll have to ask Mimi if she has spoken with her."

"So what can I do for you today, dear?" CC asked while flipping through a notepad on her knees.

"I think my boyfriend is going to ask to marry me very soon."

"Isn't that good thing, dear?" She stopped flipping and looked at me like she was confused.

"It is, but I'm unsure about a few things," I admitted, looking down and then back up at her. "I just don't know if I will be happy long-term with a guy who makes significantly less than I do."

"Have you asked him how much he makes?"

"Not directly," I explained. "Normally I would have by now, you best believe... But I was trying to back off of my m.o. after Dexter. But he has a Honda Accord. His apartment is tiny. We've never been anywhere very expensive."

"Are you paying for your dates?"

"No, he has paid for everything," I said.

"Maybe he is frugal? At any rate, you need to stop making assumptions and have a serious talk about money before you marry him, if you choose to do so. Also, having money does not ensure that you will have a happy life together. There are countless examples of that. So what are the other things?"

"Baby mama drama," I said with a laugh. "Wendell has a three-year-old daughter, and of course, his daughter has a mother that he co-parents with."

"And they are causing problems for you, dear?"

"No. His daughter is very well behaved, and her mother doesn't seem to have a problem with me. It's just the idea of having to share Wendell. I have two older step-brothers from my father's first marriage, and I know what that is like."

"So what is it like?"

"I don't know anything different, but I guess I just wanted something different for me. I wanted to be the mother of my husband's first child. If I decide to have children, that is."

"I can understand that, but you may end up alone if you insist on having everything you want instead of focusing on what you need. Sometimes what we need isn't handed to us on a perfect platter, but over time, we see that it is perfect for us."

"Funny that you put it like that, a perfect platter," I said with a smile. "My mother says that too."

"And your mother is in a happy marriage?"

"She is," I admitted. "It's not necessarily what I want for myself, but they are happy."

"Your marriage doesn't have to be like your parents' marriage, but marriage is always about two imperfect people coming together to create what is perfect for them. Does that make sense, dear?"

"Yes, it does."

"Considering what you have told me, Wendell may be a good match for you," she said, taking off her glasses. "But don't marry him if you are sure it will make you miserable. You have a lot to think about, but I know you will make the decision that is best for you."

Destination Wedding Meeting #20

Unable to get in touch with Jarena, and with Mimi unavailable for their August meeting, Senalda had the perfect opportunity to discuss marriage with Whitney. Especially since Whitney and Richie's marriage was the one she wanted for herself. She knew her friends were going through some struggles, but every long-term married couple she had ever known had struggles at some point. They were the quintessential SpelHouse power couple with their achievements in their respective careers and respectable pedigrees. She wanted to know if being a power couple was all it seemed to be from the outside looking in, particularly since Wendell was not the one she expected to fall in love with.

They met at No Más! Cantina and Hacienda in Castleberry Hills for lunch.

"Hey, Bossy!" Whitney said cheerfully as she hugged Senalda. "Look at your hair! You're wearing it curly! I could never do that! Necesito margarita pronto! Isn't that how you say, 'I need a margarita immediately?'"

"Más o menos! Muy bueño!" Senalda said with a laugh.

The hostess approached them then and showed the ladies to a table.

"I can't see the menu," Whitney remarked while removing her oversized black shades. "It's too dark in here."

Senalda silently observed that Whitney's eyes were surrounded in puffiness and that her skin had a sallow look. She chalked it up to Whitney's long work hours. After ordering, the two relaxed in their chairs, exchanging what had been going on their lives since they had last seen each other.

Finally, Senalda asked, "What is it like to be married? I really want to be married, but is it worth it to merge your life with another human being's? Is that even possible?"

Whitney took a long sip through the straw in her margarita. It was so long, Senalda wondered if she even intended to answer.

"In the beginning," Whitney started, her eyes brightening to Senalda's relief, "it's wonderful and hard at the same time. When Richie and I first got married, every day I would wake up surprised that this gorgeous and great guy wanted to wake up to me every morning. I'm gorgeous and great too, but you know what I mean. I felt like I would never have to be alone ever again.

"And then it's hard because you have to consider someone else's feelings when you make a decision, and I wasn't so good with that in the beginning. And Richie is having issues with that now."

"So what is it like to be a power couple?" Senalda continued to probe. "It must be wonderful to have the same outlook on life, the same drive to achieve, the same education, the same or similar income."

Whitney's initial joyful reminiscence gave way to an unsmiling muteness. Senalda scrambled inwardly for something to say, but before she could, Whitney spoke.

"I've threatened to divorce Richie because he is totally disregarding my feelings." She carefully wiped tomatillo salsa from around her mouth with her napkin before plunging a tortilla chip into more salsa. "And all he said was if I couldn't accept him for who he truly is, then whatever I needed to do was okay with him."

"Are you serious? Why didn't you tell me it had gotten so bad? So what are you going to do?"

A white couple at another table rubbernecked Senalda as her shrill voice rose above the festive mariachi music playing in the restaurant.

"You really cannot accept that Richie wants to be a photographer instead of a doctor?" Senalda asked, quietly this time, although the shock of Whitney's news continued to reverberate in her head. She questioned her ability to make a marriage with Wendell work if a perfectly matched couple like Richie and Whitney couldn't make theirs work.

"I love him, so I'm going to attempt to stay with him, but it's true what they say about that seven-year itch." She munched on more chips before completing her statement. "I feel like he is going through a midlife crisis, and if I just stick it out, then maybe he will come back to his senses."

"But what if he never decides to start practicing medicine again?"

"I don't know, Senalda," she said breathlessly, as if she was very, very tired. "I deserve to be happy, and I'm not happy right now. I haven't been for months."

"Excuse me for being too nosy, but are you guys having money trouble?"

"No, we're fine for now," she said, "but I didn't sign up to be the primary breadwinner. We have some investments and everything, but I just don't want to be married to a photographer. I'm sure you understand."

As Whitney continued to justify her complaints, Senalda thought about her relationship with Wendell. She had said similar things to herself. But in that moment, she decided that maybe her definition of a "power couple" needed to be reworked. Maybe the power came from two people loving and being willing to support each other, not trying to live up to the image of what some people defined as successful.

CHAPTER 22

September

🔔 Destination Wedding Meeting #21

SENALDA DIDN'T BOTHER CONTACTING Mimi or Whitney about meeting in September. And they didn't contact her, either. And as Jarena still had not returned any of her voicemail messages since their July meeting, on the Saturday afternoon that she wanted to host the meeting, she determined rereading her now favorite relationship book, *Why Men Marry Some Women and Not Others*, would have to do. She zeroed in on the section about abandoning "princesshood" behavior.

As she reread the section, it made sense to her this time. *I've got a man who loves me very much and wants to marry me. He is responsible, has a good job, and is a great father. So what if I make more than he does? So what if I am more polished than he is?*

That night she was meeting Wendell at Jackson's at midnight to celebrate her birthday. As he didn't have Sunday, her actual birthday, off, he asked if they could celebrate after his Saturday shift was over. She recalled her birthday the year before, and a feeling of terror overcame her.

She frantically texted Wendell. "I hope you're not planning a surprise birthday party for me, because I hate them."

Then she texted her friends. "If Wendell is planning a surprise birthday party for me, you better let me know NOW."

Wendell texted her back within seconds, but none of her friends responded. "A surprise birthday party is not what I have planned, purrrty."

"What should I wear tonight, then?" she texted.

"Whatever you feel is appropriate :)"

Since she had just read about putting "princesshood" behind her, she simply wore blue jeans, a red turtleneck sweater and some ankle boots. No need to dress up, she reasoned. Knowing Wendell, he was probably taking her to a midnight movie or something on that level.

She left her home at 11:30. As she drove, she searched for a good radio station, stopping when she heard Al Green's ethereal melody, "Let's Stay Together," floating from the radio. She smiled, because his songs always reminded her of her childhood. Sometimes, if she stayed up late enough, she heard Al Green crooning from her parents' bedroom. She thought about calling them, but they were probably asleep by then. Plus, they would probably call first thing in the morning for her birthday.

After pulling into the restaurant's parking lot, she texted Wendell to let him know she was there. "Come on in," he texted back. She walked to the restaurant's front door and opened it, not sure what she would see inside the closed restaurant. To her surprise, the hostess was at her usual station, stepping up to her as she crossed the threshold.

"Ms. Warner, please follow me."

Senalda braced herself, wondering if all of her friends, associates, and co-workers were corralled in the restaurant's dining room, but she saw nothing except scores of candles all over the room on the chairs, tables and ledges. A single round table with two chairs was in the center of the room. She looked back to ask a question, but the hostess was gone. Instead, a waiter appeared at her left, directed her to the center table, and pulled out her chair. From the back of the room, the swinging doors leading to the kitchen swung open and there was Wendell, his husky body ensconced in a white tux with a black bow tie and vest.

"Happy birthday, purrrty!" Wendell said as he strutted over to the table where she sat.

"How did you get your boss to agree to do this?"

"Don't worry 'bout all that," Wendell said with a cocky grin. "I got pull with management."

"I guess you do," she said with a smile.

"I hope you haven't eaten."

"I have learned to be hungry when I see you," she said with a laugh, recalling when he tried to force-feed her popcorn on their first date. "So what's on the menu?"

"All your favorites," he answered. Everything that she ordered at Manolo's was brought out to them.

"How did you do this?" she said. "This is a soul food restaurant."

"My buddy Manolo made everything and brought it over here."

"You must really have an understanding boss," she concluded.

"Let's just eat."

After finishing their meal, the waiter brought out a Puerto Rican rum cake with candles on top.

"Blow the candles out, purrrty, and make a wish," Wendell directed.

She did as instructed.

"Cut me a piece of cake," he said.

"Okay," she said, standing up to cut a slice. Just as she lowered the knife, something sparkled in the center of the golden brown Bundt cake.

"What's this?" she said. "There's something in the center!"

"Reach in and get it out!"

She thrust her hand in the cake, pulling out a diamond ring.

"Wendell," she screamed. "Is this an engagement ring?"

"Purrrty and smart," he said with a hearty laugh. "I gotta keep you."

"Is there something you want to ask me?"

"Yeah. So you gon marry me or what?"

"You didn't even get down on one knee."

"I can take the ring back, purrrty," he said, only halfway joking.

"You don't have to do that." She bent down, clasped her hands around his chin, and kissed him.

"Is that a yes?"

"Sí señor," she said.

"Now that we got that outta the way, I wanna tell you something."

She sat down then, flashing back to when Dexter proposed, and preparing herself for the worst. Did he have more children that he hadn't told her about? Was he being evicted? Did he need to borrow money? Was he bisexual, too? A dozen scenarios played out in her head in seconds.

"What do you want to tell me?" she finally asked.

"Not only am I the executive chef here, but I also own Jackson's," he said.

"What did you say?"

"This is my restaurant," Wendell said. "I'm the boss and the owner. And sometimes the janitor and erethang in between. I should have told you sooner, but I've met some really materialistic women in Atlanta, and I wanted to get to know you first."

"But you have a Honda Accord! You live in a small apartment! And you own all of this?" Senalda usually Googled everyone and or checked them out on LinkedIn but hadn't thought to do either, since Wendell didn't have what she considered to be an important job. She realized then that all of the time she spent worrying that he did not make as much as she did amounted to nothing. She couldn't wait to tell her girls!

"Yes, because I have expenses. I have a whole staff depending on me. Haven't you heard of living beneath your means, Ms. Client Manager for Wachovia Bank?"

"You are making a lot of sense," she agreed.

"Dollars and cents," he said with a smile. "I know it's corny. Purrrty, I know you like the finer things in life and you deserve them and I want to give them to you when I can afford them."

"Wow," was all Senalda could get out.

"Is that aight with you?" Wendell asked, attempting to mimic her accent.

"Ay papi!" she replied.

CHAPTER 23

October

. . . .

Jarena

IT HAD BEEN A month since I met my father, but every day since then, I relived what happened when I drove down to Vidalia on Saturday, September 10. Two weeks after Dr. Baker told me he was my father, I agreed to meet him at his office at Redemption Baptist Church, where he was the pastor emeritus. Driving onto the church parking lot, I realized two things: This was the first time I had been on the grounds of a church since being kicked out of lay ministry at Hidden United Methodist, and stumbling onto Hidden United Methodist was about finding my way back to Redemption Baptist, a near replica of Hidden United Methodist. Tears gathered in my eyes as I just knew that I would be hearing from God that day. But instead of letting them fall, I willed them to go away.

As I inched up the frayed green-carpeted steps to the front door, I felt my grandmother's spirit with me, so much so that I turned around, almost expecting to see her.

"Dr. Baker?" I called out before touching the doorknob on the door that said OFFICE.

Dr. Baker appeared. I attempted to dredge up all of the confusing anger I had been feeling since we spoke, but all of the good memories I had of him as a child overrode my attempt. He looked like the same kind man I knew as a little girl, only with deepened lines in his forehead and gray hair.

"You are my sister's twin, especially with your Afro. Your mother had a similar style of hair when we knew each other," he said. "I was so sorry when I heard she passed."

"Thank you," was all I could say.

"My office is in here." He guided me from the outer office to his office. "Please have a seat."

After we sat down, he continued. "How was your drive down here?"

"It was fine," I answered, wanting him to start explaining immediately how he let thirty-four years go by without telling me he was my father.

"You know, your mother was my secretary before you were born," he said. "She used to work in that office right there." He pointed toward the outer office.

"Prior to meeting your mother, I had been faithful to my wife, who I am still married to," he explained. "But I spent a lot of time with your mother since she was the church secretary, and we ended up having an affair. When she got pregnant with you, I was so excited, but I didn't want to lose my wife. She wasn't able to have children, and it would have killed her if I told her about you. I didn't want to lose my ministry, either. I have a long history at this church. Your grandfather was the pastor of this church before I became the pastor in 1970. So I asked your mother to pretend you were another man's child. She agreed to keep my secret, but she said she couldn't lie to you, so she moved away to Atlanta."

He also explained that the money the deacon brought in church envelopes was his money and how my grandmother sent the money to my mother because she refused to accept it from him until after my grandmother passed.

"Your grandmother was the only other person who knew what happened. She made an agreement with me that when you visited her in the summer she would bring you here. The last time I saw you was at her funeral. I think you were twelve."

I said nothing as he spoke. I concentrated on his words as if I wanted to memorize them. Everything in my life that I couldn't explain up until that moment, I could now explain. All of the times I asked my mother about the identity of my father, and she refused to say anything or changed the subject. How she always told me that men were cheaters and couldn't be counted on. Her dogged insistence that I be emotionally and otherwise self-reliant and know as much as I could. How Dr. Baker always spoke to me at church. My mother choosing not to come back to Vidalia after my grandmother died. Her not having my grandmother's funeral at Redemption Baptist Church and having it at a funeral home instead. My mysterious call to ministry and my insidious attraction to married men. And I could finally answer Mimi's question in that "dating intervention." Dr. Baker had given me a map of my life, and I could finally trace how I arrived from one destination to the next.

A lifetime of feelings I had guarded behind an emotional levee flooded out. My father got up, grabbed some tissue and sat down in the chair next to mine. He hugged me while he said, "I'm sorry; please forgive me," over and over again. After what seemed like forever, I was able to dry up my tears.

"I have something I want to give you." He went to his desk drawer and pulled out a letter.

I instantly recognized my grandmother's precise handwriting. She wrote me letters almost monthly until she passed away. In the letter, she verified everything Dr. Baker told me, and she apologized if she had hurt me by keeping my identity hidden from me.

"She gave me this letter and asked me to give it you when I decided to tell you who I am," he said. "She told me that one day I would be ready to tell the truth. That day came last month when I had a heart attack. I thought I was going to die, but I didn't. So I decided since God has spared my life, I needed to be honest with my wife and my church. I've told my wife, and I plan to tell my church tomorrow, now that I've told you."

He asked me if I wanted to stay for the next day to be there at church and meet his wife and relatives. But I wasn't ready to deal with another scandalous public revelation in a church. Since then, my father and I have been working on developing a relationship, and I've started looking for a new church.

❦ Destination Wedding Meeting #22

Senalda devoted October's meeting to wedding planning. She was the Destination Wedding project leader and a bride-to-be, she reasoned. Also, her giddy text to her girls, "Happy birthday to me! I'm engaged!!!" along with a photo of her engagement ring, had renewed their interest in meeting.

She'd been fielding congratulatory texts and phone calls from everyone since the announcement. Her mother cried, she was so happy.

And now it was time to plan the wedding! She wanted to stay true to the original goals of Destination Wedding—to get engaged and married within a year. So Senalda and Wendell chose to have a New Year's Eve destination wedding in Puerto Rico. With only three months to plan the wedding of her dreams, she hired Priscilla Preston Love, owner of Love Affairs, the premier wedding planning event company for Atlanta's black elite. Priscilla was going to be the guest at the Destination Wedding meeting, but first, she wanted to speak with her friends privately. Jarena was the first to arrive. Instead of acting funny with her as she had been for some time, she hugged Senalda.

"I'm so happy for you."

And Senalda opted to let Jarena be, and not question her about her love life anymore.

"Thank you," Senalda said, gazing at her ring. "I still can't believe it's happening to me."

"It's your time, girl," Jarena said with a smile.

Minutes later, Mimi was on her doorstep. When Senalda opened the door, the both of them simultaneously screamed, grabbing each other in a messy hug. Jarena scowled but was silent. Once her friends were seated in her living room, Senalda explained why she wanted them to arrive first.

"Ladies, we have been through so much in this Destination Wedding project, and I want to thank you for being a part of it. Mimi, since you were the first to get married, I want you to be my matron of honor. And Jarena, since your prince is still on his way, would you be my maid of honor?"

"Fa sho," Mimi said initially, "but what 'bout Whitney? She's your best friend?"

"I already explained to her that since she was just a consultant to the project, I wanted to honor the women who were actually in the project with me. But she is a bridesmaid."

"Cool. I'm honored to be your matron of honor," Mimi said. "Jarena, I'm a matron of honor! Can you believe it?"

"Not really," Jarena snapped with sarcasm.

"What about you, Jarena?" Senalda said, turning to her.

"I'm honored as well," she said, quickly morphing her downturned lips into a cheery smile. "Puerto Rico, here we come!"

And then Priscilla Preston Love made an entrance. She was everything Senalda thought and more. First of all, she smelled like she soaked in flowers. Every time she moved, the scent of them mushroomed in the air like dust. Her cascading weave of black, silky, doll hair was fashioned to one side, exposing large chandelier earrings. Her brown face was smooth, but her cheeks were rounded with filler. Her purple dress was so tight, her D-cup breasts had no choice but to try to escape. Her heels were so high, Senalda thought she would wobble in them. But she pranced in them like they were ankle socks.

After consulting with Priscilla, Senalda was convinced that her wedding would be everything she had dreamed about, even if there was only three months to execute it. Priscilla commanded her matron and maid of honor to immediately start planning her bridal shower to be held in November. She gave Senalda a copy of the personalized timeline she created to ensure that every detail was handled. Whenever Senalda doubted what she could accomplish with so little time, Priscilla would declare, "I'm a pro-fes-sional, and I don't play piss-poor service," with a snap of her fingers. She could see why Priscilla Preston Love was featured on every wedding reality show that was filmed in Atlanta.

After her girls left, the wedding planning continued.

"If you like, I can get Chula Ramirez—you know, the big star—to sing at your wedding," Priscilla said. "She was the featured soloist at another one of my weddings, and her voice is just magical."

Senalda was quiet for a moment. Given Mimi's past with Chula, her first inclination was to say no. But Mimi had been happily married to Ian for almost a year. She was confident her friend could care less about Chula anymore.

"Having Chula sing at my destination wedding would make it absolutely perfect," she replied.

November

....

Mimi

DAMN, THAT SLAA MEETING *was just what I needed,* I said to myself as I left the noon Saturday meeting. Since getting married, I attended meetings when I could, cuz it was taking a minute gettin' used to being someone's wife, plus I was working on a new songwriting career.

"Hey Mimi, wait up," Richie called. We hadn't been talking much, and I'd been hoping the drama he had been going through with Whitney for the last few months had eased up.

"How's it going, man?" I yanked one of his now collarbone-length dreads. He sighed and then smiled.

"That good, huh?" I said, checking out his weak-ass smile.

"Yeah, but we're making it, I guess," he said. He moved one of my locs away from my face. "How's married life treating you?"

"Why does erebody ask dat? One day at a time." I smiled big so he could see my teeth, even though on the inside I still wasn't as settled down as I wanted to be.

"Wanna have lunch?" Richie asked.

"I did see an Atlanta Bread Company nearby," I said.

"I can do that."

Settled into a booth with our sandwiches, I asked, "So how are the twinsies? Every time I see them, they've grown up so much!"

"They are just about the only reason I can tolerate being at home."

It was already one of those dark fall days, and the look on his face made me feel even more down.

"What you sayin'? Cheer up! It couldn't be dat bad?"

"Whit and I," he began, while shaking his head from side to side, "I don't know. I don't want to make you feel negative about marriage since you're still a newlywed, but we're just going through it."

"But y'all gon work it out, right?" I bit into my veggie sandwich while waiting for him to answer.

"We've been trying, but I keep feeling like she is trying to wait me out, like she thinks I'm having some kind of midlife crisis and life will go back to what it was before I went on this spiritual journey," he said. He pulled at the bread on his chicken salad sandwich but left it on his tray.

"Are you having a midlife crisis, fool? You a lot different since I met you years ago."

"C'mon Mimi, I thought you would understand. We're both on a spiritual journey in these recovery meetings," he said.

"I have heard that recovery will make a good marriage better and break up a bad one."

"YOU are giving marriage advice?" Richie snickered at me. "If I didn't know any better, I would have thought YOU had a shotgun wedding. You married Ian after only dating him for a few weeks!"

"Obviously, I wasn't pregnant," I shot back, a second too fast. "And I met him months before we started dating. I didn't know you were all up in my relationship like dat!"

"I'm sorry," he said with a straight face. "But you were in love with another man just before you married Ian. Being married won't keep you from having feelings for other people."

I smiled as big as I could even with a little bit of my sandwich left in my mouth before speaking. "I love my husband, and my marriage is working," I declared.

"Alright, I will leave well enough alone."

While Richie went to the bathroom, I took out my cell phone, scrolled through my contacts and stopped at Jovan's name. I thought about deleting it right then, but I just wasn't ready yet.

Destination Wedding Meeting #23

All of the preparations came together nicely for Senalda's bridal shower brunch.

"The women are simply going to adore their souvenir bags," Whitney pronounced as she positioned them at each woman's place setting. She took one last look at the contents of each bag: Bath & Body Works lotion, heart-shaped chocolates, a miniature champagne bottle with Senalda's moniker on the label, and a spa gift card.

"I hope so, with all dis money we spending," Mimi quipped.

"Thanks for hosting Senalda's shower, Whitney," Jarena said, attempting to soften Mimi's statement. "Everything looks fabulous!"

"I just want everyone to be in a festive mood," Whitney said, her eyes narrowing. She surveyed the decorating, which included crimson and crème balloons attached to matching ribbons cascading from the ceiling, crimson and crème place settings, crème chair covers and crimson floating candles on the table. The caterer was in the kitchen, but the smell of the food wafted to the formal dining room where the brunch was being held.

"What time we serving the food again?" Mimi asked.

"We start serving at noon if we can wait that long," Whitney answered. "We estimated that after the welcome, door prizes, Senalda's speech and some time built in for 'our people,' it should be noon."

"Noon sharp," Priscilla declared as she marched into the dining room with a clipboard in hand. She took bridal shower schedule copies and handed them to each of the women. "Whether our people have arrived or not!"

Mimi rolled her eyes as she looked at Jarena and Whitney.

"I'm so glad Senalda don't want games," Mimi said, folding her schedule in half. "I hate playing games at showers. I just wanna eat, drink, get my laugh on, maybe get some free stuff and go home."

"Hush," Jarena managed to get out as she giggled.

About thirty women started streaming in at 11. Wearing a crème tea-length dress that cinched at her waist and flared at the sides, Senalda arrived last. Priscilla stayed on schedule.

"Mimi and Jarena, are you ready to welcome everyone?" she said to them as the women sat at their assigned seats. They nodded while walking to the head of the table.

"Hi ladies. I recognize many of you, but for those who may not have met me before, I'm Jarena, Senalda's maid of honor, and this is Mimi, Senalda's matron of honor. Along with Whitney, who so graciously agreed to host Senalda's bridal shower brunch, we want to welcome you. We are so glad you want to help celebrate our girl as she gets ready to marry her love NEXT MONTH."

The women cheered as Jarena said the last two words. Nashaun was the loudest, belting out "Won't He do it?! Praise Him!" as she stood up at her seat. Whitney's eyes blazed as she fixed them on Senalda's assistant, but Nashaun was not deterred, doing a quick dance before she sat back down.

"To thank y'all for coming, please enjoy your gift bags, and in a minute, we'll be giving out door prizes!" Mimi said, once Nashaun was done.

The women conversed and intermittently strolled over to Senalda, cooing at her engagement ring. After the door prizes were awarded to the woman who had arrived first, the woman who had known Senalda the longest, and Senalda's mother, the bride-to-be rose from her seat and read from a note card.

"My dearest friends, thank you from the bottom of my heart for celebrating the love that finally found me." She lifted her hand in the air for all to admire her sparkling engagement ring. The luster of the ring matched the warmth spreading over her as she recounted the journey, starting with the news report with its bleak statistics and ending with her meeting the love of her life. "Mimi, Jarena, and Whitney as our married consultant, started the Destination Wedding project to defy the statistics by getting engaged AND married in a year! There were some setbacks along the way, but Mimi got married last December, I'm getting married this December, and Jarena's prince, I know, is on the way. Black women can be successful in their careers AND in their personal lives. Forget the statistics and the haters!"

Conversations erupted about the room as women discussed duplicating Destination Wedding's results in their own lives or the lives of friends. Optimism weaved throughout the chatter.

Raising her flute in the air, Nashaun coalesced the jubilance. "I'll drink to that, Mizz—I mean soon-to-be Mizzus—Senalda."

"Hear, hear," the women echoed after one another.

"Before I sit down, I have a surprise for my Destination Wedding crew." Her friends glanced at one another, not knowing what to expect. Senalda reached down next to her chair and pulled up a large Tiffany bag, handing each of them a Tiffany blue box with a white bow around it from the bag. Her shower guests reacted with "ooh" and "ahh."

Mimi opened hers first, holding up a sterling silver locket with the initials "D.W." engraved on it for everyone to see. "Girl, you spent some money on this!"

"I remember this photo of us from SpelHouse's homecoming a few years ago," Whitney said, peering into hers. "We had so much fun that day. How did you get that photo in there?"

Jarena shook her head in admiration, allowing the resentment she had been feeling lately to dissolve in a flood of good memories of their friendship over the years. "A project manager who thinks of everything! I got to give it to you. You're the boss for a reason!"

"In front of everyone, I wanted to thank you for being my best friends and apologize for any misunderstandings on my part. I know we got on each other's nerves in the process, but I hope these lockets remind each of you how much we mean to each other."

Senalda's announcement was the meaty main course, and her presentation served as the dessert, its sweetness almost too rich too digest. More than one woman found herself dabbing glazed eyes as the friends fused themselves in a group hug.

After Senalda's presentation, Priscilla guided the guests back to the scheduled events. As the congratulatory chatter continued, Jarena almost didn't hear her cell phone ring.

"Hello," she said, putting her head down.

"What you know, good J.J.?"

"Jovan?" Jarena stood up, realizing that Mimi was nearby, and walked out of the dining room. "I haven't heard from you in forever."

"What's going on there? I heard all that noise!"

"I don't know if you remember my friend Senalda, but she's getting married next month, and I'm at her bridal shower. You know women get loud when we get together. So what's up?"

"Yeah, I remember Senalda," Jovan said before pausing. "That's why I'm calling you, actually. Priscilla Preston Love asked Chula to sing at her wedding. I just wanted to let you know so you won't be surprised."

"I guess, thank you, but it's not me you should be telling," Jarena said, attempting to keep her tone neutral after Jovan's unsettling news. "Mimi's the one you need to tell, don't you think?"

"Yeah, that's why I'm calling you. I figured you could tell her. You're her best friend, so..."

Whitney eyed her, so she wrapped up the conversation.

"I'll see what I can do," she said as she passed Whitney and went back into the bridal shower.

Whitney continued to the bathroom, shutting the door behind her. While gazing at her reflection, she recalled her own bridal shower seven years earlier. Separating it from her wedding band on her finger, she examined her engagement ring, remembering how she used to hold her hand at a certain angle so the diamonds glinted. She lifted her hand, but then she frowned.

"How did I miss this crack in one of my diamonds?" she said, louder than she realized.

"What did you say?" Senalda said from outside the bathroom.

"I'm just in here talking to myself," Whitney said, putting her hand down next to her side and opening the door. "I'm so happy for you."

She hugged Senalda then, hoping she grabbed her before she saw her eyes glistening with tears.

"I'm getting married in Puerto Rico," Senalda said as they hugged. "I can't wait!"

CHAPTER 25

December

· ·

Destination Wedding

MIMI TOOK HER ROLE as matron of honor seriously, so seriously that she studied the wedding program while lounging in the lobby of Jewels San Juan Hotel. Ian couldn't make the wedding celebration because he had to work, so she hung out in the lobby as much as possible to avoid feeling alone. She nodded with approval as she read Senalda's song selections, such as "Spend My Life With You" by Eric Benét and Tamia and "There Goes My Baby" by Usher. But she almost spit her bottled water out of her mouth when she saw Corazón Ramirez was listed as the soloist for "The Lord's Prayer." She was able to swallow her water by telling herself that Corazón couldn't possibly be "Chula," but then she heard a voice she recognized.

"Baby, baby, walk slower. You're pregnant, and you're wearing heels."

In the herd of people heading toward the hotel's front desk, Mimi spotted Jovan. And next to him was a very noticeably pregnant Chula, wearing a wide-brim straw hat and a strapless golden sundress while teetering on kitten heels. As Chula's star continued to rise, Mimi noticed she had dropped her tomboy image in favor of a more feminine one. Which was probably her strategy with Jovan too: start off as his homie and friend and lure him into being her lover. Mimi fell to the carpet to stop, drop, and roll away, and she would have, except there was no way to go except toward the front desk. So instead, she perched behind a sofa, peeking above it periodically to make sure that she had really seen what she thought she had.

Once Jovan and Chula were gone, she threw away the rest of her bottled water and headed to the hotel's bar. All she wanted was to obliterate thoughts about Chula and about her own child with Jovan, which invaded her brain more than she would admit to anyone.

"A Dark 'n' Stormy, please," Mimi said to a bartender, dropping herself onto a stool and swiveling it to face the bar.

"If that drink doesn't make you feel better, I can," a man said behind her. Mimi turned her head to see who was talking.

Damn, is this dude gonna follow me around all weekend?

There had been an impromptu meet-and-greet for guests the night before in the hotel restaurant. Although Wendell's best man Nathan was married, he kept looking at her the whole time, even winking at her once. But she wouldn't have been interested, even if she wasn't married. Another one of Wendell's friends, Chauncy, a wiry, butterscotch-colored man with hazel eyes, was sorta interesting, but she was Married Mimi, not Single Mimi.

But as Nathan stood in front of her, obviously wanting her attention and as she had nothing else to do other than to try to forget that one of her best friends not only invited but included the pregnant wife of the love of Mimi's life in her wedding, she smiled.

"Oh for real?" Mimi said, winking at him. The dark-skinned, thick, muscular man took her wink as an invitation to get closer and he whispered in her ear.

"You so crazy," Mimi said. As she threw her head back in an exaggerated laugh, Senalda walked by the door of the bar, stopped, and frowned.

• • •

Mimi didn't care who was watching as she kissed Chauncy near the bathrooms in El Restaurante De La Playa. When he pulled her waist to him, she felt that he was as excited as she was. He was so strong, the motion caused them to fall against the wall.

"Let's take this to the bathroom," he said, lifting his lips from hers for a moment. With their lips still pressed together, he guided them inside the men's bathroom, where they locked themselves in a stall. As he yanked up her dress and unbuckled his pants, she realized what was about to happen.

"Wait, wait," she said breathlessly. "I can't, I can't. I'm married."

"You told me that before," Chauncy replied. "He will never know. What happens in Puerto Rico stays in Puerto Rico, baby."

"But I'll know," she said. "I'm sorry. I can't use you, and that's what I'd be doin' if we did this."

"Okay, okay," he said, backing off of her.

She pulled down her dress and pushed the stall door open. She scurried out of the men's bathroom and entered the women's bathroom. She attempted to calm down in front of the mirror. Her face was flushed, and her red lipstick was smeared. With cold water, she wet some paper towels, patting them on her face and wiping her mouth. Then she reached into her purse, fishing out her tube of lipstick to reapply it. Just after she started, Senalda stomped into the bathroom, followed by Jarena and Whitney. Rage, confusion, and disdain, respectively, contorted the women's faces.

"Just because you married someone you're not in love with doesn't mean that I'm going to let you make a mockery of my wedding," Senalda snarled, glaring into Mimi's eyes in the mirror. "Last night you and Wendell's best man were flirting and tonight, you are kissing another one of his grooms-men. This is not a Tyler Perry movie. This is my wedding! And I didn't plan it this way. And you are married, so act like it!"

Mimi rolled down her tube of lipstick before responding to her diminutive accuser.

"Why is da woman always seen as the home wrecker?" Mimi said, maneuvering her neck and throwing her long dreadlocks over her shoulders. "Wendell's best man is married too. Did you ever think he was tryin' to get wit me? I don want dat man!"

"That's a first," Senalda snapped.

"What you saying?" Mimi said. She folded her arms and cocked her head to the side.

"You've got a problem. I don't care if he did approach you first. It was obvious that you did not mind his attention. So how did you end up kissing another man tonight? Did he kiss you first, or did you just trip and fall on his lips? You're supposed to be my matron of honor and you're acting like a hoe!"

"Okay, okay," Jarena said, getting between the two of them. "Y'all, we cannot do this here. People can probably hear y'all outside. Maybe we should go back to the hotel and talk about this."

"Talk nothing," Senalda said. "I've said what I need to say except for one last thing. Whitney, will you be my matron of honor? Clearly, Mimi doesn't respect the sanctity of marriage or give a damn about me or my wedding!"

Mimi opened her mouth to speak, but nothing came out. Instead, tears fell down her cheeks as she pushed past the women and ran out of the bathroom. She rushed out of the restaurant before remembering that Senalda had betrayed her first. She turned around, marched back to the bathroom and flung the door open.

"You don't give a damn about me or my friendship or you wouldn't have included Chula in your wedding!" Mimi screamed. "I thought I put Chula and Jovan behind me but instead they here for your wedding because your stank ass invited them! What kind of friend does that?"

Senalda looked stunned. The room was silent for a few beats before Jarena spoke, her voice calm. "I didn't want to say anything, but I did think it was wrong to include Chula in your wedding when she has caused so much trouble for Mimi," Jarena said.

"Don't try to get all self-righteous now, Jarena. You knew Chula was going to be in the wedding," Senalda said.

"You knew?" Mimi asked, looking at Jarena.

"I thought Senalda was going to tell you, since y'all are best friends now."

"And I'm tired of your self-righteous minister act, too," Whitney said. "Especially when you were a mistress up until a few months ago."

"How—how —" Jarena sputtered.

"How did I know?" Whitney said, putting her hands on her hips. "Mimi's husband Ian used to date Barry's wife's older sister. And she is my line sister.

And he told her. And she told Barry's wife. So that's how I know. And I know it all, too. I've been waiting for you to tell us, and you haven't said anything!"

"Whaaat, how did Ian know?" Jarena screeched. With nothing to offer to defend herself, she folded her arms and stewed in silence.

• • •

Whitney and Senalda returned to Whitney's hotel room to find Mimi crying on Richie's shoulder as he rubbed her back.

"What's going on here?" Whitney said, charging at them. "Are you trying to get with my husband too?"

"Am I tryin' to get with yo husband?" Mimi croaked. "This is my friend. I thought you were too."

"Calm down, Whitney," Richie said. "Mimi and I both go to meetings. We are program buddies."

"Yeah, tell her, Senalda," Mimi said. "You know we go to twelve-step meetings together."

Whitney gaped at Senalda.

"What? You know my husband and Mimi have some kind of secret friendship going on and you didn't bother to tell me?"

"Well, that program is called Sex and Love Addicts *Anonymous*," Senalda said, weakly. "I didn't think it was my business to share."

"I mean…You know what?" Whitney shouted, throwing her hands in the air, "I just can't. Since you're keeping Mimi's secrets, she needs to be your matron of honor, not me." She stormed out of the room without saying another word.

• • •

The first notes of "Spend My Life With You" sounded, signaling the entrance of the matron of honor on the white runner that led to the marble gazebo in the courtyard where Senalda and Wendell would say their vows. Flanked by hanging palm trees and tropical foliage, the gazebo would shield the bride and groom and minister from the sun. Priscilla, unaware of the blowup, nudged Mimi.

"Mimi, that is your CUE," Priscilla said firmly. Mimi did what she was told, traveling down the aisle with the rest of the bridesmaids and grooms- men following. Wanting to honor their unique personalities, Senalda had them wear the same one-shoulder satin dress with an organza overlay, but the dresses were in different jewel tones. Mimi wore fuchsia, Jarena wore teal and Whitney wore emerald. The groomsmen wore tan suits with ivory vests and ties. Kailen, a princess in an ivory dress made of tulle with crystal accents and a sparkling tiara atop her curls, inched down the aisle with her head down. Every few steps, she stopped and released a clump of petals until she got midway down where she paused. Then, she just ran the rest of the way, stopping at her father's leg, to everyone's laughter.

When Senalda appeared at the end of the aisle alongside her father, who was in a wheelchair, the three friends temporarily forgot their anger and focused on the bride. Instead of her usual pressed hairstyle, Senalda's hair was in its natural state, full of curls. Her ivory dress featured a sweetheart neckline with thin flowered straps. The top of her dress was simple but the bottom was a cloud of ruffles that swished as she walked. Her features, often pinched with stress, were liberated by and luminous with love. Wendell's face contorted as she got closer to him until he finally took out a handker- chief and wiped the tears sliding down his face.

As if directed by Priscilla, the sun set behind the gazebo while the two recited their vows.

"Today, in front of my family and my friends, I promise that I will be your woman and your wife and you will be my man and my husband," Senalda started. "I will respect and love you and not try to change you. I promise to eat all that you will feed me. You are the one that I love, need, and want."

Wendell attempted to say his vows but kept wiping his face in silence until Senalda reached for his handkerchief and wiped his face clean. Then, he was ready to begin.

"Today, in front of my family and friends, I promise to be your man and your husband, and you will be my purrrty and my wife. I will protect you and love you and not try to change you. I promise to up my bougie game. You are the one I love, need, and want."

Mimi, Jarena, and Whitney agreed that they had never seen Senalda look so happy and content.

• • •

Although the four friends were still angry with one another, the wedding ceremony went as planned. But the bad feelings bubbled over with the lubricant of champagne and other alcoholic beverages served at the open bar at the reception at El Restaurante De La Playa. After the matron-of-honor and best-man toasts, Richie, who was also one of the groomsmen, stood to give a toast. As he shot up, he nearly slipped. His locs askew, he grabbed the back of his chair to steady himself.

"I want to say a few words to honor this happy occasion," he said, his words slurring together. "To Senalda, my wife's best friend, and Wendell, your new husband, I wish you all of the happiness I thought I had when I married that woman over there." Richie pointed to Whitney and continued. "I hope the two of you know yourself better than we did or else you will end up just like us: a wife who is ashamed of her husband, and a husband who wishes he was married to a wife who accepts him for the man he truly is. This woman values being a power couple over loving her man. And I'm a man who is in love with his wife's friend Mimi."

The crowd gasped in unison. Without a word, Wendell's best man shoved Richie away from the head table and out of the room while Whitney fled in the other direction. Mimi stared down while Jarena pressed a smile to her face. Senalda sat still, not knowing what to do. It was the best and worst day of her life all at once.

CHAPTER 26

January

. . . .

New Year's Day

MIMI TRUDGED TO THE hotel lobby, suffering from a hangover of the heartbreak soaked in the spirits served at Senalda's wedding reception. The sun, nature's daily promise of hope, was coming up on her last day on the island before flying back stateside on an afternoon flight.

Richie was splayed out on a couch still in his wedding suit, now dirty and wrinkled. Her first impulse was to flee, but the lobby's emptiness presented the perfect opportunity to confront him about his stunt hours earlier. And if someone happened to see them, no one could claim they were cavorting in secrecy.

"What da hell was that?" she said, thumping him on his forehead.

Richie's eyes moved under closed lids before he fell to the ground with a thwack. His head on the carpet, he opened his eyes.

"What? Mimi?" he said groggily.

A potent mix of stale breath, dried sweat, and hard liquor confronted her, causing her to move backward even as she continued to question him.

"We supposed to be in recovery from sex and love addiction, and then you say some shit like you did last night," she said. "You know damn well you're not in love wid me, and I am sho as hell not in love wid you. So why did you say what you said last night?"

She wasn't completely certain that Richie wasn't in love with her. Still, after taking inventory of her own behavior over the weekend, whether or not it was provoked, she knew that she was wrong for acting out. The SLAA program had taught her to see her part in all situations. She suspected that Richie's drunken declaration of love was simply him acting out as well, and she wondered what triggered it.

On still-wobbly legs, Richie repositioned himself on a couch, rubbed his eyes, and replied.

"For a while, I did think I was in love with you, Mimi," Richie confessed as he massaged his temples. "You understand me in ways my wife refuses to, and I'm done with trying to make her understand. After I got drunk last night, I thought that if I announced I was in love with you, she would finally get it... See why I don't drink anymore?"

"Yeah, that was a dumb as fuck idea," Mimi agreed. "I bet that's why your ass obviously slept out here."

"Yeah, Whitney kicked me out of our room last night. Like I said, I don't think Whit and I will make it, but I know this is not the way to do it. I apologize I brought you into this and for messing up the wedding reception."

"I was already mad at your wife before this happened, but she sho as hell didn't deserve that. And neither did Senalda."

"Yes, I need to make amends to Whit and Senalda, but do you forgive me? Because I'm sorry."

"You're not sorry," Mimi said with a smile, "crazy as hell, like we all are in SLAA, but not sorry. Yeah, I forgive you. We good... I got some amends to make too, I guess..."

Mimi could see the rise of the sun, its rays dispelling the anonymity of darkness, behind the sea across the street from the hotel. She silently thanked her Higher Power for its presence.

• • •

Mimi, Jarena, Whitney and Richie each nearly rescheduled their Sunday afternoon flight, to avoid having to travel together.

But Mimi missed the predictability of her husband's love. Her proximity to Jovan brought back memories—good and bad—of their relationship, and for the first time, she was able to juxtapose what she thought they had with actual love. Her love with Ian was real. She was anxious to tell him the whole truth about what happened at Senalda's Destination Wedding in Puerto Rico—and more. Of all the people she owed amends to, her husband was at the top of her ledger. She only hoped that telling him everything wouldn't injure him or their marriage in the process, as the ninth of the twelve steps warned about.

Jarena couldn't wait to retreat to the sanctity of familiar surroundings. She could handle being single most days, but now that all of her close friends were married, even if some were unhappily, she could count on her home being a buffer between her and a world that insisted on being coupled up. Whitney had to be at work on Monday and now that it seemed that divorce was imminent, her security was more important than ever. Richie was excited about a photo shoot with a big client the next day.

On either side of a wall of silence, Whitney's and Richie's ears popped as they awkwardly perched next to each other in first class until Whitney attempted to relieve the tension, asking a flight attendant if she could sit in *any* available seat in coach. Mimi and Jarena, who were also sitting together in the middle of the airplane, watched as Whitney, in a cloud of sadness, passed by them, trudging to the rear of the airplane.

"I do believe I have seen it all," Jarena said as she looked behind her. She noticed that Whitney's light skin seemed to have blanched rather than tanned in Puerto Rico as hers did.

"She right to be pissed off, though," Mimi commented from the middle seat.

"You're right to be mad at me too," Jarena said, putting her hand on Mimi's. "I should have told you about Chula coming to Senalda's wedding. Between being jealous that Senalda was taking my very best friend away and watching everybody couple up but me, I made some mistakes."

"I can't even judge," Mimi said. "If you lined up my mistakes next to yours, you know I got way more than you. And I still think somebody is gon snatch you up. You gon see."

Before Jarena could respond, a bell rang and a flight attendant passed so quickly, the disturbed air moved the tendrils of her Afro. The lights came on; the in-flight movie stopped.

"Ladies and gentlemen, we have a medical emergency. If there is a doctor or other medical personnel on board, please ring your flight attendant's call bell," a distressed voice announced over the PA system.

Richie rushed by, and Mimi and Jarena craned their necks backward. The flight attendants were clustered at the back of the plane. Richie was shocked to see his wife's still, small body on the floor. Her eyelids fluttered but she was otherwise unresponsive. As he frantically checked her vital signs, his wedding vows ran through his head. He had promised to be there for his wife in sickness and in health. It now seemed that Whitney had disdain for the "for richer, for poorer" part. But he intended to honor his pledge to her and their marriage.

Within seconds, Whitney completely opened her eyes and Richie's face was the first one she saw. Her heart wanted to retreat but her body didn't have the strength to follow her brain's commands.

"What happened?" Whitney breathed out.

"You fainted," Richie replied, his tone tender. "When was the last time you had something to eat or drink?"

In frantic preparation for the wedding, she hadn't eaten. And just before Richie made his toast, she was about to eat. And afterwards, she had been so embarrassed, food was the last thing on her mind. She had simply forgotten that she needed sustenance to exist, which made sense since she was so embarrassed she wanted to disappear.

"I didn't drink water after noon because I didn't want to go to the bathroom on the plane, and I haven't eaten since Friday," she said slowly. "How is my hair?"

"We figured that's what happened," a flight attendant said as she gave Whitney juice and crackers. "We see that a lot." Richie helped Whitney sit up, taking a seat on the floor next to her. As the rest of the passengers returned to their seats, Richie smiled at his wife.

"One way or another, you were going to get me to be a doctor again."

"I can't control you or your career, no matter how much I want to," she said to him, her heart, brain, and body in alignment. "And maybe I shouldn't have tried anyway... Could you please pass my mirror to me, Richie? It's in my purse."

They did not exchange regrets or recantations, but they recognized their words for what they were: a realization that their relationship, like their seating arrangement, had shifted during the flight. Whether or not it would survive after they reached their destination, they did not know, but they decided their wedding vows were worthy of one last chance.

• • •

After recapping all that happened to Senalda in a cell phone call, Senalda simply said, "I'm glad that it all worked out" to Jarena as she made her way in the concourse. Her new husband convinced her that despite their wedding day drama, it only mattered at the end of the day that they were husband and wife. She had arrived at her intended destination despite the detours and distractions along the way. She only hoped that Jarena would not give up on finding love, but she held her peace after careless words had threatened to destroy her own happiness the night before.

As Jarena rode up the escalator alone among the travelers at Hartsfield Jackson Atlanta International Airport, the *Spirit of Atlanta* photographic wall mural above welcomed her home. The photograph featured a little black girl clad in a swimsuit, arms outstretched toward heaven, among the fountains springing in the formation of the Olympic rings at Centennial Olympic Park in downtown Atlanta. Although there were other children in the mural, the girl was alone in the center, a visual representation, Jarena realized, of how she planned to live her life going forward from the first day of the New Year. Armored with the presence and love of God, she would be the center of her own world, because there were no guarantees that a mate would be joining her in the journey to the destination of her life.

Acknowledgments

FIRST AND FOREMOST, I have to thank God, the Creator with a capital "C" for bestowing me with the gift of creativity with a little "c." I cannot fathom how God must have felt when He created the world and all that inhabits it from nothing, but I think I experienced a bit of what it must have felt like when I created a fictional world from nothing in "Destination Wedding."

Secondly, I dedicate this book to the memory of my friend and sorority sister Sherry "Elle" Richardson who passed away on her birthday in May 2017. She was the first person that I discussed *Destination Wedding* with once the idea began to take shape in my imagination, and she encouraged me to begin writing right away! I hope that somehow she knows that I completed what I set out to do, and I couldn't have done it without her.

There were many others who encouraged me along the way including but not limited to Janell Walden Agyeman, Mackenzie Fraser-Bub, Jane Friedman, Rhonda McKnight, Megan McKeever, Tiffany L. Warren and Joy A. Williams. I thank Latoicha Andino and Stephanie Clay for reading the "Destination Wedding" manuscript in its early stages. To make sure that my characters were as "real" as possible, I interviewed several people including radio personality Sasha The Diva, Rev. Dr. Elaine Gattis, former Clayton County Sheriff Kem Kimbrough, Nelta Clements Latimore, Rev. Dr. L.K. Pendleton and Cliff Robinson. Thank you for your input! I thank David Wogahn and AuthorImprints, theBookDesigners and Erin Willard, my copy editor, for bringing *Destination Wedding* to life after years of simply being sentences in a Microsoft Word document.

To my husband, Robert L. Meredith Jr., you made my *Destination Wedding* dream come true in 2013, and I'm glad that wherever our destination, we're on the way together. I love you man. And to my parents Dr. Denzil & Mrs. Alice May Holness and all of my family which includes my Central Christian Church family, your love and support has made me who I am today. I love all of you so very much.

Lastly, if there is any name that I forgot to mention, charge it to my head and not my heart.

CPSIA information can be obtained
at www.ICGtesting.com
Printed in the USA
LVHW011808081219
639816LV00007B/35/P